DARK SILENCE
The Bound Subject Volume 1

Jay Aheer,
Love,
Kayleshaw
xxx

DARK SILENCE
The Bound Subject Volume 1

KATZE SNOW
SUSANNA HAYS

Table of Contents

Copyright
Dedication
Monster
Prologue
Chapter 1 — 1
Chapter 2 — 25
Chapter 3 — 56
Chapter 4 — 64
Chapter 5 — 74
Chapter 6 — 87
Chapter 7 — 103
Chapter 8 — 121
Chapter 9 — 132
Chapter 10 — 142
Chapter 11 — 157
Chapter 12 — 173
Chapter 13 — 200
Chapter 14 — 216
Chapter 15 — 228
Chapter 16 — 248
Chapter 17 — 265
Chapter 18 — 286
Chapter 19 — 395
Chapter 20 — 305
Chapter 21 — 319
Epilogue — 331
Acknowledgements — 335
About Katze — 337
About Susanna — 341

Copyright

Copyright © 2017 Katze Snow (primary author) and Susanna Hays (co-author)

Edited by Lisa Cullinan

Cover Design by Jay Aheer @ Simply Defined Art

This is a work of fiction written in **British English**.

All rights reserved, worldwide, and on any multiverse that is known or unknown. No part of this publication may be reproduced in, stored in a retrieval system, or transmitted, in any form or by any means, including electronically or mechanical, without the prior written permission of **both** the copyright owners. A signed contract has also been agreed between both authors and it will therefore be respected by **both** parties.

Names, characters, businesses, places, events and incidents are either the products of the author's imagination or used in a fictitious manner. Any resemblance to actual persons, living or dead, or actual events is purely coincidental.

This book is licensed for your personal enjoyment only. This book may not be re-sold or given away to other people. If you would like to share this book with another person, please purchase an additional copy for each reader. If you're reading this book and did not purchase it, or it was not purchased for your use only, then please return to your favourite retailer and purchase your own copy. Thank you for respecting the hard work of these authors.

Warning: This story is DARK. It is not intended for those who are seeking a happily ever after. This psychological, erotic thriller is meant for those who enjoy the darker side of life. It is NOT a romance and it contains graphic scenes of sexual torture in which some may find upsetting. Other possible triggers include abduction, torture, non con, manipulation, and enslavement. Please consider these warnings before entering the professor's world.

Dedication

To Raissa Phoenix

For introducing me to the world of Dark Erotica.

Love, Katze

Monster

/'mɑːnstər/

Noun

1. One who deviates from acceptable behaviour or character

2. To be cruel, abnormal, and devoid of humanity

Prologue

THE SUNLIGHT FILTERING through Claude's office was of no use here, and the explanation had always been quite simple: light did not belong in a world that cultivated only darkness.

Normalcy was a state of being that had no place in the professor's world. Not many dared to understand *his* line of work. Or rather, not many people wanted to. His theory of psychological science was of a... peculiar nature. It insulted everything humans believed to be true and contributed to everything they feared. Therefore, to such small minds, Claude's profession was a mocking subject of humanity and needed to be eradicated rather than endorsed.

They called it inhumane. Cruel. Barbaric. Genius. Professor Claude Galen was either admired or feared for his research. But there were those, like Claude and his father, who could see the bigger picture—see their study for what it was worth—whether it be with just gentle perseverance and support, or an open mind willing to facilitate their *research*.

Claude's obsidian eyes strayed to his laptop screen again and gazed at the tall, dark-haired boy who stared back at him. Twenty-one-year-old Tristan Kade from Montana. Single. Alone. Exquisite physical condition. Though the video footage had been muted, Tristan's lips were in full swing as he gushed over senseless gaming strategies to his four thousand *GamerOn* subscribers.

Claude's heart skipped a beat, taking in those perfect, bowed lips in front of the camera.

Tristan looked exactly like Claude needed him to be.

Every Sunday morning, Tristan would thank his subscribers for selecting their weekly video game, and then he'd upload the footage of him completing it, sometimes, just barely doing so. It had become a simple but compulsory part of Claude's daily lifestyle: watching the boy's uploads and imagining those sweet, bowed lips begging Claude to let him come …

A crease formed between his eyebrows when Claude's iPhone vibrated in his pocket. He sighed and pressed the side of his headset attached to his ear. "And where exactly are you this time, Dmitry?"

Dmitry cleared his throat. "I'm drinking coffee outside Starbucks," he reported. "Tristan's inside with some fella and an old, blonde chick. They've been in there over two hours. Oh, and would you believe I've actually managed to get a tan over here?"

"You'll get more than a tan if you do not stay focused, boy," Claude warned him, his black eyes never shifting from his laptop. He restarted the video and watched greedily as Tristan appeared in front of his camera, smiling and waving to his subscribers. "I did not send you to Montana to have a fucking holiday, or are you forgetting what it is I pay you for? Shadow Tristan every minute of every day, and … Do. Not. Get. Caught! I want to know everything the boy does, everyone he speaks to, and for however long. Do you understand me, Dmitry?"

"Yes, Boss…" Dmitry's voice was no longer humorous

across the line. "You sure this is the one you want, though? He's loud and obnoxious. Ugh, I just watched him pick something up off the ground a few minutes ago and eat it." There was clear distaste in Dmitry's tone. "Also, his friend smells like cheeseburgers, and you know I always report the truth. Are you sure he's the right one?"

Am I sure? Claude almost laughed into the headset. "I am absolutely certain, boy. Now, have him arrive in the UK by any means necessary. I don't care how you do it, just make sure it's done. You have four weeks to not fuck this up, is that clear?"

Four weeks was plenty of time for Claude to make the necessary arrangements required for his new toy.

Claude stretched up from his chair and approached the wall opposite his desk. The various photographs, locations, check-ins, and schedules of Tristan Kade adorned the colourless wall. They were stitched together with metal pins and string that accentuated his likes and dislikes, and exactly why they would soon be of use to Claude.

"He likes video games," Claude said, fixing his eyes on the black and white image of Tristan in his cluttered bedroom, crouched over some kind of vintage game console and takeaway boxes.

Ripping the photograph from the wall and clenching it in his hand, Claude's dark eyes roamed over the shape of Tristan's mouth and eyes. His own tongue darted along the seam of his lips as his throat tightened with anticipation. He swallowed hard and returned the image to the wall.

Sitting back down at his desk again, he added, "I suggest you use that thick brain of yours to get the boy to me by the time I arrive. And Dmitry, do not return here empty handed—or you *will* be punished."

Chapter 1

WHEN TRISTAN FOUND out he had a chance to visit Europe, of course he took it. Accepting a free ticket to the biggest gaming convention in the UK was a no-brainer, even if Tristan had to visit a science college along the way. He couldn't wait to sink his claws into all those beautiful, soon-to-be-released games. No matter whether he'd promised the British science guy, Dmitry, that he'd make a stop-off at their famous nerd school, it was *still* a vacation.

Apparently, Westside Charter University of British Science had recently opened up, and they were looking to enrol international exchange students into their 2018 programme. Tristan wasn't *entirely* against enrolling. The thought of it was pretty damn awesome, but when it came down to it, Tristan knew he loved gaming more.

Quiet and rich with medieval history, Edinburgh was a stark contrast to his hometown back in Montana. He'd never stepped out of the States before, and this certainly seemed like a good starting point for him. Plus, his and Jake's gaming channel had a ton of British subscribers, so hopefully he'd come across some of them at the convention. He could only hope they wouldn't beat his ass for trying to be funny in all of his video uploads.

His arrival so far had been everything he'd imagined it to

be. Except for one tiny, insignificant detail. Tristan had *sort of* lied to Jake's mom, Connie, who he lived with back home. While Tristan was visiting the UK for the sake of gaming, and maybe a little bit of history, he'd told Connie he was going purely to attend the interview at Edinburgh's Science College. Only he and Jake knew about the convention.

"Did you reach the college okay?" Jake asked from over the phone.

"Yeah, man, I'm looking at it right now," Tristan replied, glancing over his shoulder to make sure he hadn't gone the wrong way.

The college swelled into Tristan's line of sight, its historic stature like Hogwarts from *Harry Potter.*

"Have you seen the gaming con yet?" Jake's voice broke Tristan's train of thought. "Make sure you get lots of footage for our channel. Some chick subscriber is convinced you're really a twelve-year-old girl, so try getting yourself in some of the frames. "

"Dude, she only said that because she's pissed that I reviewed *Alucard Reigns* and said it has stiff controls and there's not enough customisation. True story. But don't worry, I'll get some decent footage all right. I just need to do this stupid interview for like, thirty minutes, then I'm outta there and in gaming heaven."

Well, in one more day. The convention wasn't until tomorrow evening, and he still had the interview to do. He'd be lying if he said he wasn't looking forward to it. But the flight home Wednesday night? Yeah that, not so much.

"I might book myself in for a tattoo tomorrow morning," Tristan said. "Maybe get the tiger with the wings from *Zaybero* added to my sleeve?" That was his and Jake's favourite fantasy game. "Or some shit to represent this city. I'm not sure yet."

"Awesome, bro. I like the sound of both, but just be careful. And make sure you ask the stupidest questions possible at the con," Jake said, though Tristan knew his best friend was excited beneath the surface. "Since it's you, that shouldn't be too hard."

Tristan rolled his eyes at the jab. "You better be thanking my ass. Our channel subscribers are going to skyrocket once we post this footage."

"Whatever, dude. Just finish that interview so we can focus on what's important."

The line went dead before Tristan had a chance to reply. He stuffed his phone into the pocket of his red sweatshirt and ran a hand through his messy, black hair. Jake was more nervous than anything, and had said something like a free tip and interview were too good to be true. He only agreed to let Tristan on the plane so long as he phoned him every morning and night and told him the hotel he stayed at.

Jake always had Tristan's back. He and his mother had even taken him in when his parents kicked Tristan to the streets for being gay. He'd only been thirteen, so obviously his parents were shitty people, and Tristan had been glad to get rid of them. Life was too short to be surrounded by those who were toxic, and Tristan had zero tolerance for drama.

Maybe, he'd return to the States with more than just a tattoo and gaming footage. A *career*. Future respects. Maybe, with a stroke of luck, Tristan would have the chance to finally start fresh in the UK and make a name for himself. No more bullshit. No more family abandoning him and having to rely on other people to save him.

He could only hope that he'd actually be able to do it.

Survive on his own. Sacrifice gaming. Go to college. Live his life *outside* of his bedroom.

His green eyes roamed over the granite façade of the college entrance—Westside Charter University of British Science. The sculpted building swallowed his line of sight, and its grounds had flyers littered everywhere about a scientist named Professor Claude Galen. He must've been a famous scientist visiting, but hell if Tristan knew who he was. All he could tell was that the college had been vandalised with pamphlets of his name and face, and students were giving out free bouncy balls branded with his initials. Was he the professor Tristan was due to meet that day?

"Here, take one," a cute guy offered Tristan as he walked through the stone courtyard.

He was slightly older than Tristan, tall and built like an overcompensated quarterback. Tristan gulped and took the ball from him. He smiled quickly before stuffing it inside his pocket, ignoring the twitch in his pants when he touched the guy's hand.

Finally locating the college front desk, Tristan spotted the receptionist already hard at work over a pile of filing.

"Hey, I'm supposed to have an interview in like... oh, uhh... two minutes. My name's Tristan Kade?"

"And who are you seeing, son?"

Tristan brought his backpack to the front and opened it, rummaging through the mess of paperwork. "Uh, let's see..." He tossed a few wadded papers on the desk and continued to rifle through his backpack. "I couldn't really read the name. I, err, spilled some water over it on the plane..." He pulled out the letter and handed it to her. "I think that's a G? And another G?"

"Is it Professor Galen?" She raised a pencil-thin eyebrow, her thick Scottish accent somewhat amused. "He just arrived today and said he was off to interview his new student. I guess that's you?"

"Yeah, I think that's the guy," he replied with a nervous smile.

"He's on the third floor," she said to him, glancing from her computer screen to Tristan. "Room three hundred and twelve. Usually has his tea break about now. Will you be okay?"

Tristan nodded, stuffing the crumpled papers back into his backpack. "Thanks."

He walked away from the front desk and to the stairs, unsure whether or not he was headed to the right place. The college was *big* and no one talked to Tristan, although he received a glance here and there from students in the hallways.

He looked at the letter Dmitry had given him and read the

opening paragraph, eyes pouring over the elegant handwriting.

'To whom it may concern,

I received written communication from a colleague who is based in Her Majesty's British Embassy in Washington, informing me that you may be interested in my psychological science programme.

Fortunately, a position has currently opened for an international exchange student, and I would be delighted if you could please join me at Westside Charter University of British Science in Edinburgh, Scotland, for an informal interview. All expenses will be paid (see attached expense form for your attention). This interview will be a chance for you to discuss the remainder of my letter in detail, and ask me any questions, but more importantly, to familiarise yourself with our renowned campuses…'

Tristan scrunched up his face. *Renowned campuses, huh?*

Westside Charter was one of the most prestigious universities in the UK—specialising in psychological science, which Connie always had a keen interest in. When she saw Dmitry and his letter, she was ecstatic that Tristan had a chance to 'better' himself. Wasn't like anyone would take on a kid who'd been held back nearly twice in high school. So she encouraged him to go and told him there was no harm in checking out their offer. It sounded legitimate to her, and if Tristan felt unhappy with it, he didn't accept it.

Jake, on the other hand, had been nervous but stoked about the gaming con, *Night Vision*, happening in the same city. As long as Tristan was to be safe, he pushed for him to focus on what Tristan truly loved more—gaming.

Who needs college when there's talking wolves and blood-thirsty Orcs waiting for him?

Tristan, however, just wanted a break. The letter was a once-in-a-lifetime opportunity, and even *he* wasn't stupid enough to deny that. Anyway, it wasn't like he didn't have a backup plan. He'd get his tattoo done tomorrow before the convention, and then maybe do some sightseeing before his flight home on Wednesday morning.

He couldn't wait to add to the half-sleeve he already had on his left arm, although, it mostly consisted of the black wolf from *Zaybero*, trees, and a raven carcass. Perhaps he'd add something that would reflect Edinburgh City. A mask to represent the plague that once devoured its dingy chambers? Or the castle or some shit like that. Maybe even a highland cow.

Ultimately, he'd make sure to have some fun as well as attending the interview—just like he'd promised Jake and Connie.

Tristan walked up the stone staircase, jumping two at a time, and wandered through the semi-crowded hallways until he found room three hundred and twelve.

With a sharp intake of breath, he knocked on the already-opened door. "Hey, anyone here? Is this where I talk about the student thing?"

Claude's Monday was not off to a good start.

Not only had his ten o'clock presentation been cancelled at the last minute—erasing all of the hard work he'd poured into his project for weeks now—but Derek, the school's mind-numbingly, uninteresting dean, had requested that Claude accompany him to an event across the city late that night. Wasn't that good of him? Some kind of charity fundraising dinner, which wouldn't have been so awful if not for its attendees, and the fact that Claude had better things to be doing with his time.

Things that required his full, undivided attention.

At least he'd be paid for the dinner, not that he needed the money. He'd only come to Edinburgh because he'd grown restless of his seminars in Milan, and more than anything, he desired to meet his new student.

Unlike his last one, Claude hoped that this boy would be willing to learn from him.

"Hey, anyone here? Is this where I talk about the student thing?"

A young boy knocked on Claude's office door. He stood there alone with a worn-out, black backpack slung over his shoulders; even though Claude was at the other end of the hallway, he could smell the boy's cheap aftershave invading his senses. He knew straight away who the boy was and why he'd ventured into Claude's office.

The professor cleared his throat and halted beside the boy, who turned around like a deer caught in the headlights. Considerably larger than him, Claude's shadow swallowed Tristan up.

My poor, helpless boy.

"I do believe the last time I checked," Claude said to him coolly, "doors were incapable of a response. Are you lost?"

The boy glanced up, and his eyes were a startling shade of green. Sculpted by a mop of thick, unruly wavy hair and a pale, jutted-out jawline, Tristan shook his head.

"Err, I was sure this was room three hundred and twelve." He glanced down at a scrunched-up pile of paperwork in his hand and scratched the back of his neck. Noticing the plaque nailed against Claude's door, Tristan tapped it rapidly and exclaimed, "I was right! This is the right room! I'm looking for a Professor Jalen? Dude, can you help me out? I'm not really from here, as you can probably tell. Spot the newbie, eh?"

"Well, first of all, it's Galen," Claude corrected him with a clear, precise English accent. He sipped his latte and swept by the boy and into his office. *Dude?* Just who did this young man take him for? The boy rushed in after him, stopping at the threshold. "And as with every teacher in this school, you will address me as Professor—or Sir. Now, to what do I owe the pleasure of your visit?"

As he veered confidently towards his desk, he was no longer looking at the boy, but he could see in his peripheral vision that Tristan was blushing immensely. A thought that brought a smirk to Claude's face.

So this is the real Tristan Kade, hmm? He is absolutely exquisite. Yes… he'll do splendidly as my new student.

Claude sat down on the corner of his desk and leant

casually against its rich mahogany. The room was old and typical of Edinburgh—stacked with countless old books which, probably, no one had or would ever manage to read, and it smelled particularly of parchment and lavender polish.

Claude did not despise the city, but he would be glad to see the back of it once he returned home. As soon as he'd taken care of his new… responsibility up north, he could elope to London once again and then rest.

If things went according to plan, that would be quite soon.

"Oh, well, I got this"—Tristan pulled out a letter that had been crumpled up numerous times, and had coffee stains on it—"and I was told about some placement or something?" He paused for a moment, and then blushed, "Sir? Dmitry, the embassy guy who spoke to me, didn't tell me a lot. But he said you guys were keen to take on new students since the college just opened up. So… here I am," he added hastily, sparing a bashful smile.

Claude's dark eyes never moved from Tristan. After a moment, he regarded the paper with a nod of his head. "Yes, your invitation letter. I'm delighted to see you managed to hold it together." The clear tape and coffee stains brandished over the letter did not go amiss as he held his gaze for a moment. And then Claude glanced into Tristan's eyes again, which pierced into Claude's in utter defiance.

He's untamed…

Claude had already noticed how worn out the boy's Converse were and that his shirt poking out from his red hoodie was clearly not ironed.

Like a puppy just begging *to be trained.*

"Anyway, I have misplaced my manners," Claude said, offering him a tight smile. "Would you like a drink? Edinburgh at this time of year does not have the best climate. In fact, Edinburgh at any time of year doesn't have the best climate. So, tea? Coffee? Hot chocolate?"

Although the boy didn't know it just yet, Claude's hospitality was not something to be taken for granted. Tristan would soon learn that.

"Uh, hot chocolate would be nice, please," the boy paused and added, "Sir," before he took out an obnoxious blue-coloured bouncy ball from his pocket and started fiddling with it. His attention now seemed more focused on the ball rather than Claude.

"So, tell me, Tristan. Are you familiar with my *malleability theory*?" Claude asked, and Tristan shook his head. Claude had already expected as much, and so he steeled himself. "It's a fascinating study, Mr. Kade, however, not one very well known. But should you agree to study here, I could teach you its concept in such riveting detail that you'll never again look at the world the same way—almost as if you have been reborn."

"But I already know how shi—I mean, how terrible the world is." Tristan rolled his eyes and gave out a huff of air, which made Claude tense. "I'll have sugar with that, too, I guess. Thought you English people put it in everything, anyways."

My, my, my. Such appalling behaviour. Claude merely

grinned at him. "I'm a complex man, Mr. Kade, and I would be cruel to delude you into thinking otherwise. For example, just because someone asks me for something does not mean I grant it. Take what you are given." Claude narrowed his eyes and a smirk tugged at his lips. "Sugar in something that is already sweet is unnecessary. Would you not think of it as an overindulgence?"

Already, Tristan had failed one of his tests.

Such a pity.

The boy's lips pressed into a line, but his ears and neck flushed an astonishing shade of pink. "Fine, then I won't take the hot chocolate," Tristan huffed out in that same childish manner of his. "I'll just have water or something."

The boy's reaction amused him, but it was foolish. Claude leant over his desk and tapped at his intercom.

"Ms. Helens, a hot chocolate and fresh latte, please. Extra shot."

"Yes, Professor!"

By all accounts, the poor widow would do anything to be inside his office. She frequently altered his flowers there, or asked if he needed any water, even when he repeatedly told her not to disturb him. In spite of his profession, he simply was not the sociable type.

He had never been.

Claude sat back and pressed his hands on the edge of his desk. "I have a tour of the university planned out for you, Tristan. Before we do that, I thought this would be an opportunity for us to have the interview. Highly informal and it should not take very long—merely enough time for you to ask any questions about the student placement, and for us to get to know each other. Put a face to the name, if you will. What do you say?"

Tristan leant back and crossed over his arms, and though it looked casual, Claude knew it was a defensive pose. "Sure," he said quietly. "What about this malleability theory, then? What's it about? Unless you want to talk more about sugar and hot chocolate."

Clearly meant to be a taunting jab, and not one that Claude appreciated. He told himself to remain calm and slowly wet his lips before beginning. "Human beings, by nature, are malleable creatures. Like many others, Mr. Kade, I believe the human brain can be conditioned into something that is infinitely greater than originally intended. We are always evolving. Always adapting to our environments. So, why can't we condition the mind to alter a person entirely? That's the malleability theory. That's what I teach and have done so for nearly twenty years now."

"Sounds interesting enough," Tristan replied, feigning disinterest by the way he unfolded his arms and tossed the ball into the air so he could catch it. "So, what about you? What are you like? I kind of want to know if we're going to be a good fit and all that before I make my decision. If I can't get along with my teacher, then it's not going to work out, no matter how cool your theory is."

Claude chuckled dryly. "Well, I do teach malleability for a living, Tristan. As long as you do what I say and always obey my rules, then I think we'll get along splendidly."

Tristan laughed, too. "Uh, *all* of them? I mean, they're not like strict rules, right?"

"That all depends on perspective." Claude winked at him, and at that moment, Ms. Helens rushed into the room and placed their drinks on the middle of Claude's desk. They remained silent until she left, but while Tristan's eyes fixed on their hot drinks, Claude's were on him. "Go on, help yourself."

Claude nodded towards the hot chocolate, but Tristan didn't take it. Instead, his gaze went right to Claude's as if he were testing him. "Not thirsty anymore, Sir. But... uhh, thanks."

This one will require a lot of training. Claude couldn't help but smirk at that. "Do you recall what I said earlier on?"

Take what you are given.

When Tristan refused to answer, Claude felt his jaw clench. He was not a man known for self-centeredness, but he did, however, receive mail on a weekly basis begging him to spare students a second glance. Work experience. Keynote engagements. Dates, for heaven's sake. This boy's demeanour... it was completely off the script, which irked him.

Perhaps he'd gotten off on the wrong foot with Tristan, which wouldn't bode well if they decided to *work* together. He hadn't meant to test Tristan right out of the gate, either, but the boy's apparent disinterest had irritated Claude.

He picked up Tristan's hot drink and extended him it.

"Drink up before it gets cold," he said firmly. "I've not got two heads, Tristan. I am not a monster. I'm simply trying to get to know you. If I offended you before, then I can only say that was not my intention. How about we skip all the formalities, and you tell me about your hometown." He nodded towards the hot chocolate, which Tristan still hadn't taken from him. "And by the way, there was already sugar inside it. I was merely testing you, which I happen to do quite often. It's how I come to understand what people desire. How they function. I'll admit, my father did always say I often push people too far. You'd think after thirty-eight years I'd have learned."

This time, Tristan took the hot chocolate from him and drank it, the tension in his shoulders ebbing. "Well, my hometown's nothing to write home about. Just some middle class area where my best friend's mom took me in after my parents couldn't deal with me anymore." He shrugged, taking another sip. "Troubled teen and all that."

"Do you still keep in contact with these people?"

"Nah, they have three other kids, and I'm the middle child anyway. Didn't really care about me. Besides, I can manage on my own. I mean, look at where I am now."

"Indeed." Claude sipped his own drink, relieved Tristan had loosened up a little, and that his own anger had abated. "Had you always had a keen interest in psychological science?"

Claude crossed his arms and leant against his desk again. Tristan shrugged and bounced the ball up and down, eyes following it instead of Claude.

"I don't know. Maybe? Guess I just wanted to know why I had to be the bad kid while my brothers got to be the good ones. It's the main reason I came here today. I'd like to explore it more, you know, broaden my horizons. I just don't know where to start. I mean, the only thing I'm good at is video games, really."

"I see great potential in you, Tristan, and not just with gaming. Included in the response letter you sent back to me, I saw you'd originally had an interest in studying herpetology, particularly lizards. I'm sorry to say that studying with me would not afford you to do that, however, I do have associates across the country who'd gladly allow you to shadow them for a day or so. What would you say to that?"

"That'd be cool," he replied, shrugging his shoulder. But Claude could see those beautiful, green eyes light up with exhilaration, despite the boy trying his damnedest to hide it. "I used to have a pet lizard named Borg. Took him to school with me and everything... I miss that creepy lil' guy."

A smile tugged at Claude's stubble. "I'll keep this conversation in mind, then. As for the basic legalities of the placement itself, all expenses and student loans will be paid for under our International Exchange Student scheme. May I ask how old are you again?"

"Tw—" the boy paused for a moment with wide eyes and a hard swallow. "Eighteen... I'm eighteen. Probably too young for this programme, huh?"

No, but you are certainly too old to be lying to me. As if Claude didn't know already that Tristan was twenty-one. Pity. He had given the boy a chance to be honest with him, and he failed. It would no doubt be the first of many.

"On the contrary, you just made our cut-off for the placement. It was only open to eighteen to twenty-year-olds." Claude saw disappointment flash over Tristan's face. He continued, "One thing I do need to know, Tristan, is your next of kin? I know you've said that you don't keep in touch with your folks, but for legal purposes, I need to know who to contact in case of an emergency. There must be *someone* out there who looks out for you. Wonders where you are."

"Uh, I kind of don't really have anyone." His cheeks dimpled into a grin, humouring Claude. "Everyone I knew died last week in a terrible tornado accident. Cows were flying and everything." Tristan's little smirk sent waves of anger through Claude's body. The boy was mocking him; there had been nothing in the media lately about catastrophic tornadoes. "I hope that doesn't ruin my chance of working with you."

"Oh, my. What a terrible ordeal you must've gone through with the tornado. Such a brave, young man you are," Claude shot back dryly, and this time Tristan snorted, throwing the bouncy ball into the air and catching it again. "But I should warn you that having a sense of humour may get you into trouble. Naughty boys do not often last long in my class, Tristan."

Tristan smiled at him tightly, but again, it had evidently

been forced. He wanted to slap that insolent grin right off the boy's face. But that would not bode well so early on. Claude knew he had to feign flirtation to keep the boy from running away from him.

It wasn't Tristan's snarky attitude that angered Claude so much, but rather it was the way he looked like he truly didn't *want* to be there. He didn't *want* Claude. He was the first to not want any of it. To not want *him*.

"Truthfully, I only have my best friend and his mom," Tristan explained. "But I'm moving out soon, and they're pretty eager to have their spare room back. So, it *is* just me."

Claude gulped, his throat turning dry. He unfolded his arms and ran a watched hand through his dark, slicked back hair. "Once you see the school and its facilities, I'm sure you'll see exactly why studying here—with me—can enlighten you. I travel a lot, you see, because every university I am welcomed into is a way for me to open my research to new, like-minded individuals. The journey can often be overwhelming. Intense. Utterly fascinating. But if you are willing to learn and do as I say, Mr. Kade, then I guarantee you'll have a lot to gain from what I have to offer you. I simply need someone who is loyal, obedient, and knows when to take what they are given."

Tristan tensed, shoulders hunching forward. "I'm not really any of those things. Look, I'll level with ya; I only came here because Jake's mom really wanted me to. I'm kind of the opposite of everything you just said. I mean, I put stink bombs in the principal's office until I was fourteen… and the resume and references you asked me to email you? You saw that I've never had a job, right? Well, I sort of lied about that. I've had five of them and got fired from every single one." His face fell slightly, but Claude could see that he was telling the truth—because Claude had already known. "Honestly, you'd be an idiot to accept me."

"Honesty is a curious thing," Claude said to him, "and is something that I encourage my students to be with me at all times. But honesty, just like compliancy, is something that is taught. As your mentor, I can show you how to adapt, how to obey, how to truly push your boundaries, and to become malleable in every way, shape, or form. That's the art of my theory—to condition one's mind in a way that never seemed possible to them before. But, let's talk more of this later."

He stood from the edge of his desk, picked up his coffee, and extended his gaze towards the door.

"I have a feeling you'll be surprised by what this school has to offer. Shall we begin the tour, Mr. Kade?"

The boy gulped, and then he followed Claude out of the office.

"Over here, we have our student accommodation halls. Down the corridor from that, there is a private gym, sauna room, and a pool. Do you like to swim, Tristan?"

Tristan jumped out of his stupor. He'd been too fixated on the professor's elaborate hand gestures to realise he was asking him a question.

"Uh, not really," he answered.

"Well, I am aware that swimming lessons take place every Thursday evening, so if you ever wanted to learn, it would be included in your placement. Everything at the university is free for our ideal student. In return for enrolling in our exchange program, we take care of everything for you, including your tuition fees."

"Is there a gaming room here?"

The professor nodded, the sun's rays slicing over his sharp features. "An entire floor dedicated to it." He stopped and glanced at his watch, then looked ahead. "Ah, I do believe I should show you the main fire exits first. Boring, but necessary procedure. In total, there are forty-one of them, but the most important one is next to the cafeteria. Oh, speaking of which…"

Now that they had reached the cafeteria, Claude paused next to the coffee machine at the salad bar. Tristan was surprised to find the cafeteria almost empty. No students ditching class or studying there like he was used to. Just the janitor mopping up a spillage next to the *Healthy Eating* campaigns: a collection of notice boards about why veganism was better.

Yeah, right! Bacon was Tristan's life.

"I do believe it's time for my second one," Claude said with a ghost of a grin, and the way he slapped the side of the vending machine caused Tristan to jump. "The cups get jammed inside," he explained to him when Tristan dipped down to peer at the coffee pouring into the paper cup.

"Yeah, the vending machine at my school was like this. I found a cat inside it once."

"You found an animal inside of a vending machine? How on earth did that happen?"

"Beats me. But me and Jake, my best friend, we managed to get her out and took her home." Sadness laced the boy's features and his lips pouted into a frown. "I miss that dopey cat."

"What happened to her?"

Claude retrieved his coffee cup and gazed at Tristan softly.

"She ran away two years later. She used to constantly attack Connie's vases... Hmm, now that I think about it, maybe the front door being open was no accident at all."

Mirth had returned to the boy's voice, and Claude found his body swelling with warmth. "Yes. Perhaps not. Would you like to see the science department?"

"That would be awesome, yeah."

They continued their tour and Tristan listened to more of Claude's stories of his achievements and even some reminiscence of his childhood in England. The way he spoke and used his hands a lot reminded Tristan of one of his favourite high school teachers. The only teacher who had ever made his history class fun.

Despite the whole scene with the hot chocolate, Tristan found himself warming to Professor Galen. He was way too intelligent to be talking to someone like Tristan, not to mention attractive—if Tristan was into older guys, that was. But still, he enjoyed Claude's company and *actually* considered taking the placement.

Sure, he was a bit eccentric, but weren't all scientists? If anything, Tristan found it endearing, especially when the professor went on and on about the theory he and his father had been carrying out.

"You seem pretty close to your dad," Tristan said. He couldn't help but smile when Professor Galen spoke and used those elaborate hand gestures. "You two must get along well."

The professor hummed to himself, then a tight grin crossed his lips. "He certainly shaped me into the man I am today."

"He *must* be a good man then. I mean, you've achieved so much."

Professor Galen chuckled at that. "Compliment taken, Mr. Kade."

Tristan's face and ears heated. He wanted to know more about the professor outside of the school, but he couldn't bring himself to suggest such a thing. The professor probably had a girlfriend, anyway.

Tristan's heart plummeted at the thought.

"So," Professor Galen started, as they reached the reception desk where Ms. Helens waited patiently, "what do you think about working alongside me?"

Tristan stared at him for a moment. "I... I don't know.

This place is really far out and I'm just not sure yet."

More like he didn't want to drag the professor's name into the ground with his own stupidity. Plus, the gaming con…

"If you were truly uncertain, Mr. Kade, then you would not be standing here today." Claude finished the remainder of his coffee and threw the cup in the rubbish bin. "Fortunately, you have until Wednesday to decide on your final answer before I'm forced to seek another candidate. You know what I have to offer you. So please, take your time thinking about it, and let me know what your decision is in a few days' time."

Did Tristan fall into the *Twilight Zone* or something? What the hell did the professor see in him? Tristan couldn't even say the alphabet backwards, never mind name all the elements on the periodic table.

Professor Galen's eyes darkened as they pinned Tristan under that inscrutable gaze. Tristan allowed himself the fantasy of imagining it was lust in those dark chocolate orbs.

"I'll think about it," he said, squirming under Claude's gaze, knowing full well it was impossible.

Claude nodded, a gentle smile tugging at his pressed lips. "I do believe Ms. Helens is here to show you the way out." He nodded over Tristan's shoulder, where they could hear Ms. Helens' heels clicking against the floor. "Perhaps I will see you in the meantime? But if not, I will look forward to our next encounter." He offered Tristan his hand, who took it hesitantly, and they shook, their eyes burning into each other. "It's been a pleasure, Mr. Kade. Until next time."

Tristan visibly shuddered. "Yeah," he muttered quickly. "Until next time, Professor…"

Chapter 2

TRISTAN STAYED IN his hotel that night, thinking about his meeting with Professor Galen. Intriguing, but intense. *I mean, that whole sugar thing? What the hell was* that *supposed to mean?* It didn't matter, anyway; Tristan did not belong here. It was clear from the beginning that he was wasting Professor Galen's time, and he didn't know why he got the letter in the first place, or why Dmitry asked him to fly over. He did what he could to turn Galen off—even lying about his age, in hopes that saying he was eighteen instead of twenty-one would have made Claude think Tristan was too immature to be a candidate. But even during the tour, the professor seemed eager to have him.

Maybe he should have brought up being held back in tenth grade, but that was something Tristan had been self-conscious about, especially since he had always been the oldest in his class and that Jake graduated before him. It was Tristan's incompetence that made their graduation trip never happen.

It wasn't that school was hard for Tristan, but he stopped doing his homework when he got wrapped up in the wrong crowd that year. Then he stopped going to his classes, which sank his once average grades even lower. Not even touching on his clear *mommy and daddy issues*, really, it was a miracle

Professor Galen had given Tristan the time of day.

And Tristan acted like such an *ass* at the beginning! He hadn't intended to, but the professor just brought a side out of Tristan that he'd been so long without.

Lust and longing.

He longed to make a future for himself, but his dick lusted for Professor Galen.

Why was his brain so fucking stupid? He'd just met the guy, who was totally out of Tristan's league. But Claude was kind during the tour, and patient, which made it all the harder to convince Tristan he was barking up the wrong tree. Claude would talk about things Tristan had no idea the meaning of, and then he'd ask him a question, and Tristan had to bullshit his way out the best way he could.

Not to mention he'd talked about his vending machine cat story, and then walked into a glass door.

Twice.

Apparently, winging it had become Tristan's immediate fallback in life—just like Jake's mom always said it would.

"None of us know what we're doing in the world, Trist. We just get on with it and hope we somehow survive."

Connie had been right. She was *always* right. When it came down to it, Tristan did like the school, even if he knew jack shit about the professor's unique malleability theory. With Claude's patient smiles and his equally patient pauses, it was clear Tristan had answered a lot of the professor's questions incorrectly. But he was still so encouraging with Tristan, prompting him with answers and explaining every aspect of the school and its International Exchange Student Programme. Tristan had nodded and smiled, even though he'd known nothing about the school except from what its webpage had told him, which Tristan's goldfish memory had forgotten by the time he arrived in the country.

He could at least remember what it looked like, though the pictures didn't do it justice. *Tickle me pink and call me Harry Potter* had been Tristan's first impression of the school—school being a total understatement. It was like a castle. From the marbled tiles in the hallways, the grand staircases, brass pillars supporting every classroom, and immaculately groomed courtyard, to the stained-glass windows in the canteen and bell on top of the domed building, it was like a dream come true for some.

He could see himself having a real future here, working alongside some of the greatest minds in the country, and being mentored by their scientific *God*, for Christ's sake. That's what Ms. Helens had called him. Claude Galen was really something in the science world. Tristan felt stupid for not knowing who he was or any of his malleable *whatever-the-fuck-they-were* theories.

Claude seemed happy to fill Tristan in about the school, and the more he talked about his study of malleable transcendence, the more Tristan grew engrossed by what he said, and he wanted to learn more. Was he choosing this over gaming?

It seemed possible.

But when you peeled back his surface, Tristan wasn't

qualified enough. That was the biggest downside of all. He liked science, but it wasn't like he had good grades back in high school. Chemistry was his best class with a measly B-, and he didn't think that was enough to be Professor Galen's prized, international student—regardless of what Jake's mom said.

Well, at least he got a free trip to Europe, so there was always that, and the convention was tomorrow. *There* he was in his comfort zone and actually knew what he was talking about. And he had Jake and their channel to think about.

Tristan reached over to his nightstand and grabbed his ridiculously old cell phone, then looked at the screen. He should call Jake to make sure everything's okay back home, but he figured it'd be the middle of the night for them. He'd sent Connie a text earlier, anyway, saying he'd been to the college, and it'd gone well. Tomorrow, he planned to visit a tattoo parlour two blocks away, and then he'd hit the *Night Vision* and start filming.

Tristan's stomach flipped with excitement, butterflies gathering at the thought of being there. He knew by the way his body reacted to the con and a tattoo, as opposed to the placement, that gaming was where he truly belonged. It was the one thing that had always been there for him as a kid, and he was never tested on it.

In the end, he'd realised that he'd rather pursue gaming than go to college. He knew in the back of his mind which was the most logical option.

The college.

But at what cost?

The fact that his body twitched whenever he thought of Professor Galen, and that he jerked off thinking about him while he took a shower in his room late that night, spoke loud and clear that it would cost him more than just his soul.

The next day, Tristan walked down the cobbled roads that were crammed behind his hotel, and he searched for the tattoo parlour he'd been recommended to online. It had a five-star rating, and it accepted walk-ins as long as they knew what they wanted and paid the amount in full.

He'd been thinking about it all night—along with other things, or rather, other people—and he finally decided on what he wanted. Something dark and cool but also reflective of the medieval city he was in.

A plague doctor seemed to be the most fitting. While the pandemic had been eradicated over five centuries ago, the City Chambers, where victims had been left to rot and die, still existed today. Reading an article about it had caused goosebumps to break out over Tristan's body. He loved to learn about things that sent shivers down his spine and caused his skin to crawl. The beaked mask would look perfect next to the raven skull inked around his elbow.

Thankfully, the weather wasn't as bad as Tristan anticipated. He'd been forewarned that the British climate was among the worst, and he hadn't looked forward to wintertime in Scotland. But that day, it wasn't raining, and the sky was devoid of any clouds. A beautiful winter's day shrouded in thick snow, Tristan wrapped himself in his favourite red sweater, jeans, Converse, and leather coat, and then tied Jake's turquoise scarf around his neck. He somehow managed to follow Google maps on his cell phone, and after only getting lost twice, he found the right tattoo place.

Yang Tattoo Parlour: *Walk-ins and dugs welcome!*

He hoped the tattoo and convention would take his mind off the college. The offer had been tempting, but now that he'd slept on it, something about the interview had come across off to him. Professor Galen, in general, set Tristan on edge, and he couldn't shake off the uneasy feeling that crept inside of him whenever he thought of Galen… Guilt about wasting his time, and then an undeniable surge of desire that prompted him to crash his lips against Claude's mouth.

Sure, the guy was intelligent. He knew his shit straight off the bat, even if Tristan had no idea what he was talking about. But those dark brown eyes, shaded by his dark hair and impeccably ironed shirt and pants, made the man appear godlike. It was impossible not to feel mesmerized or intimidated by him. He wanted to know more. He *wanted* Claude Galen! But he wasn't good enough for the program, or for him. Tristan was a nobody, and gaming was his only outlet.

He'd decline the offer tomorrow. Right now, Tristan pushed open the parlour door and stepped into a room adorned in expensive leather. The sofas in the waiting room flanked the entire left wall, whereas the right supported a dark wooden desk adorned in leather skull heads, burning incense, and various memorabilia. From what Tristan could tell, the place appeared empty, and when he peered over the reception desk, a pile of artwork had been scattered all over it, spilling over the counter and down onto the chair and dark-carpeted floor.

"I'm gonna close up, cutie," someone called from the back room, appearing through an archway that was shrouded in dangling rosary beads. "I gotta nip out, so no walk-ins for at least an hour."

Tristan assumed by the amount of tattoos and piercings on the guy's body, he was the parlour owner. He only looked to be in his midtwenties. His latex-gloved hands held onto a piercing gun, and when Tristan's eyes roamed up from the gun to his grey eyes, he jolted.

"Oh, that's cool. I just wanted to like… see if you could sketch a tattoo for me." Tristan fumbled through his jeans back pocket and withdrew a bunch of rolled-up British notes. "I can pay in cash?"

The bearded Scotsman gave Tristan the once-over. "What d'ye want likes?"

"I sketched it down for you. Thought that might be better. Uhh... but I can totally come back. I don't fly home until tomorrow."

"I'm fully booked 'til then. If you want something done, now's your chance before I go on a lunch break. Are you visiting from America?"

Tristan nodded, a little bashful under the man's penetrating, but kind stare. This was the first person outside of the college that Tristan had spoken to in Scotland, and his husky accent was beyond attractive.

"Yeah, I'm just here a few days, but I really wanted something to reflect this city. I thought a plague doctor's mask on my upper arm, next to my raven tattoo, would be cool."

He blushed again, and the owner smiled. "Name's Scott. Sit down back there"—he nodded to the back room, where Tristan could see nothing through the gothic beads that dangled from the doorframe—"and we can start the outline. How big are you thinkin'?"

"Just an inch or two," Tristan said, grasping his left arm. "I've already got a half-sleeve, so I guess we could just extend that. Uh, if that's cool with you."

"When did ya get the sleeve done?"

"Err..." Was it three years ago? He'd gotten the first part of the sleeve—the raven's skull—at a house party when he was eighteen. "Three years ago, I guess. It's not super faded."

Scott nodded. "Well, let's see what we can do in a couple of hours. Once I'm done, you can sit with me for lunch if you want. Nothing fancy, but I figured since you're new 'round here you'd wanna hang out with some of the locals. I'm as Scottish as you can get." Scott reached out and flipped the sign on the door to *closed*. "Offer is there, cutie. You can take it or leave it. The place does good bagels, though, and it's near that geek con I bet you're going to."

Tristan laughed. "Am I that obvious?"

"You have a Tardis on your school bag."

Tristan followed the tattooist to the back of the parlour, a smile creeping onto his face.

Had he just been asked out on a date?

"Oh, and by the way, what the hell does *dugs* mean?"

Scott snorted and glanced over his shoulder. "Let's just say it's hairy and has lots of teeth."

❦ ❦

"The café's just down there," Scott said, pointing his tattooed hand down a cobbled, one-way street. Edinburgh was full of them, though sometimes it was hard to see the potholes on the roads because of the snow. And there had been a *lot* of them. "Vegan, but I swear, this shit tastes amazing."

"You've tasted shit before?" Tristan probed, raising an eyebrow.

He'd grown immensely comfortable in Scott's presence over their two-hour bonding session back at the parlour. Tristan's arm tingled with the aftermath of the needle, but it was a pleasant sensation. Or rather, an accomplished one, like he'd actually done something productive.

"Don't you think you can stay for a little while longer? There's still so much to see. I get bored of it because I see it every day, but I could show you around Calton Hill, Arthur's Seat—everything. All the good bits. You'd enjoy it, kid."

"Sorry," Tristan said with a too-wide smile. "I want to, but my ticket only lasts until tomorrow."

However, he thought he could visit again sometime. No harm in making friends over here. Plus, it was a truly beautiful city, and he was beginning to have fun with Scott. Maybe they could exchange details after his lunch break.

"Well, what if I kidnap you and hide you in my room?" Scott's eyes glinted with mirth, a smile pulling at his bearded cheeks. "You can be my secret boyfriend."

"I can't have Jake do the channel by himself. Even though he thinks he's good at games, he sucks. He'd burn our channel to the ground. Trust me."

But still, I could always accept Claude's offer and stay here, hang out with Scott more, and I'd get to see the professor more...

The placement tempted him, but it wasn't enough to work with a guy that sent shivers up his spine and restricted his breathing. His gut lurched whenever he thought about Claude Galen and those sharp, penetrating eyes. A prestigious university and renowned professor, wanting to take Tristan on because some Dmitry guy at the British Embassy invited him to their school? All inclusive? Yeah, what was the catch? Would Tristan have to sell his soul or some shit? The more he thought about the offer, the greater he suspected it was too good to be true.

On the other hand, if he *did* accept the offer and it turned out to be legitimate, it wasn't like Tristan had anything to lose.

"How's your arm now?" Scott asked, opening the door to the artisan coffee shop.

Tristan had been too lost in his thoughts to realise they'd

arrived. He rubbed at his bandaged arm, his skin hot beneath the strong winter sun, and sweaty under the cling film Scott wrapped around the bandage.

"Uh, good. I can't wait to see it once it's healed. You did an amazing job, dude."

He really did. The mask looked awesome next to Tristan's raven skull.

"I don't think I ever had someone grab my arm the whole session," Scott said with a lopsided grin. "That swear at the end was quite impressive, and I canny say I didn't enjoy it. You young *brats*," he teased, pushing Tristan's playfully. "Can't take the pain, eh? It wasn't *that* sore. Or were you just trying to flirt with me, cutie"

Tristan's ears heated, and his head turned around defensively. "I wasn't flirting!"

"Come on, don't break my heart," Scott winked at him, stepping over the wooden threshold. "Not when we've bonded so much already."

He swept by Tristan and over to the cake display where two baristas steamed milk and ground coffee beans mechanically. Tristan smiled faintly. Usually, he turned defensive whenever his sexuality was questioned, but Scott was so easy to talk to and clearly interested in him. Why else would he ask Tristan out for coffee and also refuse the tip he had offered for doing his tattoo in less than an hour? Scott was exactly Tristan's type: tattoos, piercings, beard, and a killer laugh.

Then why was Claude Galen, a man who was probably

old enough to be his *father*, swarming his mind?

But as for the vegan café he'd taken him to... that remained to be seen. It was Tristan's idea of *hell*. However, he was in a new country, and he was willing to try different things even if it meant no bacon or milk. He ordered a raw *Shamrock Shake* made up of mint leaves, spinach, bananas, and cocoa powder, and a flapjack consisting of freshly crushed-up dates. Once he and Scott sat down in a dark wooden booth, Tristan found that his food didn't taste too awful once he got over the initial shock of *no hot chocolate or real cake*.

A quirky, male waiter brought Scott his bagel and cup of tea. There were two sachets of sugar on the side of the saucer, and Tristan remembered the interview again. His stomach sank at how he'd soon be declining an opportunity of a lifetime.

Claude Galen's intense, dark stare...

Tristan's fingers blanched white around his smoothie, and he tightened his legs together. *Damn it!* The professor's gaze was etched into him, sending jolts to areas of Tristan's body that he hadn't felt in... fuck, forever.

Why was his body reacting like this whenever he thought about the professor? Sure, his whole personality was somewhat hypnotic, but Tristan couldn't *actually* be into someone he just met, could he? Was it because Claude reminded him of Mr Simmons? The only teacher who ever gave a shit about Tristan and saw potential in him.

Shit. How would the professor handle his rejection?

He did say something about being forced to seek another candidate, so the guy clearly had a list of students waiting to be mentored by him. Maybe he needn't worry about how the professor would react, or rather, how Tristan would tell him. *When* was more important. After the convention? That would be cutting it close, and the college might be closed.

"You okay?" Scott probed him, glancing up from his iPad on the booth table. "You're totally spacing out on me."

"Yeah," Tristan said absently, and his stomach grumbled through the swamped café. "I mean, *no*! I'm just *still* hungry, is all. *Hungry*, not spacey," he winked at Scott, grabbing the waitress' arm as she buzzed by their table.

She was a petite girl with messy, auburn hair tied into a bun on top of her head. It flapped around like a donut as she smiled and took his order. His dinner at his—what was the hotel called again? Ah, Premier Inn—wasn't the most appetising. For some reason, Tristan couldn't bring himself to eat anything after his meeting with the professor. But now he was starving, and the cake hadn't been enough. He ordered a basket of mixed fruit, hoping it'd settle his nerves.

Maybe he could call the college *before* he headed to the convention in a couple of hours. It'd be enough time to think of how he'd say it—how he'd throw away the biggest opportunity of his lifetime, according to Connie. While it wasn't the most logical solution, it felt the most right. And as much as he hated his parents, they'd taught him to always follow his instincts.

His instincts told him to steer clear from the college.

"Beautiful weather, is it not?"

Tristan looked up and couldn't believe his eyes. Professor Galen was sitting two tables away from them, latte in one hand and a book in the other.

"If you like the snow, I guess," Tristan replied, his smile too tight as his face and ears heated.

Why did Professor Galen make him so nervous? He was handsome and kind, clearly, but there was *something* about him that made Tristan's heart race and his palms turn sweaty—more so than Scott did. Even more than Joe Manganiello did.

The professor's smile—it made Tristan's stomach flip flop in ways he hadn't experienced before.

Scott glanced between Claude and Tristan, putting two and two together. He picked up his iPad.

"Ah, well, I was gonna nip to the gents anyway. Gotta drop the kids off at the pool."

"Ew. You're disgusting," Tristan teased, and Scott snorted his way towards the restroom.

Tristan's heart hammered in his chest, all too aware of Claude's presence down from him, and that if Tristan didn't speak *now*, he'd feel like an ungrateful ass forever.

"I was actually going to the college later..."

Go sit next to him, you idiot!

He cleared his throat and nervously stood up from the booth, dragging his backpack with him, almost dropping it. *Get ahold of yourself, Tristan! You're acting like you never saw a hot guy before.*

"Is it cool if I sit with you, Sir?"

He gestured the seat across from Claude, who inclined his head with a soft smile. "Of course. Can I get you anything more? Extra cake? They do wonderful scones here."

"No, thanks," Tristan said, tone more clipped again. None of his joking like with Scott. No. Claude felt way too formal for that kind of approach, despite the faint glimmers of normalcy he'd shown during the interview, and Tristan's heart hammered too loudly for him to focus. He could only imagine what Claude was like in the bedroom. So dominating and powerful. *Focus, Tristan!* "I had plenty earlier on. I've never had raw smoothies before, but they're... not half bad. I'd eighty-nine percent recommend the Green Shamrock Shake."

Claude nodded, then picked up his paper cup. "That's a precise recommendation," he said, and Tristan could smell the coffee oozing over the paper rim. "I prefer the old-fashioned stuff, Tristan, much to Ms Helens disapproval. Anyway, have you thought more about my offer?"

"I'm declining," Tristan said softly, then he unzipped his backpack and pulled out the paperwork. He tilted them on the table towards Claude, who still sat there with a smile not quite reaching his eyes. "Sorry, it's just, I'm not cut out for it. I really do think someone else will benefit from it. Someone more experienced than me. I'm sorry, but... I'd like to thank you for your consideration. And your colleague, Dmitry. I really did appreciate it, man, but professional gaming is what I've always dreamed of doing. I'm actually hitting the convention later on tonight, and I'll hopefully figure out how to open those kind of doors for me, you know?"

Would it be rude to ask Claude to come to the convention after declining a once in a lifetime offer? Fuck, Tristan certainly wanted to.

Claude smiled patiently again, however, something about it had been... false. "You have some time to decide. Perhaps you should wait until—"

"I'm getting on an early flight tomorrow morning, so I thought it better to just let you know as soon as possible, face to face. Listen, I'm super thankful, but I don't think this course is for me. You've got the wrong guy."

They must have.

But the look in Claude's eyes spoke of a different story. They changed to something sinister, and it made Tristan's heart thud in his chest. Then the look faded to a dead expression that was somehow more terrifying than the look before it.

Now, he looked superficially calm, but Tristan had a feeling that wasn't the case on the inside.

Come on, Tristan, you're reading too much into this.

"I'm sorry you feel that way," Professor Galen managed. It was all he could say because Tristan was rising, leaving the papers on his table and was back at his own booth—cramming his fruit and cake into his backpack.

His face and ears were on fire. He wished the floor would just swallow him up whole. He had to get the hell out of there, and fast.

"I'm sorry to disappoint you, Professor," Tristan repeated, leaving the remainder of his smoothie and a five pound note. His hands were trembling, his nerves getting the better of him as he began to hyperventilate.

Sorry Scott, but I've gotta get out of here!

His eyes met Claude's one last time, light green into dark brown, as he made his way towards the door.

"Thank you for your consideration. I really am sorry I can't accept it, but I wish you all the best!"

His legs sprang into action, thrusting him out of the café and into the cold, biting air outside. He practically jogged halfway down the street and didn't stop until he got a stitch in his stomach, and he had to crouch over to catch his breath. His heartbeat pounded inside his chest, anxiety kicking his ass to Timbuktu.

He'd done it.

Thrown away the offer.

It was either the bravest or stupidest decision he'd ever made.

Connie certainly wouldn't be happy about it, but at least, Jake would be pleased. And hopefully with time, Tristan would be too. He had chosen gaming over science.

❦ ❦

"Thank you for your consideration..." Claude murmured, somewhat stunned as he relayed the images of Tristan's flustered expression in his mind. Those rosy, dimpled cheeks tilted into a frown, green eyes sorrowful and clouded by lust at the same time.

After Claude finished his soya latte, he calmly dragged out his cell phone from the inside of his suit pocket and hit speed dial.

"Yes, it's me. Where are you?"

"Outside the hotel, just like you told me to be," Dmitry said, his voice an unpleasant sound to Claude's ears.

"Then, I will leave my dog in your care."

"Are we really switching to plan B, Boss?"

"Yes, it would seem so. Contact my students and have the boy delivered to my holiday home by midday tomorrow. I'll be returning in the evening to begin his training, but I expect him to be there before I arrive—untouched and placed inside his kennel. Do you hear me?"

"Yes, Boss. But what about the money? The guys who are helping me expect more after the last time."

"They'll get it, boy, as soon as my pet is delivered to me safe and sound."

"Okay, okay," Dmitry said to him, just as the waitress began clearing away Claude's coffee cup and jug of water.

Claude stood up from his chair and walked outside into the snow, which fell around his shoulders in thick, white lumps, and he breathed an irritated sigh. Tristan was nowhere to be seen nor was that buffoon of a man who had accompanied him.

That had certainly been interesting—the feelings of lust and envy that had risen in Claude's body when he'd spotted

Tristan conversing with another man. His stomach heaved at the memory of it.

Soon, Claude would become Tristan's world, and not some worthless brute who had lacked the skill to keep his pets from absconding into darkness. Oh, the irony.

"But what if Tristan puts up a fight like the last one, Boss? That kid had Oliver on his arse and knocked out three of Emit's teeth if you recall."

"Then use a fucking muzzle on him!" Claude spat, and he ended the call without a further word.

His breath shot through the midday air like a stream of smoke, disappearing into the clouds gathering overhead. He watched them sail away until his anger faded and the blood decreased from his face, his heartbeat calming.

He had hoped things wouldn't have to be like this, but the thankless boy had given him no other choice. Tristan hadn't a clue of the things Claude was capable of and had been planning for him for the better part of a year, and he'd be damned if the boy was going to deprive him of that. Tristian would become his; it was only a matter of time.

For with pleasure there also comes pain, and Tristan Kade would soon learn that.

❦ ❦

Tristan went over his suitcase again, making sure he had everything. The sooner he got the convention over and done with, the better he'd feel.

In all of his twenty-one years, he had *never* had someone do this to him—make him become so dishevelled that he could hardly recognise himself.

The worst part of all: Tristan wanted to explore more of the new feeling. He wanted to get lost in Claude Galen's dark gaze and let the man… do what to him, exactly?

Tristan hadn't finished his perverted fantasy to allow room for an answer.

When Claude Galen looked at you, it wasn't just a glance—it was a firm, calculating stare that ripped you of everything, and left you naked and shivering. Guilt stabbed at Tristan when he thought of Claude, and it only worsened when he stewed on the fact that he'd finally declined the offer and abandoned Scott in the café.

Luckily, Tristan still had Scott's business card in his backpack. After the convention, he'd text Scott and apologise. Tristan glanced at his cell phone again and saw it was nearly four-thirty p.m.—one hour until the convention started. He'd better hurry, or he was going to be late. He could just imagine Jake telling him off over Skype…

He threw his cell onto the bed and then rushed towards his suitcase. He reached for his camera, but stopped when he heard someone knocking on his room door. He assumed it was the front desk sending him complimentary room service again. Fuck knows why they did it last night, but Tristan hadn't said no to a free meal. He'd thought maybe they'd sent it to the wrong room. However, this time, he didn't want to get billed for it.

"I didn't order any room service," Tristan said, unlocking and pulling open the room door. "As much as I love pizza, you've got the wrong room. But if you want I'll—"

The words were driven from Tristan's lungs before he could finish.

One moment he was standing at his room door, and then the next he was pinned against his bed by two men wearing grotesque Halloween masks. Tristan's body jerked into panic mode, and a whisper of a scream escaped his lips. Then one of the men clamped his hand against Tristan's mouth, nearly suffocating him as he fruitlessly tried to wiggle free.

Useless.

His breath came out ragged against the sweaty palm, and he fought the urge to cry out in pain when one of the men leant too heavily on top of him, confining him underneath his thick body.

"You get the legs. I'll make sure the little fucker doesn't move."

"What the fuck are you—"

But again, words were ripped from Tristan when the man pressed his hand against his mouth.

Instincts ripped through Tristan. He was by no means a strong man, but as his legs flailed and his fingernails scratched at the clown masks above him, Tristan managed to knee the smaller henchman in the gut, who let go of his legs and cursed.

It wasn't long enough for Tristan to kick the other man away and make a break for it. Zip ties were fastened round his ankles, and his arms were pinned to his sides. Still, Tristan fought them. He had no idea what the fuck was actually happening to him, or how he should act in a situation like this, but all he could think of was survival. Every fibre in his being told him to kick and scream and scratch and thrash his body as much and as fast as he could.

When one of the henchman got their fingers too close to Tristan's mouth, the lights catching over his silver-toothed grin, Tristan bit down hard—hard enough to draw blood.

"The fucker bit me!"

A fist came down and punched Tristan on his jaw, snapping his head sideways with the force. His cheek swelled like an inflated balloon, blurring his line of sight. But he could still hear... still *feel*.

"You want your pay docked, Emit?" the bigger one snapped. "Just tape his mouth shut and get on with it. No fucking touching."

"Whatever you say, Big Guy."

Emit pulled out some duct tape and taped Tristan's mouth shut, despite his struggling and attempts to keep it open. Then he threw a bag over Tristan's head, and though the material was thin, Tristan couldn't make anything out— just pitch-black darkness and monsters groping at him.

"Even if we did touch him, it isn't like the boss would know," Emit groused under his breath. "Plus, this little bitch deserves it for biting me. I'm still fucking bleeding!"

Tristan continued to kick and flail even when his hands and feet were bound and darkness enveloped him. Why were these men in Tristan's hotel room? And why the *fuck* was he being kidnapped by them? Tears sprung furiously into his eyes. *Talk about a welcome to the UK!*

"Listen to me, you stupid little *fuck*!" The bigger guy grabbed Tristan by the throat and pressed his knee against his groin, their noses just inches apart. Tristan could feel his breath panting against the bag. "You move those legs again and I swear to fuck, I will fuck you in the ass so hard you'll feel my cock sliding off the back of your teeth. Then my buddy here will have a go, then his mates will all take turns on your ass, and there ain't nothin' you can do to stop us. Trust me, I ain't kidding. It's up to you whether or not you make this journey easier or harder on yourself. So, you can either come with us willingly, or we'll fuck you unconscious and take rounds on your cumbucket ass. Your choice."

Although the men themselves wore Halloween masks, Tristan could hear him just fine, and what he said petrified him. They were going to fucking *rape* and kidnap him? Tristan mumbled his protests through his taped-over mouth, but he kept his legs and arms perfectly still.

"Good boy," he said. "You're not as stupid as you look." Something sharp pierced his thigh then, and Tristan cried out at the needle forced into his flesh. "Just a precaution," he added coolly, pumping the liquid into Tristan's veins. "Don't want you getting any ideas once we get outside."

Tristan tried to fight them again, but he was outnumbered. Before he knew it his limbs stopped working, and he floated on the bed as if he were on a sea of clouds. He heard Emit fumbling around the room, opening cupboards and doors, and then he zipped Tristan's suitcase shut. The other guy slung Tristan over his shoulder and carried him out of the room.

"You're late," a female voice stated in the hallway. "My staff were beginning to wonder why I dwindled here."

"Yeah, well, we had a reluctant participant on our hands."

"Reluctant's a bit of an understatement," Emit grumbled. "You really own this hotel? You're just a brat. Don't you hang around our uni?"

Tristan could only assume the female arrival was the hotel manager. Her accent definitely sounded familiar. Then it dawned on him... *She's the chick who brought me the room service yesterday...*

With the blood rushing to Tristan's head, he couldn't gather an accusation. He'd never hit a woman before, but he sure as fuck wanted to knock her pearly-white teeth out and throttle the bitch. She was in on it, too. How *dare* she!

"This way," she said curtly. "You have sixty seconds to get the fuck out of here, or else we're all in the shit."

She ensured that the path was clear before leading the men to an emergency exit at the far end of the hallway. Once outside, Tristan was adjusted over the man's shoulder, and the woman chuckled.

"Two hundred quid, just like we agreed," the Big Guy muttered. "Not a penny less."

"There should better not be. Now piss off, and I don't want to see you back here."

"You said that last time," Emit teased her, just as the fire exit doors slammed shut.

Droplets of snow soaked through Tristan's shirt as the men unlocked a car door and tossed him over the back seat. Their heady smells of alcohol and cigarette smoke wafted Tristan's nostrils as their bodies pressed in after him, one at either side.

"Buckle him up tight," a man growled, who definitely hadn't been in the hotel room.

How many men were there inside the car? Three? Five? Hell, it could be a limousine full of twisted fucks, and Tristan would have no idea. His body swayed numbly because of the drug, and his sight blackened. He could see nothing. No faint slithers of moonlight catching the monsters' features. Nothing but darkness.

Someone leant over Tristan's lap and pulled a seat belt around him, the touch almost gentle.

"Did you apply the drug like we wanted, yes?"

"As doped up as a crack addict," Big Guy confirmed, tightening the seat belt with one final tug.

"Then let's go already," Emit groused, his shoulder pressing into Tristan's side. "I'm hungry."

"Easy there, Emit," the driver warned him. "Remember who's in charge here."

But the car lurched into motion all the same.

Someone switched on the radio, and Tristan's mind screamed for him to run. But he couldn't move his body. Every time he tried, the world spun and his senses became overwhelmed with a wave of nausea. Even if he didn't have the bag over his head, it was unlikely he'd be able to tell where they were headed.

He was a foreigner here, alienated from everything he knew to be right. He didn't belong in this country. It wasn't his home.

And yet, he could do nothing about his abduction besides slump in the back seat and work his fingernails into the rich leather in the hopes that someone—anyone—would know that he'd been here.

This was the car used to kidnap him—TK.

Tristan Kade.

As the car drove forward, he thought of all the things he'd ever done in life that could've led to this. All of the moments he'd argued with someone, even fought, betrayed, and fucked over. Amongst the hammering of his heartbeat and dizziness of his mind, Tristan panicked over every minuscule bad decision he'd ever made: running away from home, ditching school, stealing candy at the local convenience store…

He wasn't perfect, but nothing was deserving of this. It was like a living nightmare—something he'd only ever heard about or watched on TV. But he hadn't done anything to even remotely instigate being abducted.

Tristan hadn't spoken to anyone since he arrived, except for Ms Helens, Claude Galen, a few airport staff, Scott, and a taxi driver. So, it wasn't like he'd started an argument unintentionally. He hadn't argued. He hadn't done anything other than live his life and keep his eyes fixed on the pavement as he walked.

Scott…

A horrible feeling sank in Tristan's stomach, his heart clenching at the thought. Scott wouldn't have arranged something like this because he'd ditched him at the café. There was no way he was capable of hiring these asshats—even if he *had* just met him. Scott seemed far too genuine to do something like that.

But then again… just like Connie used to say, you can never be too sure when it comes to other people.

"When he's not fighting like a little bitch, he's quite the cutie," Emit spoke up, his boozy breath and cheap cologne suffocating Tristan.

Bile rose from Tristan's stomach, multiplying when Emit leant against his shoulder and caressed the side of his waist. Tristan cowered from his touch, but Emit didn't stop. He cracked his neck from side to side, and for a brief moment, streetlights sliced through the car window and captured his silver tooth. Bag over his head or not, it was impossible not to see it flashing against the lights.

The large hand abandoned Tristan's waist and snaked down to his inner thigh, cupping his bulge. *No!* The word caught in Tristan's throat, screaming louder in his mind when the cold fingers slipped into his jeans.

Tristan's body betrayed him. He shouldn't be enjoying this. He should be kicking and screaming, fighting with all his power, but… he was terrified, not to mention paralyzed by whatever the fuck they'd pumped into his veins. It was as though his body had completely shut down, and now all he could do was sit there, frozen, while a masked stranger molested him in the backseat of a car.

A whispered *no* poured from Tristan's lips, then a moan as the hand stroked harder, circling around his sensitive head. Tristan's cock hardened more in his pants, and he bit his lips to stifle another groan.

He had never been touched by a man before. From a young age, Tristan knew he had been attracted to men, but he'd never done anything about it. Never touched a man or felt his touch in return. He was still a virgin, for fuck's sake, and now he was about to be *raped*!

Why can't I fight him? Why won't my arms move? Where am I?

Tears rolled down his cheeks, and in his mind he protected himself by clenching his legs. But in reality, they stayed wide open.

"What the *fuck* are you doing, Emit?" Big Guy spat, turning his attention from the driver and to Tristan who twitched on the back seat, strangling his moans. "We're not supposed to touch him. Get your fucking hands off!"

Emit's hand paused, only for a second, then he went back to work on Tristan's cock, squeezing his base to the point of pain. "Just playing a little. Calm down, bro, and let me put on a good show." Tristan whimpered a protest, and Emit laughed under his breath. "Did you notice how beautiful his eyes are?"

"Emit." It was the driver warning him now, his British accent firmer than the others.

He clearly held some kind of authority. As soon as he uttered the name, Emit stopped touching Tristan's cock and returned to his cheek. Tristan kept still, not wanting to entice the man further. He gulped and squeezed his eyes shut, trying to ignore the fingers stroking his face.

Just get through this, just get through this, just get through this… just… get… through this...

The car ride had lasted hours until its engine cut off, and the doors swung open. Strong arms carried Tristan out of the car, up a dozen steps, and through a stifling hot building. Glad of the bag still tied over his head, Tristan's world no longer spun… but fear threatened to suffocate him. A door creaked open, and the smell of clinical bleach burst through Tristan's nostrils. His body floated upward, then to the side and back again, his feet unable to touch the padded ground. He realised hazily that he was being suspended from the ceiling, and that hands were groping at his body, ripping off his clothes.

The touch of the intruder's hands were ice-cold against Tristan's skin. He hissed as they forced into his jeans, dragged them down to his ankles and then discarded them with a cruel tug. Nobody said anything, but he could feel their breath against him, their hands slithering around his body, tearing his clothes apart as if they were drowned parchment. A rough hand unhooked Tristan from the wrought-iron suspension, freed him of his zip ties and the hood over his head, then dressed him in a thin hospital gown that spilled to his knees.

Without a sound, the men left him, slamming and locking a white-cushioned door. Once it closed, it just looked like another part of the wall. Tristan choked back a sob and collapsed onto the padded floor, unable to keep his strength.

His trembling fingertips peeled away the tape from his mouth, allowing room for the strangled sobs to escape him at last. His eyes tumbled over colourless walls, straining against the fluorescent lights, hoping to find *something* he could recognise. But there had been nothing inside apart from a mirrored wall and a heavily bleached futon and padded table in the far corner. No windows. No doors. No escape. Nothing.

"H-hello?" Tristan tried, but nobody answered him. The drug was so powerful that it kept him on the ground, latching greedily onto his limbs and throat. *I've got to stand up...got to run... gotta get out of here!* "Anyone… anyone there? *Please…* Someone help me!"

More lights switched on above his head, and they bled into Tristan's oversensitive eyes. He squinted against them, but his hands felt inept of shielding his burning hot eyes. A high-pitched humming noise pierced through his ears, then it steadily grew louder and Tristan began to feel nauseated. He squeezed his eyes shut, actually wishing for the blindfold back, but nothing lessened the agony.

A deep, disembodied voice filled the room. "One."

It was too mechanical—too garbled—for him to know if it

was a man or woman's voice, or, if it was even human. With a glimpse between his fingers, a beetle-sized camera attached to the mirrored wall seized his attention. The screeching grew louder then, the white lights more excruciating.

Tristan concealed his body as much as he could, but the noise continued to throb against his eardrums, his temple bursting with veins, causing sparks of pain to flash across his eyes. If the noise and lights kept going, like nails clawing frantically at a chalkboard, he swore his head would split open.

"Two," the voice said, after what had to be five minutes of nothing but sheer torture.

The lights seared his skin, and the noise escalated into a shrilling cry, his whole body shaking from it. Hoping it would cancel out that fucking din, he screamed out, but to no avail; his pleas were no match for the deafening volume. *Please, stop!*

"Three."

This time, it had to have been an hour before that mechanical voice reappeared. Tristan was so close to vomiting that the bile from the back of his throat now foamed down his chin and neck.

And then everything stopped.

The lights switched off, and the noise ended.

Nothing but complete silence and delicious, pitch-black darkness surrounded him.

Chapter 3

"SIR, THE MEN placed him inside the isolation room," Dmitry reported. "He's been there for over six hours now. No food, no water, no sound, no colour. Nothing, just as you instructed."

"Good." Claude's attention fixed on his tablet and he watched the footage of Tristan inside the White Room. The lights had been deactivated as a way to confuse the boy. Now, they were in full swing again, and Tristan wept at their existence. "Feed him some boiled rice in the next couple of hours. Nobody talks to him. I want him confined in absolute solitude and for his senses to be deprived for at least two more days. Wear padded shoes so he cannot hear you, and should the subject attempt to sleep, you may suspend him from the ceiling until I say otherwise. Am I clear, Dmitry?"

"Crystal."

"Get to it, then, and do not disappoint me like last time."

Claude ended the call before he received another of Dmitry's pathetic excuses. It was because of Dmitry's negligence that Claude's last subject escaped him before he'd even set foot into the White Room. Admittedly, Claude had underestimated the boy, and the Russian ex-marine had managed to outrun Dmitry and two of his henchmen at the Parisian airport.

In the end, the student had to be killed, and weeks—if not months—of Claude carefully selecting his student were thrown to the wind. An unprofitable investment was Claude's greatest displeasure, so in order to prevent wasted endeavours, Claude had instructed his men to use the sedative.

After all, a dead subject was of no use to Claude Galen.

But from what Dmitry had reported upon his arrival, only a mild sedation was required, for Tristan hadn't put up much of a fight. Claude's university subordinates, Cas and Emit, had managed to subdue him with a simple pep talk at the hotel.

Claude scanned his tablet again, and reclined slightly in his first-class chair. After six months of constant travelling, he was flying north of Scotland for a much-needed break. For the first time in years, he couldn't wait to arrive. Excluding his apartment in London, his mountain home in Aviemore was the most beautiful location he knew, and he was well travelled, thanks to his father. Aviemore also happened to be the most secluded. The prime location for experimenting with his research.

He watched one of his men enter the White Room, covered completely in white, clinical overalls, just like the rest of them. Just like Tristan. The boy definitely wouldn't forgive him for capturing him like this. He'd resisted as much as possible to begin with, and Claude had watched three of his men haul Tristan into the White Room like a scolded animal. But he did not cry. Did not weep. Not yet, anyway. It was still too early to fathom how far Claude could push Tristan until he eventually cracked. That was the best part of his experiment.

He'd let the boy endure the White Room a little longer — until his ears bled out, and his legs collapsed from exhaustion.

Only then would Claude's training begin.

Only then would Tristan become his.

When Claude's private car pulled up outside of his luxury log cabin, a giddy feeling lurched in his stomach. He stepped out into the snow, and surrounded by acres of secluded white land, he practically hopped onto his doorstep. Despite the whereabouts of his 'holiday home', the building was opulently modern, with an impressive sheet of glass covering one face of it.

Tristan had been placed in the soundproof laboratory at the back of the building — the same facility Claude's father had designed and extended to the cabin in utmost secrecy when he purchased the place. Damn human rights groups always trying to fruitlessly shut down his experiments. As if that was enough to stop them.

He glanced at his tablet again, and saw that Tristan had been silent for the most part of an hour, no longer screaming or swearing or *moving*. He whispered a little mantra to himself, though Claude could not hear it. He assumed the boy was repeating his own name so that he wouldn't forget it. His subjects often did that. Their identity was the last thing they held onto before their entire world crumbled and they broke.

He'd give the boy another hour or so, and then it was time.

Time for Claude to claim his prize.

In the meanwhile, he entered his home and glided straight through to his kitchen. A tall glass of red wine and a newspaper already sat on his marble breakfast table. Claude dropped into one of the leather stools and took a small sip. Cracking his neck back and forth, he thought of what he'd have for dinner.

He could certainly think of *one* thing on the menu that he desired, but he knew he had to be patient. Tristan was not ready for that yet. Claude's ex-slave turned live-in subordinate, Oliver, had gone hunting with that useless mutt of a dog he kept in the attic with him, so until he or Dmitry returned, it'd just be Claude and Tristan. Not that he needed to worry about Tristan escaping—the boy was perfectly confined.

He'd have something light, perhaps a tuna salad, and then do some work in the lounge. Both rooms were amalgamated together, separated only by an extensive, marbled fireplace that ran down the middle of the room, making it a pleasant area to work. Claude rarely had the fire off. He found the heat and crackling embers to be welcoming once he returned home after a long journey.

After Claude had eaten, he walked into the living room and finished off his wine while reading the newspaper Oliver left him. His body sank into the lushness of his fabric corner suite, and in comparison, he could only imagine how uncomfortable Tristan was downstairs. Claude wanted to go to him, wanted to see those sweet, full lips and sorrowful, green eyes. But the boy had elected a different course of action. Instead of working with Claude willingly, he'd chosen to resist, and to resist the inevitable was foolish in Claude's eyes.

Now, restricting the boy's communication as well as his senses was an imperative part of his training.

He had to bide his time. Wait until Tristan had shrunk to such a level that the boy would be *begging* him for human contact.

All Tristan wanted to do was sleep.

His thoughts drifted, his body floated, and he didn't know who or where he was anymore. He wasn't even sure if *he* was real. Nothing but unwavering numbness surrounded his senses, and that was *without* the drug in his system. The high-pitched frequencies and shocking whiteness were enough to render Tristan's consciousness into a misshapen ball of snivelling pleas. Prayers that purposely fell to deaf ears, leaving his empty calls hanging in the air.

Tristan tried to sleep, but every time he closed his eyes, the mechanical voice would speak again and unleashed that godawful noise—a noise so deafening that Tristan felt as though his skull had cracked open multiple times already.

The one thing that existed clearly in his world was the unaltered, silent whiteness.

And then a door, hidden somewhere in the wall, opening and closing. The visitors who entered the White Room never spoke to Tristan, they only checked for his pulse. If he somehow managed to fall asleep, they suspended him from the ceiling and then left him.

He just wanted it to stop: The visits. The silence. The agony.

Please, just stop!

Curled up in the corner, he buried his head into his hands and tried to drown out the noise and light. It was a futile attempt as it was just too blinding and too strong. Tristan was weak, so weak that he just wanted to crawl up somewhere and die.

Something light thudded down onto the floor next to him. Tristan opened his eyes a little, and his blurry vision fixed on a plastic tray of bland, colourless food. Boiled rice, chicken, and a glass of water. Just like the other times. Tristan clenched his eyes shut, his retinas too damaged to keep them open any longer.

The most frightening thing of all was that he didn't even *feel* hungry. He had no recollection of how long he'd been trapped in the White Room or the last time he ate or slept. He had nothing but his agony and thoughts to comfort him and the never-ending voice, piercing through his skull.

As always, nobody spoke to him. They delivered the food

and then slid through the door, repeating the process every now and again.

Tristan closed his eyes, and for a hopeful moment, he thought sleep had taken him at last. Either that, or he had died, and by then he really hoped for the latter.

He eventually drifted into darkness. He couldn't tell how long had passed until his next mute visit arrived, but he could feel somebody touching him this time. He must have fallen asleep. They grabbed onto his tender shoulders and hauled Tristan onto his feet, holding him as if he weighed nothing. While Tristan was no athlete, he had been lean and tall enough to consider himself toned and in shape.

He doubted he was anymore.

Had it been days since he'd last eaten, or only minutes? The whiteness had drowned out his sense of time. His sense of *everything*.

The arms held Tristan in the air, and something cold brushed by his shoulder. The shackles. The iron trailed down his arm and slithered around his wrists, clanging together. Somewhere amid Tristan's delirium, he laughed.

The iron tightened around his flesh, and strong arms grabbed onto Tristan's waist and lifted him. As soon as he hung from the hook, the hands withdrew, the door closed, and he was alone again.

"One."

The voice broke the deafening silence. Tristan's body twirled a little, but his tiptoes were too far off the ground to steady himself. He opened his eyes and grimaced at the reflection staring back at him. It was the first time he'd glanced into the mirror intentionally, and he hardly recognised the chained boy dangling from the ceiling. He was a slab of meat left to bleed dry in the back of a butcher's shop, forgotten and no longer alive.

"Two."

If Tristan were still in the UK, or back home in the States, he had no idea. He could be in Thailand for all he knew. The only thing he recognised was the boiled rice they kept on bringing him, over and over again, not that Tristan ever touched it.

"Three."

The noise began again.

Tristan screamed, and this time, he did not stop.

Chapter 4

CLAUDE SLANTED HIS tie, ran a hand down the black coat draped over his navy suit, and cracked his neck from side to side. Standing opposite the mirror that gazed into the White Room, Claude's stomach flipped with what he suspected to be excitement. But the more he thought about it, the greater the feeling equated to distaste.

This could be his one and only chance to gain Tristan's trust.

He couldn't afford to let him slip through his fingers again. His favourite subject—student, experiment, pet, whatever you wanted to call them—had stayed with Claude for over two years. He had been reluctant to sell Joshua, but like with all his subjects, he hadn't much of a choice once his father began to probe him. Researchers were created to *train*, not to *desire* their subjects, and favouritism had been forbidden.

Thankfully, Joshua had afforded Claude quite the profit in return for his obedience, and his father hadn't been made aware of it. Since then, Claude had trained many subjects but none of them had compared to sweet Joshua. It had been months since Claude tasted the result of his handiwork, since he had felt the flesh of his creation quiver beneath him. Now, it was time for him to train his new subject, though Claude had no intention of letting this one go.

Sorry, Father, but Tristan will not be for sale.

He belonged to Claude, and he would pound that into the boy's skull until he fully accepted that. After all, Claude Galen never accepted anything less.

His reflection swelled up beside Tristan, a stark contrast of black against white. Claude mussed up his dark hair, shirt, and suit jacket before he emerged into the White Room.

Still as tempting as ever, Tristan had been suspended from the ceiling, drooping in his wrought-iron chains. It was such a shame that things had come to this, but Claude was a man who would not accept defeat. He'd resort to desperate measures to achieve his desires, and in this case, it was Tristan.

Thank you for your consideration…

Claude approached Tristan with slow, steady strides. The boy had only spent three days in solitary confinement, but Claude knew that was enough to drive even the strongest of men to insanity.

Claude rushed over to him, his boots sliding over the cushioned floor.

"Tristan! *Tristan!*"

He clutched onto Tristan's waist, lifting him upward effortlessly. He'd done this a million times before—hands unhooking the boy from his chains, and then laying him gently on the ground.

"Can you hear me?" The concern in Claude's voice was palpable; a ruse he had become masterful at. "Please,

Tristan—*look* at me! *Talk* to me!"

Tristan's head lulled backward and his body, twitching with the aftershocks of his treatment, fell limp in Claude's arms..

"Ga...len..."

Tristan's voice was so weak, so vulnerable...so heartwarming.

"Is...that...really...you?"

Claude clutched him to his chest. "Yes. I've been searching for you for days. Hush now, it's okay. I'm here for you. I'm here, Tristan." He sounded deceptively sincere. "You're safe."

"Please, help me...please," Tristan sobbed, clutching onto Claude's suit. "I need your help...someone...please, Professor! Get me...outta here..."

Claude squeezed him tightly in his arms. Tristan's eyes had closed and his head fell hard against Claude's pounding chest again. He could hear the boy sleeping—it was the first he'd slept in days, the poor baby.

Just as Claude planned, he carried the boy to the bedroom across from his own and laid him down on the bed. His body was so light and clingy that Claude didn't *want* to release him. But he had to. He pulled the covers over Tristan's body, tucked him in tight, and then stepped back. He sat in the armchair next to the bed and swiped open his tablet.

He'd wait there until morning.

Until the boy woke up and saw his world in a new light.

Tristan opened his eyes to a beautiful world of colour. It was excruciating at first, and he nailed them shut again, unable to take them in for more than a minute. His retinas were so used to white, that the browns, greys, and blues in the illustrious bedroom stabbed at his skull, and an urgent need for darkness consumed him.

But he kept on trying. He peeled his eyelids apart, closed, and then repeated the process at least half a dozen times. Various attempts later, he saw the bedroom was wide and spacious, and Tristan nearly wept when relief flooded his veins. After being starved of colour for so long, he realised how much he'd craved it.

Craved *normality*.

He turned his head and noticed someone had eclipsed the bay window. The rich mahogany drapes had been pulled aside to let in the sun, and its rays cut over the man's shoulders and bathed the room in glorious hues of silver and gold, every scant of their light sculpting his slender frame, almost as though a halo had been wrapped around him.

"Professor Galen?" he rasped out, nearly whispering the words as his voice came out hoarse. "Professor...?" he tried again, this time louder and clearer, though his swollen eyes struggled to remain open.

His body still trembled underneath the duvet, from exhaustion or pain, he no longer knew. His head felt as though it were sinking into a bed of clouds over a calm sea, heaven against his muscles. He tried to move his limbs, but even still they wouldn't budge. He tried to sit up but couldn't convince his body to listen to him. Had he been drugged again? It certainly felt like it.

His weak gaze fixed on Claude standing in front of the window. He looked beautiful with all that colour around him and not a hint of white—except for the lit cigarette he held between his fingertips.

"Please do not try to rise," Claude told him, turning around slowly. His expression looked normal, neither happy nor sad, although the bags underneath his eyes spoke of late-night exhaustion. "Doctor's orders," he said calmly. "Can I fetch you some water? Or some orange juice? I even have some hot chocolate here. Plenty of sugar this time." He walked over to the ottoman at the edge of the bed, picked up a breakfast tray, and lay it gently next to Tristan. "All organic." He nudged the tray forward and waited patiently for an answer.

Tristan smiled, and then laughed. Odd to be laughing with all the shit that had happened to him. But he just couldn't believe his eyes. Professor Galen—in the same room as him—after he'd been kidnapped and tortured to near insanity? How? Why? Where *was* he?

"Thank you, Professor..." he replied through a pained smile. "I'm so glad to see you—*someone*—these men, they...they kidnapped me and put me into this room... It was all white and there were noises and I couldn't—I couldn't get out!" He winced at the memory of the noises screeching through his skull, at how he'd screamed until his lungs bled out and he could no longer see or breathe. His body *still* convulsed as an aftershock of the torment, and he flinched when the counting voice invaded his memory. He couldn't erase them. Couldn't run from them. Couldn't even *hide* in that White Room; there had been nowhere for him to go. *"They're going to kill me!"*

He tried to push out of bed, but Claude stood beside him and steadied Tristan with his strong hands.

"It's okay," he hushed him, gently squeezing Tristan's arms.

But Tristan's mind screamed for him to run, to find an escape, fresh air... *I can't breathe!* His body clung to the professor's as though he were an injured child and he just wanted somebody to chase away all his pain.

What was happening to him? His body felt so weak and vulnerable that he didn't recognise the pathetic excuse of a being he'd transformed into. All in the matter of... what, days? Weeks? It had been like an eternity in that horrific White Room.

"I promise I'm here for you," Claude soothed him again, gently caressed his shoulder. "Here to protect you. Don't cry, Tristan, it's all over now. You're all right. I saved you. I found you, and I saved you."

"Y-you saved me?" Tristan sobbed, grabbing onto Claude's shirt sleeves. His hands clung to him so fervently that he had almost mounted the professor's lap. "But *how*? How did you find me?"

The professor shushed him again, rocking his body from side to side. By now, he had climbed onto Claude's lap, and it might've been to Tristan's imagination, but he was certain he felt something harden against his back.

"I'll explain all of that when you're better," Claude said. "Right now, you need to sleep. You're in my house. You're safe here, I assure you."

Tristan looked up at him, desperation gnawing at his soul as he took in those dark, chocolate brown eyes. "Scott…" He sobbed, unable to restrain his thoughts. "It must've been… I don't know… I left him, and I shouldn't have. It's all my fault, Sir. I just wanted someone to—to—I should've *known*!"

"Deep breath, Tristan. Breathe in for me, through your nose and out your mouth. That's a boy. Keep doing it, and I promise you'll feel better. I'm not leaving you, okay? Just please calm down."

After a lungful of air, Tristan breathed through his mouth. "Will you please stay with me, Professor?" On the verge of tears now, Tristan's body trembled within Claude's strong hold. "I don't… I can't be alone… please…" His words faded into an airy whisper as he shook his head, his lips quivering. "I'm sorry, I just…"

Somewhere in his mind, shame flooded him to have been reduced to such a pitiful state. Crying and begging in the professor's lap, and then to be asking for help from the man who had already saved his life? Just who in the world had Tristan become?

He had so many questions burning within him that he

didn't know where to begin. Why had those men abducted him? How did the professor find him? Was Scott behind all of this, and if so, was Tristan really safe?

All he could think about was exactly that—being safe.

For some reason, Claude's arms offered him that. Even though he was the *last* person Tristan had expected to see, he was just glad to see *somebody*. To not be alone. To still be alive.

He rested his head back and closed his eyes. Finally, after a moment of clarity, he asked, "Can we go to the cops? Scott might still be out there..."

Fear clogged his throat. He bit his tongue and waited for Claude to speak. Through the mid-morning sun pouring through the window, a solemn expression flitted over Claude's stubbled face. His nearly black eyes locked with Tristan's, and he saw his Adam's apple jerking up and down.

"I found this in your hotel room." Claude reached into his navy suit pocket and retrieved a black and gold business card. Tristan clocked the tattoo parlour's logo on the front of it. "Once I discovered it was Scott who abducted you, I had him and a vast majority of his men taken care of. Think of me what you may, Tristan, but men like them do not deserve a second chance."

He clenched the card in his palm, and then carefully placed it back inside his pocket.

"So... so it was really him?" Tristan's voice sounded small. "Scott?"

"Yes," Claude answered. "Their gang is notorious for abducting foreigners studying in Britain. Twice in the past three years, but the police could never locate them, and they'd never find the students in time. I thought they had escaped abroad, but I was mistaken. We all were. When the police found the tattoo parlour completely empty, I had to take matters into my own hands, otherwise I would never have found you alive. They'd never have stopped hunting you. When I checked your hotel room, I found the card on your bed, and I knew I had to find you."

When a gentle hand softly caressed Tristan's back, he shuddered. "I... It just feels so good to be around someone again," he murmured, the words falling from his chapped lips. A single tear trickled down his ashen cheek. "It feels like I haven't... haven't been around people in years, and everything feels... It's just all so crazy. How long was I... trapped there for?"

"A few days," Claude said, "but you will never feel that kind of pain again, Tristan. I promise you. I saved you. You're okay now."

His voice had been so comforting to Tristan that he wept and buried his face into his hands, violent tears gushing through his fingers.

He'd never experienced that kind of torture before.

The lack of physical contact made Tristan half-demented; it made him feel like he simply no longer existed, as if his soul had been ripped from him. He craved, more than ever, the touch of a human's skin and the sound of their voice. He needed to be assured that this was real, that he wasn't dreaming or suffering from delusions and aftershocks.

"Do you trust me?" Claude asked him, his voice deep and hoarse, while his arms cradled Tristan gently.

Despite his unsteadiness, Tristan nodded, and Claude shuddered against his back.

Chapter 5

SILENCE... WHAT HAD recently been Tristan's nightmare had now become his blessing. He'd never anticipated, in a million years, that he would be thankful to hear absolutely nothing in the world. None of its bullshit traffic, people squawking at each other on their mobile phones, kids throwing tantrums in supermarkets, or people yelling over who hailed the cab first.

For once, silence had given Tristan a pleasure that he had never known existed, and he never wanted it to end.

His hours at Claude's home eventually grew into days, and during that time, Tristan had managed to eat and drink as normal again. He *even* managed to look at the sun without cringing, but most of all, he'd managed to process what had happened.

He'd been abducted, violated, and for days deprived of his senses.

Tristan Kade had come to Europe seeking new horizons, but what he was given was something entirely different: pain and fear from the mindless fury of a colourless world and the incessant noise that came with it.

Physically, he was able to walk around Claude's mountain home. He still couldn't process *that*, though—the professor who had saved his life and brought him to his private home as a place of refuge. Claude Galen had manifested from a reputable scientist into a surprisingly hospitable saviour in the space of a week.

But why had it felt like an eternity to Tristan?

A horrible sensation flipped in Tristan's stomach, causing his heart to clench against his ribcage.

Gaming convention.

Jake and Connie.

He couldn't possibly call either of them just yet. What would he say? *I've just been kidnapped, tortured, and now I'm cooped up in some stranger's home while I recover? Sorry, Jake, but I missed the gaming convention because some asshats fucking abducted and threatened to rape me?*

They'd be worried sick about him, and that was the *last* thing Tristan wanted to do. He didn't want to be a burden anymore. He'd wait until he had recovered fully and then he'd call them, given there were any telephones in the house. Tristan hadn't seen one in the bedroom, and Claude only ever used his cell phone... There were no laptops or computers, either, from what Tristan could gather.

Until Tristan contacted them, would they be worried sick? Had they been calling a dead mobile in the hopes of making sure he was safe? He had told Jake that the last place he went was the Yang Tattoo Parlour, so at least the kidnapping could be linked to Scott. He hoped, with a small ghost of a chance, they were looking for him. Until then, Tristan focused on healing and mapping a way back to them. Maybe he could start fresh once he got home—go to a different gaming convention, and he and Jake would continue their channel as if nothing had happened.

Maybe this doesn't have to be the end.

One week after Tristan had been rescued, Claude's servant brought him breakfast again. He was tall and bear-like with sharp blue eyes, and he had a thick mane of auburn hair and a beard that jutted out from his strong jawline. Similar to every other time he arrived with food, he never said a word to Tristan, and his silent demeanour set his teeth on edge.

He reminded him of the man who'd often come into the White Room, thrown him his meals, hung him to the ceiling, and then left again. Tristan knew it wasn't him, but the silence made his fear of it palpable.

When Claude entered the bedroom, Tristan had been nibbling on his pancakes and bacon. The door clicked shut, and Tristan froze, but for once he did not quiver. He *trusted* this man. He owed his *life* to this man.

Just keep going.

"How are we today, Tristan? Feeling any better?"

It had been nearly two weeks since he met Claude, and yet so much had changed.

Tristan nodded, then he watched Claude stride over towards the bed. He sat down on the edge of it and smiled at Tristan softly, resting his hands calmly across his lap. He was clearly just heading off to work, dressed in that impeccably pressed grey suit of his, and his cheeks were clean shaven; his collar shirt buttoned to the neck

"I feel… better. More like myself, Professor."

"I've told you to call me Claude." He smiled at him, raising an eyebrow joyfully. "And how is your head? Still tender?"

"Yeah, although your servant brought me painkillers with my breakfast. They're kicking in now."

Claude beamed at him again. "I'm relieved. Unfortunately, I must head to work now, but please be assured that my staff are close by and will be on hand should you need anything. You are perfectly safe here, okay? Stay here as long as you want."

"Okay."

He could manage little else. His hands clenched into a fist on top of the bed sheets, and he tried to conceal their shaking.

Was he really so weak that the thought of being alone now petrified him?

Claude's fingertips trailed lazily towards Tristan's hand and picked it up. He brought it to his mouth and gently pressed his lips against the back of his hand. Tristan's heart hammered, a painful rhythm coming alive inside his chest. *Fuck*. His lips felt… *good*.

It was so, so, *so* good to be touched again.

So *real*.

"Enjoy your breakfast, and don't forget to drink your milk."

"Yes, Father," Tristan teased, and it was the first he'd joked since… well, he couldn't remember.

His memories were hazy at that point, as though he

peered at them through a mirror in a distant dream. Once the professor had gone and Tristan finished his breakfast, he walked gingerly into the en-suite bathroom, showered, brushed his teeth, and then crawled back into the bed. It was the most he could convince himself to do.

The breakfast tray was gone by the time he returned, the room blissfully dark due to the blackout blinds, and Tristan fell into another dreamless sleep. He was certain in a few days' time that he'd be ready to go home. At least, he could try to, and he'd ask Claude to explain what had happened to Scott. Even if Tristan couldn't go to the cops, even if his entire world had been flipped upside down, he'd find out precisely what had happened to him, and why.

He'd return back home. But somewhere in the back of his brain, he knew he didn't want to. He was happy here. *Cared* for. And for the first time in his life, he felt safe.

But things were not meant to be that easy for Tristan. He'd always known that in the back of his head. While recovering at Claude's home, he had realised that he couldn't feel comfortable with the professor's hospitality because deep down, he knew it wouldn't last forever.

It was like moving in with Jake all over again. He was a burden to the professor. Tristan was *nobody*. Just a guy who'd found himself hitting rock bottom, and then selfishly clung to the only person he could find. Unfortunately for the professor, it had somehow been him.

Guilt stabbed at Tristan's chest, but the fear of sacrificing his security quickly overpowered it. He couldn't bring himself to leave Claude. He'd done it to his parents, practically done it to Jake and Connie, and now… to someone who'd saved him from the brink of death no less?

There was ungrateful, and then there was *that*.

He'd convinced himself that he just couldn't do it. Not until he'd fully recovered and could thank Claude properly.

The weeks drew on at Claude's winter-swept home, and with every passing moment, he found himself increasingly anxious to contact Jake and Connie. He couldn't suppress the urge to hear their voices again. He wanted to prove that he still lived in the same world as them, and this wasn't all a nightmare.

Tristan had mentioned it to Claude not long after he'd come to after the White Room. He hoped the professor would let him use his cell phone; he always kept it in his pants. "Can I at least call them?"

Claude had shot him a pained smile. "I'm sorry, Tristan, but I can't risk your location. You're the only student alive who knows what Scott's underlings looked like. They could easily intercept the phone lines and track you to here. Besides, would you really want your loved ones to hear you in such a state? For now, I think it's best if you focus on being able to face the world again one step at a time. You want that, don't you? More than anything?"

"Yes, Professor… so much."

But facing the world again wasn't going to be easy. Tristan's nightmares were plagued by the men in clown masks, the blinding White Room, and the noise—the noise that never seemed to fade from him, making it impossible to forget. Even when he was wrapped up within his beautiful, dark silence, it never ended.

Always present.

Claude told him that he could stay with him as long as he wanted. They were still in the UK, but he didn't even have to accept the college placement; though Claude admitted, once Tristan was back on his feet, he hoped Tristan would reconsider. They would be able to research together, and he would be safe with him. Claude really *did* want to show him the world. He'd probably even give him it, too, if he asked nice enough.

He'd acknowledged just how fastidious the professor was beneath that contemptuous exterior of his, and just how wrong Tristan had been about him.

He'd offered him the placement simply because he was kind—nothing else.

And yet, he couldn't quench the hunger that drove him to seek justice against the men who'd kidnapped him. Against Scott. He wanted—*needed* to know what happened, and how Claude had truly found him. There was no way it'd been by sheer coincidence, and the desire for vengeance burned so deeply in his core that Tristan vowed never to let it go.

He needed to find Scott's minions, and then he could go home. Then he could find closure.

It was the only thing that kept him going.

Each day when Claude went to work, Tristan would ask

the cleaning lady (Ethel, he thought her name was) to bring him a newspaper. Just like every other servant who had entered his room, the woman refused to talk to Tristan. But she would nod and return some moments later with a folded-over newspaper.

Tristan used it to see whether or not his kidnapping had been discovered—always hoping but never seeing anything. Not even a single headline about assaults at Westside Charter University, never mind his kidnapping. Oh, but there were tons of coverage about the success of the 2018 gaming convention in Edinburgh—the one Tristan had been robbed of.

Hopelessly, he'd wait for the servant to bring him the British newspapers, and every day he checked, and every night he fell into abject misery. Nobody was searching for Tristan Kade, and his assailants had gotten away undetected.

He'd considered calling the police, but what Claude disclosed soon came rushing back to him. He'd had Scott and his gang taken care of? Tristan couldn't even begin to think how… and he certainly didn't want to land Claude in prison. After everything he'd had done for him, he couldn't betray him like that, no matter how sick the thought of killing someone made him.

Furthermore, who would believe him?

Had he hard evidence to go on other than what the kidnappers looked like, the hotel he'd been stolen from, and where he'd been seen in public with Scott? Would they think he was making it up for attention? Just some tourist wanting to make it in the newspapers?

To Tristan, the whole thing proved just how little his existence mattered to the world. Or how little it mattered to himself.

All he could do was keep himself sane until he could go home. He'd been told not to leave the house for at least another few days. Claude hadn't found the rest of Scott's men yet, and they could still be after Tristan.

Tristan tried not to contemplate that, although it had been highly impossible. They'd managed to kidnap him out of a hotel, drug, molest, and torture him. Coming back for more wasn't unrealistic when it came down to sick fucks like that. And worse yet, if he did call back home, they could trace Tristan *and* Jake and Connie.

Even looking at his tattoos brought his fear flooding back to him. He tried everything in his power to keep his eyes from glancing at the plague doctor, recalling the memory of the tattoo session and the lunch date. Hadn't Scott said he could kidnap Tristan and make him his secret boyfriend?

Scott… that twisted motherfucker!

He clearly hadn't been joking.

At least Tristan had free range of the house during the day, a stark difference to the confines of the White Room. Claude went to work for the most part of the day, and the staff were practically non-existent. Tristan usually spent it in the gym or watching movies in his bedroom. Anything to keep himself busy. Usually, Claude didn't get home until late at night so Tristan mostly ate alone—not that he minded. It was nice to be around people and feel safe again, even if they never spoke to him.

He'd seen from the windows that the cabin was in the middle of nowhere. Utterly secluded, all Tristan could see were acres of trees and mountains shrouded in thick blankets of snow. No people. No cars. Not even any birds or street lamps from what Tristan could see.

Nothing but nuclear whiteness.

He'd always prepare dinner himself in the evening. He wasn't the best cook in the world, but at least he managed to not burn spaghetti after the freakishly tall lumberjack chef, Oliver, had showed him the ropes around the kitchen.

He wanted to make Claude dinner as a thank you for letting him stay so long, but it was weird trying to accustom himself to the kitchen facilities when the head chef refused to speak to him.

Three weeks at the cabin and not a single word.

The guy could really hold his tongue.

The clothes that had been placed in Tristan's bedroom were a godsend, though. He probably liked them way more than he should have. He guessed having different coloured things made him feel... human again. No more itchy, white gowns and bland food.

Sometimes, he found himself wanting to wear something tight just to catch the professor's eye, which he often did. And his heartbeat soared every time. He'd even considered waltzing around the house naked, so that Claude would see him through the glass walls when he returned home from work.

Deep down, he knew he just wanted his attention. The house was so damn quiet during the day, and Claude was the only one who bothered to talk to him. The only one who *ever* talked to him. Tristan suspected that Claude wanted his staff to give him space, but in reality, it drove Tristan crazy.

Fortunately, Tristan always settled for a simple button-down shirt and jeans, which fit him perfectly. In all honesty, it was like Claude had the wardrobe customised for him. The shirts, the jeans, the Converse—all designer brands that Tristan had never been able to afford. He usually stuck with Jake's hand-me-downs. He'd always been used to that since he could never hold a steady job and pay for new clothes.

Tristan heard a car pulling up in the gravelled driveway, and somewhat nervously, he set the plates down. He quickly removed the candles on the dinner table at the last minute—*too obvious*—and waited by the sleek black table, his heart thumping as a goofy smile crossed his face.

"Good evening, Professor," he beamed when Claude finally entered the kitchen, probably on his way to make his usual evening coffee, and then dump his briefcase down on the breakfast table.

"Tristan…" Claude paused at the table and surveyed his surroundings, almost as though he didn't quite understand what was happening.

The log fire in the middle of the room had been organised by Oliver, prior to him retiring to his bedroom in the attic, and its embers crackling in the silence was a beautiful addition. Claude ran a hand through his black hair and shook away the snow that clung to him.

Tristan's heart thudded with anticipation.

He didn't normally ask for the fire to be lit, but it'd been cold, and he hoped it would've comforted Claude after a long day at work. It was a silly idea, he'd realised then, but he hoped it would express even a fraction of his gratitude.

"I, uh... I made it myself." Tristan lowered his gaze, still smiling. "I figured it'd be a nice thank you. Or something like that, I guess." He kept his eyes fixed on the pasta dishes leaden on the granite breakfast table. He was unable to look at Claude without getting a little *too* excited.

Why all of a sudden? The last thing Tristan wanted to do was ruin the evening with an unwanted hard-on.

"Thank you," Claude said, a hint of a smile tugging at his full lips. "You really didn't have to. Oliver could have prepared the food for you."

This time, Tristan did look up, and Claude's dark eyes were rooted on him. He felt strangely vulnerable at that moment. No longer could he hear the crackling of the fire or the winter winds outside. The only thing he could hear was Claude's shallow breathing as he licked his lips slowly, eyes trailing from Tristan's eyes and down to his lips, which were still slightly chapped from the cold weather.

Tristan stepped around the table and closed the gap between them. "I wanted to thank you for saving my life," he said to him, heart pounding against his ribs. "It's not much, but I hope you're hungry."

Normally, he'd roll his eyes at using such a cliché, but they were in their own world now where normalcy and clichés didn't matter. Tristan could say anything—*do* anything—and it wouldn't matter. All that mattered was seeing that hungry look in Claude Galen's eyes, and knowing it was because of him.

Chapter 6

IT WAS AMAZING what kindness could achieve.

In the space of a month, Tristan had changed from an obnoxious child to Claude's perfect boy, and all he'd done was afford Tristan the things his parents never did. His time. Attention. Love. Those were rare things, indeed, but all part of Tristan's training.

First, Claude had to gain Tristan's trust. They'd got off to a rocky start to begin with, as much as Claude enjoyed fucking with the boy during his interview, but now it seemed they'd established some sort of relationship. If things carried on like this, then Claude might not have to punish Tristan at all. At least, not as much as the others had been.

Hopefully, Tristan would be his last subject. Only time would tell, though; Claude had to be careful not to push the boy too far. He was still pining for his old life, thinking that he *actually* stood a chance returning to it, as if Claude would ever allow that to happen.

He'd come too far just to let the boy fly away from his grasp.

"And you cooked everything yourself?" Claude raised an eyebrow at him, and watched the boy blush under his gaze. He took off his navy cooking apron, slung it over the countertop, and then busied himself over a bowl of salad on the table.

"Yes," he replied, swallowing hard, the bowl shaking in his hands. "I know I'm not a famous chef, but hopefully it's edible," he added with a quick and nervous laugh.

Claude gulped. He could feel his body swelling with pride.

Much too early to be feeling like this, Claude. Control yourself.

But pride consumed him so badly that his dick hardened in his trousers, and all Claude could think about was laying Tristan over that dining table and fucking him until he begged him to stop.

He sat down at the table, and noticed that it'd been laid out beautifully. Rich, velvet tablecloth, polished silverware, champagne and ice bucket, and candles that, for some reason, had quite recently been blown out judging by the poignant smell of vanilla.

Tristan brought out the spaghetti, almost dropping one of the plates as he fumbled to pour an even amount onto it.

"It's meat sauce," he mumbled, so low that Claude could hardly hear him. "Hope you're not vegetarian. I tried making the meatballs, too, but I couldn't get them to stick right. Figures. I *suck* at cooking. So, it's just mince, peppers, and a shit ton of tomato sauce."

The boy was so close that Claude could smell the sweat and nerves under his aftershave and deodorant. *Delectable.* His hooded eyes watched Tristan closely—how his slender body quivered in front of him, how his attention darted nervously around the room, refusing to meet Claude's gaze.

He pulled out a seat for Claude, and once he sat down,

Tristan picked the chair to his left. Not at the other end of the table? He smirked at that. Claude's subjects *never* sat at the same table with him unless it was a reward, or during their Primitive stage—the first phase of Claude's research, which rarely lasted longer than a month. It was similar to a mother bonding with her child. Or more accurately, an owner and their new pet.

Quite soon, Tristan's Primitive training would begin, and that's when the fun would begin.

He'd have to speak with Oliver, though. There was no way the boy had prepared the meal all by himself, and his staff were under strict instructions *not* to communicate with him. Claude was to be his only source of communication. To become Tristan's world, he had to completely eradicate his old one, and he wouldn't be able to do that with Oliver or Ethel interfering.

Tomorrow, he would dismiss Ethel and delegate her responsibilities to Oliver. That would keep him busy, and also keep Ethel out of the picture.

Claude let the boy fuss over him, serve him dinner, pour him some red wine, and then he nibbled cautiously at his meal. Tristan didn't say anything to begin with, but Claude could see how flushed the boy was next to him, and though he was no super human, he could hear Tristan's heartbeat fluttering like a caged butterfly.

"So, I was thinking," Tristan began, clearing his throat, "maybe we could watch a movie after dinner." He took another spoonful of spaghetti, clearly biding his time for whatever he wanted to say next. Finally, after finishing his bite much slower than how he usually did, he added, "or something else, if you'd like. I'm fine with anything." A too-casual shrug when he took a drink of water, but Claude hadn't missed the boy's cheeks reddening. "I just thought it'd be… nice."

"Perhaps, if you are a good boy." Claude winked at him, eating another mouthful of spaghetti, which wasn't half bad.

Thankfully, the boy wasn't as awful a cook as Dmitry, who had destroyed more than one of Claude's ovens. As a result, his live-in subordinate, Oliver, had obtained the household responsibilities.

Tristan closed his eyes and shuddered, his free hand turning into a fist on his lap. "Aren't I always?" He smiled that goofy smile of his, attempting to mask his nerves.

Claude could smell the boy's fear and arousal like a lupine catching wind of its prey. No matter where it eloped to, he could always smell it from in the shadows, and he would devour it.

"You are a good boy, Tristan," Claude said evenly. A month of social deprivation usually resorted to frantic behaviour and escape attempts, but not so much with Tristan. Claude had convinced him of otherwise. Tristan was *safe* with Claude. He was *better off* with him. Scott's men were *after* Tristan. Claude smirked and swallowed more of his food. "Well done organising all of this. I'm really impressed, and it tastes good, Tristan."

He clearly appreciated the praise by how those beautiful,

green eyes lit up. "Thanks," he beamed, eyes raw with lust and gratitude. Clearly, Tristan wanted to push their relationship to the next level, but the boy knew better than to initiate the first move. "So, uh, any movie you want to watch?"

"I understand there's Netflix in the living room. Why don't you decide?"

"We could see *A Kiss at Midnight*," he mumbled, barely audible. "I, uh, like an actor in that." Obviously a lie, but Claude let it go in favour of seeing Tristan squirm and struggle with his breaths. "It might be stupid, though. The rating was only a six point five online."

Claude had never seen the film, but he knew of it. Numerous universities he'd been to have promoted it because it was apparently a big step for the LGBT community—with the famous lead actor playing a gay character.

"Are you perhaps attracted to men, Tristan?" Claude asked him, completely deadpan.

He already knew the answer. Not only was the boy gay, but a virgin, too.

Claude had carefully selected him based on those factors. He'd studied the boy in America for over twelve months. He'd known from that blistering hot summer's day, when he discovered Tristan's gaming channel, that he wanted him— and he would become Claude's at any cost. Dmitry had been tasked with ensuring that such an outcome happened.

At least he's good for something...

Now a flash of panic sprung into the boy's eyes. "I'm sorry," he breathed out, dropping the fork. "I'm... we can watch something else. Anything else. You pick." Tristan was breathing rapidly now, close to hyperventilating. His endearing nerves never ceased to amuse Claude. "There — there are some action flicks going on, too. We can watch those instead. Lots of men and guns and guy stuff, you know... Blood and gore."

Claude's dick twitched in his pants. He nodded, and stood up from the table. "Then, I'll leave you to it. Food was delicious, Tristan. You did splendidly tonight."

He swept by Tristan's chair, ruffled his dark brown hair, and climbed the stairs to the master bedroom so he could change out of his work clothes. If only such pleasantness with Tristan could remain forever. But Claude was wise enough to know better. He mustn't get attached to the boy Tristan was now, for soon that boy would no longer exist. Not by the time Claude was finished with him.

Anything can be remade, Claude, even the most impenetrable of minds can be altered. You simply have to be patient, and above all, disciplined.

Yes, Father.

His father had been right, after all. Even the most stubborn and darkest of human minds could be moulded into something greater — *better* than they'd ever hope to be — with but a firm hand and patience.

It was only a matter of time.

And Claude couldn't wait to begin.

Tristan couldn't believe how much of a fucking idiot he was.

He'd never asked Claude about his sexuality, if he was homophobic, or even if the man would be remotely interested in Tristan.

No one back home had known he was gay—besides his parents, who kept that under strict lock and key since the day he told them when he was thirteen. His home town wasn't the most receptive to *his kind*, according to his mother and father.

So Tristan kept that side of himself hidden in fear of losing any more of his loved ones. Not even Jake knew Tristan was gay. What if it destroyed their friendship? What if he questioned Tristan's intent whenever they roughhoused? What if he'd be too afraid to hug Tristan again after learning the truth?

Are you perhaps attracted to men, Tristan?

How was he going to explain any of this to Claude? It was like his deepest, darkest secret had been ripped out of him again and was exposed for the world to see. And the only person he could blame for that was himself.

He'd said *actor*—not actress! And the main guy was famous for being a hot, straight man playing a gay, single father who had the hots for his kid's teacher. If the title didn't give Tristan's sexuality away, then Google certainly would once Claude searched for it.

Damn Tristan and his favourite fucking movie slipping off his tongue. Why didn't he just suggest *Terminator* and be done with it? He'd clearly been much too nervous in Claude's company to hold his tongue.

He changed into a T-shirt and pyjama pants, and then walked into the theatre room across from the gym; he suspected that was where Claude would meet him. It had a huge flat-screen TV and a sleek white sofa, which was surrounded by at least a dozen or so reclining armchairs and slots for popcorn and juice.

It was... astonishingly cosy, with the light brown walls and a thick carpet and faux-bear rug. In the far right corner, Tristan saw a small bar, and on the opposite end of that, a dartboard and pool table. It was more a game room than a theatre.

Tristan sat down on the sofa and switched on the TV, scrolling through generic action flicks on Netflix. He had to make sure it was all testosterone and nothing romantic in the slightest; he couldn't chase Claude away with his earlier mistake. For all Tristan knew, Claude was against gay rights, and Tristan would be out on his ass by midnight. He'd be vulnerable again; a sitting duck until Scott's buddies finished off the job.

He shook his head, plopped down onto the sofa, and selected the most popular action flick he could find. Claude finally entered some moments later, wearing matching black pyjama pants. His muscular, toned body still glistened from his shower, and his damp hair had been slicked back to the side.

When he smiled and sat down next to Tristan, he could smell the minty soap Claude had used in the shower—so fresh and organic, like peppermint spring water.

"This doesn't look like the film you suggested," Claude said with a quirk of his eyebrow.

"Yeah, that was a stupid suggestion... Sorry." Tristan ducked his head and kept his gaze on his lap. "This one's better. All manly and shit."

"You have nothing to be ashamed of, Tristan. I endorse equal rights, not suppress them."

Tristan's throat tightened and his eyes stung. Fuck, was he really going to start crying now? And in front of Claude? He grabbed the remote and started the movie, distracting himself. "Just forget about it, honestly."

"You never answered my question, however." Claude looked Tristan straight in the eyes, clean face unmoving. "Are you gay?"

"Do I look gay? I was just messing around," he tried to joke, but that dark gaze pinned him down, making his mouth dry. "The Antonio guy really is a good actor."

"This is a *yes* or *no* question, Tristan," he said, tone clipped and eyes narrowing. "Are. You. Gay?"

That sharp gaze suffocated Tristan as a few rogue tears fell. This wasn't something to cry about, but the way Claude spoke and looked at him... it was too intense, too like the time his father had gritted his teeth, demanding the same answer.

Hesitantly, Tristan nodded, but when the atmosphere around them grew heavier, he said, "Yeah, I am."

The room became lighter all of a sudden as soon as those simple words were uttered.

Claude's eyes softened, a smile tugging at his lips. "See. That wasn't so hard now, was it?"

"No," he admitted, wiping away the tears and laughed. "I guess not."

Truth was, answering that question was the hardest thing he'd ever fucking done.

It was silent between them for a few minutes, and Tristan focused his attention back to the movie. It was an awful film about surviving in the wilderness and how there was a killer beaver on the loose who was actually an alien trying to brainwash the human population.

Tristan glanced over to Claude, who had a dumbstruck expression slapped on his face, mingled with an odd look of fascination. When the plot line somehow grew stupider, Tristan paused the movie.

"Uh, maybe something else?" he suggested through a grimace.

"Put on the romance one you suggested before."

Tristan's heart jumped. "Are you sure? I mean, after what I said and—"

"Go on. There's no need to be ashamed here."

He found the movie and played it, the heat already gathering in his cheeks. Should he scoot further away to give

Claude more space? He didn't want to make it awkward between them after what he said, but Claude smelled so delicious from his shower, and he was so warm and kind and patient and *safe*. Tristan didn't *want* to move away.

"Are you a virgin?" Claude asked in a too-casual tone.

The movie had barely started yet, and Tristan startled. "What?"

"Simple *yes* or *no* question, Tristan. Are you a virgin?"

"Yes," he croaked out, body tense. What a strange question to ask. "Are you?"

Claude actually laughed. It was the first time Tristan had heard him laugh, and it was a beautiful sound. He couldn't explain why it sounded so soothing to him, it just did.

"Come over here," Claude ordered him, and the way he said it, for some fucking reason, caused his dick to swell. Tristan gulped and scooted towards him. He thought Claude was just going to be casual with him, maybe swing an arm around Tristan's shoulders, but he was wrong. So wrong.

At first, it happened so quickly that Tristan hadn't a moment to register it.

Claude kissed him on the lips.

His mouth melted against Tristan's in a hard, powerful kiss, and his strong arms slithered around his waist and lifted him on top of his lap. Tristan, lost but so alive, felt how rock hard Claude's cock was against his ass.

Because of him—Tristan Kade!

Tristan cringed inside, willing his thoughts, his heartbeat, his *everything* to calm the fuck down and focus. But he couldn't. His senses reacted so wildly to Claude's touch that he lost himself completely.

"This is much better than alien beavers," Tristan breathed out as he pulled away from the kiss slightly, enough to gasp air.

But Claude said nothing. His eyes had darkened, if that were even possible and were fully intent on Tristan's lips. He pulled him forward again and covered his mouth with his, snaking a hand down Tristan's arms until they landed firmly on his ass. He gave it a tight squeeze. Tristan gasped, too wrapped up in the moment to realise Claude had pushed him back onto the sofa and now leant on top of him.

His sculpted body and sheer size engulfed Tristan's line of sight, making his breath hitch in his throat. An unusual sense of vulnerability wrapped itself around Tristan's shoulders. Not the kind that sensed something bad might happen to him, but that he was so easily entranced by this man that he was frightened he'd never want to leave him again.

Tristan's teeth caught Claude's bottom lip as he tried to pull away.

Only slightly breathless, Claude chided him. "Behave, Tristan. I thought you said you were always a good boy?"

"Well, that all depends on your perspective," Tristan shot back, grinning at him. Claude smiled this time—just barely—before he stretched up onto his knees and tugged down his pants.

Claude was a glorious sight indeed. His groin was

impeccably groomed and his well-endowed cock glistened as it leaked with pre-cum.

"I want you to suck it," Claude ordered, his gaze fixed intently on Tristan. "Don't tell me you've never sucked dick before, Tristan?"

Tristan *burned*. He could feel his blush claiming his cheeks, his neck—his whole body, for fuck's sake, as he stared lustfully at Claude's engorged cock with his teasing, English accent shooting through his mind. No, Tristan had never sucked a man's cock before, but damn… He'd certainly give it his best shot.

"I…I haven't." Why was he breathless? "I'm sorry." Why was he apologising?

Claude stood up from the sofa and pointed to the middle of the floor. "Hands and knees on the carpet. Now," he ordered firmly, and Tristan realised how to the point Claude could *really* be.

Tristan did as he was told. He knew obeying Claude would work wonders for him. He also knew that Claude wanted it—for Tristan to be a good boy and listen to him. Ever since the day he met him, he knew Claude was the kind of man who demanded respect, outside and within the bedroom, and hell if Tristan didn't love that.

It was why he'd been so unsure of Claude to begin with.

Until this moment, he couldn't understand how Claude's presence could reduce him to *this*.

Kneeling on the floor, Tristan waited for Claude to approach him. But he didn't. He raised a finger and curled it inwards, twice. Shit… Tristan's dick was a swollen bulge inside his pants, throbbing beyond his control. He crawled over to Claude, who stroked his own cock up and down slowly, his eyes never leaving Tristan.

"Open," Claude said, inching his dick towards Tristan's mouth. "Suck my dick until I tell you to stop. If you bite me, Tristan, I will punish you."

Mission accepted.

Tristan sucked that dick until his jaw ached. He even used his tongue and frequently twirled it over the head's sensitive slit, back and forth again like the porn videos he *so* hadn't watched back home. His endeavours brought shudders and moans of appreciation from Claude. Tristan licked, sucked, and bobbed up and down until his legs turned raw against the carpet, and his own dick brushed excruciatingly against his jeans.

Fuck… He tastes so good!

So good that Tristan told himself he could suck Claude's dick all day long and never get bored of it. He did what he thought *he'd* like someone to do to him, and he cupped Claude's balls and pressed into them tightly.

The professor moaned once more, and Tristan hummed along his shaft.

"Yes, that's it…good boy," he breathed, and Tristan was glad to hear the professor was breathless. "Keep going, Tristan…Use your lips and tongue for me more."

It was hard not to. Claude was practically fucking his mouth now—forcing his dick down Tristan's throat whether he wanted it or not, barely allowing him time to breathe before he rammed it back in again. It wasn't the most comfortable feeling in the world, but he'd endure anything to hear Claude Galen moan for him.

Was he going to cum in his mouth? And would Tristan swallow it?

He glanced up at the professor through his hooded eyes. The brown eyes, which always seemed to darken whenever they latched onto him, never left Tristan's face. He burned just thinking about that.

Claude had been studying Tristan the entire time.

"That's enough, Tristan," Claude breathed out, grabbing hold of Tristan's hair and pushing him away. "Turn over and hold your ass up in the air for me."

He didn't get it. Claude hadn't cum yet, so why were they stopping? Did he do something wrong? He did as instructed, though, and heard Claude come down to the floor with him. After Tristan had faced the other way and lay on his hands and knees, he wondered what would happen next, but was startled when Claude yanked his pyjama bottoms down and exposed his ass.

Were they really going to do this? Tristan's breathing quickened as he prepared for Claude to enter him. He knew it would be painful, but he'd endure it. It'd feel good soon, so good, that the pain would slip away from him. He just hoped Claude would prepare him first.

"Forehead against the ground, and then spread your legs apart."

Fucking hell. Claude's voice was so heavy with lust that it was impossible not to squirm.

Tristan placed his head against the polar bear rug, turned slightly on his cheek so he could still see Claude, and widened the gap between his legs. His cock dangled between them, painfully neglected. If he could just… touch himself… even the littlest bit.

But before he could say anything, something warm—*wet*—licked over his hole.

"What the hell was that?" Tristan gasped out, and then moaned when he felt it again. It was odd, but pleasurable.

"You'll take what I give you, boy, and enjoy it. No more talking."

Tristan squirmed again, wriggling against the slippery intrusion, even more so when he realised it was Claude's tongue lapping at his hole.

The way he had snapped at him—he sounded just like the day Tristan had met him. Cold and demanding with no sense of humour in his tone. And *boy*? Fuck, if that didn't rile Tristan up—for all the right, and possibly wrong reasons.

He kept still and let Claude devour him. It was a strange sensation at first, but then it started to feel good. Tristan's cock leaked more pre-cum as the tongue-fucking gathered momentum. He couldn't take it—he moaned and squirmed again. *More!*

"Stay still," Claude snapped at him once more, and his breath trickled over Tristan's exposed ass. He was still breathless, still turned on from what Tristan could see from the gap between his legs.

The professor's dick bobbed between them, thick with arousal.

"But I—"

"It was an order, Tristan. Do not make me punish you — because I will." Claude slapped him on the ass, and his response was a mixture between a strangled sob and a moan.

Why was this turning him on so much?

Claude went back to work, and Tristan held motionless to the best of his ability. He panted and moaned but kept as still as possible. The sensation sent shivers through his overheated body and Tristan's balls were aching, begging for release.

He tried to think about other things to calm him down for a few seconds or else his brain would explode with pleasure from overstimulation, but he couldn't with Claude's ruthless tongue fucking his tight hole.

"More," Tristan whimpered aloud, remaining still. "Please, Claude."

"I'm not done with you yet, boy. Do not move."

Claude retrieved his tongue and faced away from him. His hands came down again, striking Tristan's ass in time with the movie's first kiss.

Oh, the fucking irony!

Tristan bucked his hips forward with the second and third spank, and then he moaned as Claude caressed his raw ass cheek.

Before Tristan knew it, Claude was pushing inside of him

with no other preparation except from a little spit. And Claude wasn't holding back anymore. The thrusts were so painful that Tristan cried out and his cock withered. He dug his nails into the carpet and gritted his teeth, but the pain soared through him; there was no way in hell he could do this.

"Stop!" he screamed when a flair of pain consumed him. "It hurts! Please, stop!"

It was like fire ripping through his body, slitting his bones in half—a white-hot, agonising pain that he'd never prepared for. Never contemplated. Not *this*! He tried to push back against Claude, but it only made the pain worse.

"Please, Claude... I said *stop*! I don't want to do this anymore!"

He felt desperate—*sounded* desperate. There was no way this pain could be normal, not at the speed Claude was thrusting into him, or the way his body seemed to shrivel up and want to die. Why wasn't Claude stopping?

His fingertips dug into Tristan's lean waist, pinning him still. Even when Tristan cried out again and again, or he tried to claw away to safety, begging him to stop, Claude didn't. He thrust so hard that Tristan saw stars, and his body soon slumped towards the floor.

He didn't scream anymore—because he couldn't. Tristan passed out just as the blood began trickling down his thighs.

Chapter 7

CLAUDE RAN THE bathroom tap and washed his face. He let the cool water rush over his features, breathed in its ice-cold fumes and closed his eyes.

I couldn't hold back...

For the first time since Claude began researching, he found himself in an unfavourable position. For twenty-two years he had broken, trained, and remade people more times than he could count. But he'd never found himself breaking in the process.

Not like he did last night.

Something had evidently come over him. He didn't know what it was to begin with, but he knew now that he had to get rid of it, and fast.

He realised the boy had lost consciousness when he ejaculated into him and saw that Tristan was no longer twitching or fighting underneath. While the sight of his subject covered in blood was not an unfamiliar one, seeing Tristan bathed in it—when Claude had intended to go gentle on him—startled him, and he'd never before seen his world crumble so quickly.

Fear as well as obey, Claude. Heal as well as punish.

Luckily, Claude's father had prepared him for moments such as this: those dark, hidden moments when Claude lost his grip on the world and delved too deeply into darkness.

He carried Tristan to his guest bedroom, laid him down gently on the bed, and then rushed back into the kitchen. Pouring warm water into a basin mixed with antiseptic, he picked up fresh linen, a packet of cotton pads, and then trailed through to the bedroom.

Tristan hadn't moved.

Claude placed everything down onto the floor beside the bed, turned Tristan over gingerly, and inspected his wounds: evidence of clear internal bleeding and a tear to the boy's anal canal. He gulped and tentatively began wiping away the excess blood that soaked the boy's hole. At least the bleeding had stopped since Claude had pulled out of him. But it didn't make the cleanup any easier. Not to mention that the state of the boy's ass was because of his lack of self-control.

He'd had such a perfect virgin hole, and Claude had torn it to pieces.

Why?

Because he was simply incapable of controlling himself? Such restraint had been basic, elementary-level skills of being a researcher, and yet Claude had completely disregarded every single one of them, all because he didn't want to *remember*.

Remember *him*.

That part of Claude's past had been locked up long ago — nearly twenty years, to be precise. Tristan reminded him so much of Benjamin, but he couldn't afford to think about the past. It was gone. Forgotten. *Done*.

Once he finished cleaning the boy, Claude left him alone in his bedroom and then called for the doctor.

Next time, he'd have to be more careful.

But for now, he needed to calm the hell down.

He turned left at his bedroom and veered towards the gym.

❦ ❦

The early autumn sunlight that poured through the window bled into Tristan's eyes. He clenched the tartan duvet into his palms, and after he managed to convince his muscles to soften, his head sank back into the soft pillows.

He was in Claude's guest bedroom again, and more pillows than he was used to cradled his body. Two by his side, and another lodged underneath his legs, propping him upward.

He turned his head and peered at the clock resting on top of the nightstand. It wasn't even seven a.m. yet. Strange to have woken up this early; Tristan was not an early riser, and morning people baffled him.

Next to the clock, there was a glass of water and a couple of white and blue pills.

Realisation dawned on him: Claude wouldn't stop, even after Tristan had begged and *begged*. He'd felt as if he were being ripped open, and now, the sharp, stabbing pain inside his body made him gasp out in agony.

It throbbed as he made even the slightest movement, and

Tristan knew those pills were meant to take away the pain. Hell if he was going to take anything Claude had prescribed him. Not after what had happened in the theatre room.

He *trusted* Claude, and look what happened! He'd be damned if he was going to make the same mistake twice. So Tristan grabbed the pills and pushed them between the shallow, dark wooden headboard and memory foam mattress. *Welcome to your new home, evil pills.*

He wanted to go home.

His eyes dipped closed, but then the bedroom door gently swung aside, and they shot back open. Claude emerged carrying a breakfast tray. The smell of French toast flooded Tristan's nostrils, cancelling out the pinewood smell the room normally had, and for a split second, even the pain between Tristan's legs.

When Claude walked over to the bed, he flinched from him like a beaten animal. He didn't want to be anywhere *near* this man and sure as hell didn't want Claude *touching* him again. He wanted to scream that into his face until he was purple with anguish, but when he parted his lips, nothing came out.

"I made it myself," Claude said gently, placing the tray over Tristan's lap. "French toast with strawberries, cream, and chocolate. I've also added a couple bits of bacon, and the orange juice is the freshest in the country. Produced not fifteen miles from here, actually." He smiled that familiar, gentle smile of his, and Tristan fought the urge to gag. "Go on, eat up," he added when Tristan stared blankly at the plastic tray, refusing to touch it. "You need your strength, Tristan, and I bet you are starving."

"You hurt me," Tristan whispered, his voice painfully hoarse. It sounded more like an accusation than a statement. It *was* an accusation. "I told you to stop… and you didn't. You just kept going!"

"Tristan..." Claude's face hardened as he stared into his unblinking, green eyes. "Words cannot express how ashamed I am. You are so very, *very* special to me, Tristan, please believe that." His breath became uneven as his eyes fluttered shut for a moment, and then opened. "I lost control, and I'm so… so sorry. This is not something that's ever happened before. You see, you're not like the others, Tristan. You do things to me that no one has ever done, and it... terrifies me."

And that's supposed to make everything okay, you fucking asshole?

He remained quiet, but gasped slightly when Claude caressed his right cheek with gentle fingertips. Tristan jerked his face away, refusing to look him in the eyes, too hurt to even swear the man out or yell at him. He squeezed his arms into his sides to make himself smaller under the covers—to make this entire encounter seem ignorantly untrue.

"I called a doctor in to look at you while you slept," Claude's continued in a low, unaltered voice, though Tristan could see him tapping his fingers against his suit trousers. "He said there is no permanent damage, and you should be well in a couple of days. You are to get plenty of rest, and I assure you that next time things will be much different. I promise."

Like there's going to be a next time, asshole!

Tristan was done. Claude knew what had happened to him—hell, he was the one who *rescued* him, for fuck's sake! He knew Tristan was a virgin and that he'd never come out to anyone before but Claude.

If the professor couldn't keep his shit together, then he should've stopped himself *before* ordering Tristan to crawl on the floor like a dog. He should've stopped when Tristan fucking told him to. He should've stopped!

"Eat your breakfast," Claude said, his features tightening into a frown as he rose from the bed. He straightened out his powder-blue tie, no longer looking at Tristan, and made for the door. "I must attend a seminar in London, but when I return, I hope to see you in high spirits again." He stopped at the archway, semi-turned around, and then opened the door. "Do not forget to take those painkillers you hid beside your mattress, Tristan. Get some rest."

Then he was gone.

Still unable to move, Tristan spent the following hours recovering in bed, feeling utterly betrayed. What did he ever see in Claude? The guy was clearly a psychopath, but Tristan had been too blind to see it; he was too busy viewing Claude as his damn saviour.

He had his first time with a guy who couldn't *control himself.*

The more he thought about what happened in the theatre room, the angrier he became. He adamantly refused to lay in bed like a fucking invalid while Claude spied on him through hidden cameras.

How else had he known about the painkillers?

Soon after Claude had left, Tristan forced himself out of bed. He winced, he stumbled, but he held his head high as he thrust open the en-suite door and forced himself to shower.

Even when droplets of blood poured out from his ass and splashed against the tiles.

His lower lip quivered a little—God, he was in so much *pain*—but he told himself enough was enough. If he wanted out of here, he'd have to do it himself.

Nobody else was going to help him, and he was no longer safe here. He'd have to think of a way around the cameras, too. Could he perhaps find them himself? Cut their wires like he'd seen in movies?

He dried carefully, pulled on a thick red sweater and a pair of navy jeans, sneakers, and faced the bedroom door.

He was ready to see the world again.

He had grown well accustomed to the ashen walls and granite sculptures of the cabin. The beautiful herringbone floorboards, exotic plants, and the overabundance of windows and mirror picture frames stacked against the walls. So many areas for the cameras to be hidden, and yet he couldn't see them.

He'd search some of the other hallways. There were so many doors he hadn't opened yet, hadn't even *thought* of opening yet. The mountain cabin was monstrous compared to the ones in Montana, and the acres of frozen land surrounding it were probably owned by Claude. A realisation that caused Tristan's heartbeat to stutter and his stomach clench into knots.

Getting out of here without any problems? *Yeah, as if, Tristan.* It was as if *Brokeback Mountain* had come across *Misery*. Tristan had only been there for a month, but it felt like forever to him; decades since the wind blew against his pale skin, since he saw Jake and his mom, or even talked to somebody that *wasn't* Claude.

None of the staff ever spoke to him. Oliver, Ethel, and the outside guards never even acknowledged him. They went about their lives day to day, and sometimes, they made a point of not crossing Tristan's path in the hallways.

Up until that morning, Tristan hadn't thought anything strange about it, other than Claude wanting to give Tristan some space. But now, something in his brain had clicked, and he wasn't entirely sure.

He felt more like a hostage here than a guest.

Moreover, he no longer had it in him to care about invading Claude's personal space. Compared to the guest bedroom, Claude's room was upstairs but at the opposite side of the building. It even had a balcony that looked over the living room and kitchen with a perfect view of the front entrance.

Tristan climbed the staircase and pushed open the metallic door. It wasn't even locked. Gingerly, he stepped into the bedroom, and his heartbeat pounded in his ears. The room was impeccable. Much like the rest of the house, everything was varnished flawlessly: the carpet squeaky clean, furniture a brilliant shade of white, or occasionally black, and the air stunk of polish. His sleigh bed and padded headboard in the middle of the room swallowed up a whole wall. Of course it would.

And was Tristan surprised to see there was a mirror above it? Not really—not after last night.

Other than that, nothing suspicious in Claude's room so far.

The balcony gripped his attention. He pushed onto it and was unsurprised to see how closely it overshadowed the living room. Tristan could spit and it'd land on the corner sofa, maybe even the oyster coffee table, if he put enough force into it.

Tempting...

He leant onto the glass railing and truly debated doing it, but he knew poor, old Ethel would be the one left to clean it up and not Claude.

He swallowed his spit and walked down the stairs again. Slowly wandering through the cabin, his senses absorbed the clean and modern feel to it. Everything was a little *too* clean, now that he looked closer, and empty, as though someone hadn't lived in the house for several years.

Tristan walked through the open-planned living room, past the gym and theatre room, and emerged into a dark hallway. He'd never ventured that far into the cabin before.

Its lack of sunlight and bolted-up door had always deterred him, reminding Tristan of a cliché horror movie. He'd suspected that Claude held his research facility back there, so he'd always made a point of avoiding going down there in the past.

Now, however, his instincts urged him forward. Although it was midday, the hallway had been completely stripped of its existence. No lights. No windows. Everything was dark. He pushed onward, swallowing his racing heartbeat, and he approached one of the bolted-up doors.

Locked.

He tried the next one; that, too, was locked.

His curiosity saw him at the end of the hallway. His eyes registered three unbolted doors: one white, one silver, and another one, black. Tristan's eyes fixed on the white door.

White... A shrilling noise pierced his skull, evoking a crippling wave of nausea that briefly blinded him. *So white, so blinding... Please, somebody help me!*

Tristan chose the black door instead — the safer option — and tried the handle. Locked, just like the others. His hands found the silver door knob and twisted it, surprised to hear it pop open.

Once inside, it looked to be some kind of industrial sterility room, a laboratory, which made sense with Claude being a scientist. But the granite, windowless room caused Tristan's veins to freeze and his hairs to stand on end. The room was too sterile for his liking, too white, and there were syringes — *why are there syringes?* — including a mess of equipment and tools that laced the wall, objects that Tristan didn't recognise or even *want* to recognise.

He gulped hard and tiptoed deeper into the room. The overpowering smell of acrid chemicals reminded him of being inside a hospital operating room back home. He found the light switch and flicked it on; a soft humming noise engulfed the silent air, deafening to Tristan's now sensitive ears. A fume hood flickered in the far corner, on and then off again, buzzing with exhilaration. Now that everything appeared clearer, Tristan registered how clinical the room *really* was. How bland and colourless, filled with ominous instruments, medical carts, countertops, and computer chairs that were sprawled around a stripped-down hospital bed.

The leather straps attached to the bed frame did not escape his attention.

Tristan's skin tightened around his muscles as he crept around, and a sickly sense that he shouldn't be in there overwhelmed him. He inspected all of the instruments laden on a steel countertop beside the bed, bringing each upward and into the light. Crucible tongs, syringes, metal clamps, and mouth props. The further he scrutinised, the more frightening they became.

The floor swayed underneath his trainers, and he grabbed onto the cart for support. He brushed aside the pain that stabbed at his body, at the wetness he could still feel trickling between his ass, and turned his head toward the large, tinted mirror ahead of him.

His green eyes focused not on the glow of his reflection

swelling into sight, but on the red light switch beside it. He flipped it on and almost stumbled back.

"What the *fuck*!?"

It wasn't possible.

It *could not* be possible!

As he stared into the White Room—*his* White Room—his heart plummeted to the pit of his stomach. It had to be a trick, or a hallucination, or some kind of figment of his imagination. Or, perhaps it was some other lab room intended for something else—Claude's research, something—anything that didn't weather the unspeakable kind of torture he'd been put through.

But it wasn't. Fear permeated his body as the flashing images came flooding back to him. Tristan was in that room long enough to recognise every little crack in the wall, the exact spacing between the foam tiles for the floor, and the lights on the ceiling. He knew the one in the upper right corner was a little dimmer than the rest, and how it'd frequently flickered off and on during his torture. He knew one of the tiles in the far left corner had a tiny groove in it, so small that no one else probably noticed aside from him. But Tristan did. He knew everything about that room, because it was *his* room.

Tristan's head throbbed as the painful memories ripped through him, and realisation kicked into his gut until it snatched his breath away.

Claude was the one behind everything. Not Scott. *He'd* been the one who tortured Tristan. He'd sent those creatures in with the bowls of rice, who'd starved his body of physical contact, of nutrients, of comfort, of love and strength.

Of everything that had once been Tristan.

His body quaked with sudden fury as he recalled all of the kindness Claude had shown to him and realised it'd been a lie. He'd cared for Tristan and made him feel safe. He had nurtured him and said he was important, and that he had potential and he deserved better, and Claude had avenged him by taking care of Scott.

But all of it was a lie!

"I'm a prisoner here…"

It hadn't been Scott who'd done this to him. It had been Claude—all of it—*Claude fucking Galen*. Tristan was now trapped in this house with a psychotic monster, forced to play a game he had no chance of winning. He couldn't gather any more thoughts or emotions thereon; he simply ran.

His legs charged down the hallway, past the kitchen where Oliver prepared lunch, and then outside the front door. He kept on running and dismissed the throbbing in his body, and the blood that trickled down his legs, begging for him to stop and reconsider.

It was still cold outside when he fled down the yard, but he wasn't staying another minute in that damn house. Snow, thunder and lightning, or not, he'd keep running until his feet bled, turned black with frostbite, and he could no longer walk because of the agony.

He'd head straight to the police station and then back home. Jake and Connie were waiting for him. Claude had calculatedly twisted Tristan into believing his every lie. But he would not be fooled by the sick freak's callousness any longer.

Tristan had no idea of where he was—if he was genuinely still in Europe— but he knew there would be cops nearby. He was certain if he kept running south, then he'd find a station.

He'd find *help*.

Freedom.

His old life again.

They were so close that he could almost taste it—almost see Jake and Connie within his sight.

The biting wind had turned his fingertips numb, but the pain didn't matter so long as he got out of there. He ran across the driveway, down the snow-ploughed road, and into an area of fir trees and tangled shrubbery. Tears raced down his cheeks as he tunnelled through the snow and the frozen moss and leaves that snagged at his jeans and shoes until he saw an archway in the trees, and he fled for it.

But just as he reached the other side, a car rammed forward and blocked Tristan's escape. Tristan puffed and he wheezed, his lungs on fire with exertion, as a door thrust open and someone stepped out. Oliver pointed a gun between Tristan's eyes, his face scarlet and eyes wide, daring Tristan to move.

Already knowing that it was futile, Tristan pivoted and ran back through the woods again. He couldn't surrender himself after finally making a break for it. But the trees convinced Tristan otherwise. He knew nothing about forests or the wilderness or even which trees he could climb, except from the ones in *Fangorn Forest*.

Gaming, he could do. But real-life running for his life…?

He wished he had his cell phone again, but he'd never seen it once Emit bagged his belongings back at the hotel. Claude had probably swiped that too, along with Scott's business card, all so he could isolate him.

You're such a goddamn idiot, Tristan! How could you not know he was keeping you hostage?

Tristan bolted down the forest path again, the branches grasping at the loose threads of his sweater and hair, and this time he turned right—the opposite direction to the cabin. He tripped over woodland debris and exposed roots, but quickly picked himself back up again, despite the ache coursing through him and the bullets that were now flying over his shoulders and into splintered tree trunks.

His terror tripled when they started to use guns, and he felt like prey being hunted by a wild predator. Except, he knew it was Claude's men—probably Claude himself—who were chasing him.

They're trying to kill me!

Tristan kept on running, hoping he'd find a way out of the woods and into civilisation, but instead, he found himself stumbling when a sharp pain shot through his right leg, dragging him down to the earth. *Please, God, please let me live!*

He wailed as the pain had him doubled over in agony, and he looked down at the hunting trap clamped around his ankle.

Chapter 8

"YOU WERE UNDER strict orders *not* to harm him. And what do you fucking do? Hunt him down like a damn *animal*!" Claude's grip tightened around Dmitry's throat, and though he didn't verbally express his discomfort, his eyes watered with anguish, and his face turned an alarming shade of purple. The stupid fuck had been wise enough to silence his protests.

"But Boss, the boy was askin' for it when the eejit broke away from us," Oliver spoke up, his thick Northern Irish accent breaking the delicious silence of Dmitry's suffering. "We only reacted, jus' like ye told us t'do if he bit back."

"I did not tell you to *shoot at him*!"

Claude released Dmitry's throat, and then backhanded Oliver across the jaw. The Irishman stumbled backwards with the force, but he didn't say another word. He was larger than Claude's six feet, and he'd probably get a run for his money should he retaliate, but his men knew better.

Dmitry remained kneeling on the living room floor, his eyes averted toward the floor as he massaged his throat.

"Which one of you fuckers are going to do it first?" Claude growled, and they knew exactly what he was referring to.

The men tensed and shot each other a nervous glance.

Claude puffed an exaggerated sigh, grabbed a knife from the plastic holder in the kitchen, and stabbed it into the chopping board.

"One thing I do not tolerate is sloppiness. You're lucky I'm willing to settle for just a finger today, men, because next time, I'll personally cut off something much smaller. Do *not* fucking go against my orders again. Do you understand me?"

They answered simultaneously. "Yes, Boss!"

Claude spared them a final glance before he walked past the kitchen and to Tristan's bedroom. This time, Claude's private doctor hadn't been dismissed straight away. With such an extensive wound, Claude knew he needed the old man's expertise for a little while longer. He needed Tristan to be perfect. Not scarred, not broken... not yet.

"How is he?" Claude inquired, striding by the doctor and to the armchair placed beside Tristan's bed. He was still unconscious from his loss of blood, but the doctor had also given him a strong sedative.

The doctor straightened from leaning over Tristan and shrugged his shoulders. "Hard to say. Are you referring to the tear in his ass, or the metal embedded into his foot?"

Claude tensed. "Both, Munro."

"Well, I had to completely re-stitch his anus. You'll abstain from fucking the boy for a while, unless you want him to be permanently damaged. As for the trap wound, nothing vital was torn. Mostly, just damaged ligaments. Luckily, the trap only snatched onto the edge of his fibula, which can now be mended with plenty of rest and medication."

"How long will he be bed-bound now?"

"He shouldn't have been out of bed in the first place, Galen." Munro's beady, scornful eyes flickered something accusatory, and Claude tensed. Although Munro was the best in his field, and taught at a top-class university in Central London, he despised that smug look on his face. "If you actually want this boy to heal, then my advice would be to leave him the hell alone. Have one of your men cater to his needs. But as for you? Steer clear of him." Munro stood up, packed his briefcase, and then threw on his coat. "At least until he's recovered, then you can do whatever you wish with him."

"Very well," Claude heard himself say, though it felt like razors on his tongue. Staying away from Tristan was torture. He wanted to feel his body again—to be deep inside of him and protect and encompass him. But he just kept going about it the wrong way. "I trust you'll return tomorrow for another check-up?"

"Do I not always, Galen? Look, you know how I feel about all this… business. Why you keep roping me into it, I'll never know."

Claude rose up from the chair, his shadow towering over Tristan and the doctor. "Just who exactly bought one of my subjects not three years ago? How is he, Munro? Still got those beautiful, doe-like eyes, and that sweet little whimper of his? I recall you had a soft spot for American boys, too.

Jocks, if I am not mistaken. How is he?"

The doctor's face darkened. He didn't say anything else then; he couldn't possibly. After keeping Joshua to himself for over two years, Claude had sold him to Munro, and in return for keeping the transaction between them both, Munro offered his services free of charge. While Claude hadn't desired to let Joshua go, having a senior medical professional at his beck and call made Joshua's departure a small price in comparison.

"I'll see myself out," the doctor spat, his lips turning into a grimace.

Claude watched him close the bedroom door before his gaze flickered toward the boy. He'd come so close to losing him because of his, and his men's, negligence. Twice. He wouldn't allow that to happen again. He couldn't afford the boy so much *freedom* next time. His training had only just begun, and yet it'd been quashed before it even had a chance to shine. He'd have to wait weeks before attempting to train Tristan again with four weeks now thrown to the wind.

His process, so far, was not going as planned.

Until the boy made a full recovery, Claude would work from home. At least, until he'd rekindled their relationship and shown the boy just how wonderful a life he could have with him.

If he would only stop running.

It had been a waste. Tristan was back in the bedroom, but now he was junked up on tranquillisers and couldn't move. Capable of only resting, the same doctor arrived for Tristan's check-up every morning for a month,

Tristan fought the doctor as best as he could, but with his body out of commission, there was little he could do to deter his advances. Claude helped the doctor, and Tristan often shouted and spat at him, flailing with every bone in his body.

Tristan had to spend weeks at their mercy and knew full well that he could not escape until his foot healed, which he'd been told yesterday would take longer than they thought.

At this stage in his recovery, Tristan could walk, but nothing too strenuous.

Like escaping from this hell hole, you mean?

Tristan had been trapped by the professor for two months now. Within that time, he could feel his sanity and determination slowly slipping from him. An escape couldn't be possible when his abductors were always two steps ahead of him. Could it?

If a bird happened to break its wing, did it simply no longer seek to fly? Or did it fight with everything it had left?

"Please, you've gotta help me." Tristan grabbed onto the doctor's forearm, unable to do anything but beg the man—just like he always did. "Claude kidnapped and tortured me and he'll—he'll do it again. If you help me escape, we—we can go to the police together, and I'll pay you for your help. Just tell me how much, and I'll get it for you. I promise. Please just help me? I want to go home. *Please!*"

God, he sounded pathetic with how his voice cracked, and how breathy his words rushed out.

It was the same scenario every day, and every day the doctor dismissed him.

He didn't even look at Tristan this time. "With the amount of rest you've had, you should be fine in a couple of days. I'll let Professor Galen know."

"I'm a fucking *prisoner*!"

Why won't you help me?

He was a *doctor*. Shouldn't he of all people want to help Tristan?

The doctor stretched up from the bed and carried a bunch of cotton buds and disposable gloves into the –en-suite. Tristan heard the sound of the trash can opening and closing as he discarded them. Once he'd inspected Tristan's foot, ass, and drew blood from him, he'd dispose the garbage in there. Then he'd clear away everything else, pick up his briefcase, and go—always locking the door from the outside. Claude must've had it installed while he'd been unconscious. He was never getting out of here alive.

To make matters worse, the doctor always wore that distinctive white cloak of his, as if mocking Tristan. The sight of it made him want to vomit all over his bed.

He kept on trying, though, every day to make the doctor see sense. When he visited Tristan some days later, he asked again for help and tried to get him to contact the police, or at least tip them off—but he wouldn't even acknowledge him.

The only thing the doctor *would* acknowledge was

whether or not Tristan was in any discomfort or pain.

"Uh, like being tortured in a white room for several weeks kind of pain? Or having Professor Galen rape me and send his men to hunt me down like a dog? Or hey, maybe the emotional trauma of being abducted by two strange men in the middle of the night, and then thrown into captivity, ripped of my life and fucking future?"

"You should be fine getting out of bed," was all the doctor said with a small hum, removing his latex gloves. "I want you going easy for at least two more days, but you've healed perfectly. No long-lasting damage."

Tristan glared at the doctor with blatant, venomous hatred. When he took the cotton swabs and walked into the bathroom, Tristan stretched over the bed and groped the doctor's bag on the armchair. He listened for the tap before rummaging into the satchel for something sharp. His heart hammered the entire time, but he was desperate and knew if he wanted to get out of there alive, then he had to take drastic measures.

He had to make sacrifices.

He dragged out a silver scalpel resting in the inner pocket and hid it in the waistband of his pants. He was still weak from whatever painkillers the doctor kept pumping into him, but he wasn't out of it like he had been with the sedative.

How easily they could overpower him.

But if Tristan had to run again, he was certain he could. He tested his legs, and forgetting the doctor was in the en-suite, he slowly got out of bed. He stood up and felt a flash of pain rush down his arms and legs. He managed to steady himself against the armchair, seconds from collapsing onto the floor.

"What are you doing out of bed?" The doctor stood under the bathroom archway.

"You said it was fine."

"Looks like Galen found an eager one." The doctor grabbed his satchel, slung it over his shoulder, and guided Tristan back to bed. "At least, rest for another hour while the tranquilliser wears off. You'll make yourself nauseated if you're too active while it's still in your system."

"I'm begging you one last time, please...please help me? You're a doctor... Isn't that why you became one in the first place—to help people?"

"Goodbye, Tristan," the doctor said, face tight and expressionless, giving nothing away. "Try not to get into any more accidents."

Tristan watched his only hope walk out the door without even a single drop of sympathy.

"Why won't you fucking help me?!" He screamed from the top of his lungs, but he was met with silence.

And the sound of his own weeping.

❤️ ❤️

There was something inexplicably soothing about winter. The stillness of it, the snow, the coldness; Claude had always believed that winter was his favourite season.

Hidden in the most secluded part of Aviemore, one could shout for help and nobody for miles would hear them. It was a comforting thought, Claude smiled to himself, to know that he was completely alone here.

Or rather, to know that his boy was.

Tristan Kade who, so far, was proving to be quite the difficult subject.

He'd never had such a tiring experience of breaking in his new pet. Never a relentless, constant, day-to-day struggle of nursing them back to health and training them, only to nurse them once again.

Normally, things went according to his plan. His subject would be selected, thrown into the White Room, and come out weeping and begging for help like some fragile, little kitten. Then, once Claude had gained their trust, he would test them. He'd watch his little lab rat scour his maze for an escape—enter the various rooms of his house—but inevitably fall deeper into his trap.

When Tristan discovered the White Room it had somewhat been intentional. Claude had wanted that to happen, eventually, just not so soon. It was Claude's mistake. He'd been the one to soil Tristan when he was at his most vulnerable. It was because of Claude's lack of self-control that Tristan later fled into the woods, which in a roundabout way, was also part of Claude's test.

Soon, the rat would discover that there was no way out. No escape.

However, Tristan getting shot at and then snatched by a

hunting trap was definitely not intentional, and as a result, it'd postponed the boy's training for at least another month.

He had two pinkie fingers to thank for that.

Claude unlocked Tristan's room door and pushed it open. An instant relief flooded him when he saw Tristan hidden under his duvet, a lump of listless bones under the thick material.

He walked over to it, drew back the duvet, but was startled to discover it'd just been a bunch of pillows bunched together

For a fleeting moment, Claude's heart sank, and his eyes searched the room frantically.

"Tristan." Claude banged on the en-suite door, noticing it had been shut and locked. "Open this door immediately, Tristan."

He could hear water rushing, and panic soared through him. He began kicking at the door, using his good shoes to mark the redwood.

"I said open this door! Do not force me to break it down, boy, because it'll be my pleasure."

Thankfully, he heard Tristan's voice speak up from the other side of the door. "It's because I'm scared you're going to hurt me again."

Claude's features softened, but his heart clogged with uncertainty. "Tristan, I promise I'm not going to hurt you. I understand you're afraid of me, but I'd never risk your life for anything... Not again. You're far too precious to me. Please come outside."

"Then why did you torture, kidnap, and fucking rape me?"

He couldn't really find an answer for that, and he despised being speechless. Finally, he said, "Tristan, come outside and we'll talk. I've brought you some hot chocolate. Tons of sugar."

Lie. But he just wanted Tristan out of there, and fast.

Why had he not removed the lock for this door when he installed the bedroom one? *Fool*.

The bathroom door slowly unlocked. Claude made a mental note to have the lock removed. Not that there was anything he could use to hurt himself, but if he was desperate and smart enough, he could inhale water from the sink.

Claude had cameras planted all over his room and throughout the cabin just as a precaution, but even then, they didn't feel enough.

One could never tell what the human mind was capable of.

Tristan pulled aside the bathroom door, and Claude almost smiled at him, but then the boy lunged at his throat. They toppled backwards with the force and wrestled on the bedroom floor, Tristan on top of Claude, and he grabbing the boy's wrists.

By no means was Tristan small, but he wouldn't be able to outmanoeuvre Claude unless he was armed. And he was. A silver scalpel glistened in Tristan's hand, and he pinned the blade against Claude's throat.

Chapter 9

TRISTAN COULDN'T BACK out now. If he was going to kill this motherfucker, he had to do it right. But he didn't know the first thing about slitting someone's throat, and his apprehensions showed through his trembling fingertips.

In a series of blurred movements, Claude grabbed onto Tristan's arms and pinned them to the side, causing Tristan to slice Claude's cheek in the process.

Deep, but not deep enough.

Before he had a chance to make another strike, Claude seized Tristan's windpipe, squeezed, and flipped him around. He pressed down hard against Tristan's groin with his knee and yanked the scalpel out from his limp grip, a snarl tugging his lips.

Tristan cried out, his partly healed ankle throbbing with pain as Claude pressed on top of him. The look of murder was in those dark, fathomless eyes, and Tristan's own widened with instant regret. He no longer thought of pain then. He thought of survival.

"Please don't kill me," he pleaded, clenching his eyes shut. "I'm—I'm sorry! I don't want to die—please don't kill me!"

"Enough begging," Claude demanded, increasing the pressure on Tristan's dick. His stubbled cheeks were flushed with rage. "You should've thought about that before attempting to take *my* life."

Tristan cried out again. "I'm *sorry*! I just want to go home… please, I won't tell anyone about any of this! My friend and his mom are searching for me, and they're going to track me to you eventually. Either way, they'll find me, but if you let me go now, they'll never know it was you. I promise…"

Claude merely laughed at him. "Do you not think I thought about them before I had you abducted?"

Tristan was silent, his thoughts racing through his mind until eventually something clicked. "Just tell me what to do, what you want, and I'll do it… I just want to go home."

He'd say anything to escape from Claude.

Anything…

When Claude didn't answer, a sob burst from Tristan's mouth. He hated the tears that began falling down his face, but he couldn't stop them. He felt helpless. Time and time again, he had tried to escape from this man, but it was futile.

There is no escape.

"I have tried to be nice to you, Tristan. I have tried to be kind and patient, and at times even lenient, but you have betrayed my trust. You threw away everything I have given to you, and on top of that, tried to kill me." His knee pressed painfully against Tristan's bulge again, this time harder. Attempting to fight Claude had been such a reckless decision. But he kept on trying to wiggle free—to shift Claude's weight off from his lean body. He just wanted to *breathe*.

"What... do you want from me?" he gasped, holding his breath until his forehead swam with stars.

"What I want is for you to obey, Tristan."

Obey Claude Galen? There was no way in *hell* following Claude's orders would be that easy—not when the man was fucking stark raving mad! But it was the only logical solution if he wanted to make it out of here alive.

"Please, give me a second chance," he said, swallowing every ounce of pride he had left. "I want to be your good boy, Sir. *Please*."

Claude chuckled dryly. "You know, I used to feel sorry for people like you, Tristan. Those who would rather lie their way out of danger than face it. It is about time you learned your true place and faced the consequence of your actions. Get up."

His hands latched onto Tristan's thin shoulders and yanked him up from the ground. Kicking the scalpel across the room, he dragged Tristan outside and into the hallway, past the kitchen, through the living room and toward the entrance staircase.

Tristan grabbed at the railing and struggled against Claude's tight grip. "What are you going to do to me?"

"You will soon see," Claude replied, digging his nails so deeply into his arm that they left bruising.

When Claude was close enough, Tristan saw his last chance; he kicked Claude's shins in the hopes of knocking him down the stairway. Even if Tristan tumbled down with him, at least he'd most likely be on top and could make another break for it—if he were lucky.

The twisted fucker must've been waiting on the attack. Before Tristan knew it, Claude had bent down and slung him over his shoulder. There was nothing romantic or humorous about their postures; Claude looked like a man set on killing, and Tristan was the prey who wouldn't go down without a fight.

Claude kicked open his own bedroom door. Everything inside had been rearranged. The king-sized bed moved along the wall to make room for something terrifyingly too real.

A cage.

"I'm—I'm sorry! Don't put me in there," Tristan begged, but it clearly fell to deaf ears.

He growled and threw Tristan down onto the middle of his bed, and his burning, dark gaze incinerated him. Gasping at the silk bed sheets, Tristan's heart pounded like a drum as he stared up at Claude, his face contorting into a bold grimace.

Claude didn't hold the gaze for long. He opened his nightstand drawer, pulled out a knife, and blood rushed to Tristan's head.

This was it. This was the moment Tristan Kade would die.

Claude loomed over above him, and Tristan instinctively covered his face with his hands. He prepared to die then, or at least have something sliced off—a finger, ear, anything. But with a quick strike of his arm, Claude ripped Tristan's shirt down the middle, and tore it off him with his bare hands.

"If you are going to act like an animal, then I will treat you like one."

Oh, God, what was Claude going to do to him *now*? More torture? More rape? More... more White Room?

"I am your Master and you will obey me. Understood?"

"Yes, Sir. I'm sorry!"

Once Tristan was naked—clothes completely shredded—Claude walked over to a black ottoman and rummaged through it. Tristan debated if he should try to run again. But did he *really* want to risk pissing Claude off even more? Risk his life again, for all it was clearly worth? The man looked seconds away from killing him, and Tristan still didn't know what he'd planned to do with him.

Killing would've been too much mercy.

Claude strolled over to him, not bothering to hide what he'd drawn out from the chest. A long, silver butt plug with a faux tail attached to the base. As Claude snaked the grey tail through his fingertips, Tristan saw the base was made of glass, and his fear multiplied. Surely he wouldn't insert *that* into Tristan's body?

He was relieved when Claude walked toward the nightstand and grabbed a bottle of lube. At least it wouldn't be as painful as without it.

Tristan could get through this—it was nothing to be scared about. Thankfully, it wasn't the White Room or incessant noises and lights. Also, Claude couldn't rape him with that thing in. He couldn't, could he? Oh, God, what if he *did*?

"Relax," Claude said, his cold voice devoid of any warmth. "If you clench up, you'll injure yourself and will have to see the doctor again. I'm not above having him hurt you this time around."

Tristan bit his lips, though a shudder and a small whimper squeezed through them. Claude walked over to where he was lying on the bed and brought Tristan's legs up, exposing his ass.

"This has healed nicely," Claude said, his voice dipping to that familiar, low level of gruffness. Tristan winced as Claude's finger gently touched his still-sensitive hole, rubbed around the swollen rim, and then withdrew again. "If you try to run, Tristan..." Claude's breath felt hot against his skin, trickling down his thighs as Claude dipped lower, and began smothering Tristan's hole in lube. "I'll keep this tail in until your ass rips indefinitely."

The bulged head was inside him, slowly inching further as Claude's breath fanned against his skin, fingers moving with sick, clinical efficiency. Pain misted his vision, and sparks of pleasure when the plug began to vibrate.

It's too big! It's too big!

"Stop!" Tristan yelped out, but kept his legs still as the large plug stretched and filled him. There was no way he wanted to cause more damage to himself—not after his last 'accidental tear'—but it was so painful that it brought tears to his eyes, and his body convulsed against the intrusion. Claude had deliberately chosen something that was too large to fit Tristan. *You fucking sadist!* "Please, I'll be good! I'll be good!"

"You don't know the meaning of it, boy." Claude stood up, walked slowly back to the chest, and brought out a pair of matching cat ears. "We mustn't forget these now."

Tristan almost laughed at how *ridiculous* this was, but Claude could really hurt him, so he settled with biting his lips again. It was just a headband—he could handle that. Claude secured the band into his, messy, dark hair, and the perverted asshat even tousled his head. "Good boy. Now, how about some milk?"

Tristan glared at him but knew if he said no, it could result in a much worse punishment than an uncomfortable plug and slight humiliation. "Yes, Professor," he replied with an obviously fake smile.

"First, we need to help build it up," Claude replied in his usual, noncommittal way.

His fingers curled around Tristan's flaccid cock, and began stroking until it hardened. Then, opening his nightstand drawer, he brought out a long, leather cage, and a pencil sized wand. He held them up so Tristan could see.

"The cage will prevent you from coming, and the wand will keep you hard. Absolutely no touching... because I will know of it and I will not be pleased."

He strapped Tristan's cock and balls inside the leather cage, and then placed the wand alongside his already-throbbing shaft. Securing the straps in place, he fastened the wand in and then readjusted the cage slightly. The wand curved at the top, and wrapped around his oversensitive slit, sending jolts of pleasure through his body.

"Hopefully, we will only need to do this for a week," Claude rumbled, still repositioning the straps. "But I'm willing to go longer if you cannot learn to behave."

Tristan shuddered at the thought. A whole fucking week?

At least it's not the White Room.

So far, his punishment was far less extreme than the actual non-punishment fucking had been.

Maybe Tristan should run away more often.

How can I joke at a time like this?

He was unable to even catch his breath, too sick with worry and dread and fear and *what are you going to do to me?*

Claude scooped him into his arms and carried him toward the cage. *No!* He began to flail rapidly, thrusting his body against Claude's iron grip. There was no way he could stay in that cage for a minute let alone a whole *week*!

"Stop kicking!" Claude snapped, tightening his grip on Tristan's body.

He stopped thrashing, and Claude placed him down into the metal cage. Tristan curled up on the wafer-thin blanket that was inside, though he'd never in a million years be able to sleep here.

Claude reached in and fastened a pair of leather cuffs around Tristan's wrists and ankles, who sobbed when they were latched onto the iron bars.

"I'm giving you the option to be quiet," Claude said, his voice harsh and clear. "If you fail to do so, I *will* gag you."

Tristan nodded, all fight evading him. However, his eyes

widened when Claude grabbed another wand from his pocket, and placed it between Tristan's balls and perineum. He secured it in place with one of the straps on the cage, and then it started to vibrate. Along with the butt plug, it had been too intense, and he yelped despite his mind begging him to keep silent.

"Do I need to get the gag already?" Claude threatened, and Tristan shook his head.

"N-no, Professor." Those words were already breathless, and Tristan knew it was on the lower setting.

"Good boy. For now, I have kept the setting on low, but there are multiple levels to this. Each time you misbehave or speak out of turn, I'll raise the setting and add a day to your edging. When I think you've earned it, you will be milked, and we'll see how your behaviour is from there." Claude closed and locked the cage, then shook a small remote. "Remember to be good, Tristan, and the setting will remain low. Pleasing me will limit your pain, and similarly, angering me will increase it. Do you understand me?"

He couldn't manage a coherent response. He simply shook his head as the vibrations moved through his body in waves, torturing him.

Claude nodded impassively. "I'll check on you later. When I retire to bed, you'll please me until you're dismissed. You're just an animal to me now, Tristan, and I'll make good use of that while I can."

It wasn't up for discussion. Tristan knew when that moment arrived, Claude would do whatever he wanted with him.

And Tristan would do nothing.

Because he *could* do nothing.

Chapter 10

TRISTAN DIDN'T KNOW what intensity the vibrations were at now, but he knew he messed up three times in one day with talking and begging.

For days, his only relief was when Claude came into the bedroom, snatched Tristan from the cage, and demanded that he pleasure him. Usually, it was a blow job while Claude fucked his ass with the butt plug, sending involuntary, intense waves of pleasure down his body, which Claude seemed to enjoy. So much, in fact, that he would sometimes take the wand he'd strapped into the cock cage, and run it over Tristan's slit; making it impossible for Tristan to focus and not bite down.

Then it happened.

Tristan was so sensitive and the vibrations were at least two notches higher, judging by the volume of his whimpers, that he'd accidentally nipped the edge of Claude's cock. Nothing hard or too painful, but Tristan knew he'd made a huge mistake the moment his teeth had come into contact with skin.

Claude hissed and thrust Tristan away from him. He landed painfully on his backside, jolting the tail plugged into his hole. Panting, he stared up at Claude with wide eyes, but he was too fixed on his dick to notice. After he inspected it for any damage and made damn sure there were no bite marks on his precious *manhood*, he spared Tristan a sharp glare.

Tristan waited for the professor to scold him, to use the remote to increase the vibrations, or pull out another awful instrument from the black chest, but he didn't. Rather, he strode over to his wardrobe, slung aside the doors, and fumbled somewhere inside. Metal clinked in his clenched palm as he swept back over to the bed, where Tristan had been on his knees.

Claude *still* didn't say anything to him, and the fear that gripped Tristan, because of the silence, held him motionless on the bed. Claude uncurled his fingers and Tristan's eyes fixed on a metal mouth prop.

"Open."

"I'm—I'm sorry...I didn't mean t—"

"I said *open*." A flash of anger eclipsed Claude's features, marred by the thin cut on the side of his cheek. When Tristan's eyes fixed on it, Claude clenched his jaw, and those dark eyes narrowed into thin slits. "I am not losing my cock simply because you're feeling spiteful. Now open that fucking mouth, or I will open it myself."

Shame filled Tristan's body, but he forced himself to open his mouth and Claude secured the wedge-shaped instrument between Tristan's lips. His saliva instantly gathered around it, and Claude hadn't even fastened the strap around his skull yet.

In some sick, perverse part of his brain, Tristan waited for

Claude to call him a good boy.

❤️ ❤️

Claude despised disobedience, and he knew that in order to redeem his subjects, he had to recreate them. Inflicting pain was the most efficient method of obtaining such a desired outcome.

Just like this beautiful, harmless mouth prop that Tristan drooled over while Claude fucked his mouth senseless.

When Claude neared his climax, he quickly pulled out from Tristan's propped-open mouth and came all over the boy's face. He used his dick to smear it over Tristan's features and into his mouth, finishing with a rough slap of his cock against his cheek.

Claude pulled back, unbuckled the mouth appliance, and watched Tristan sink languorously onto the floor, spitting the prop out as though it had been a crab latched onto his tongue.

"Better, Tristan. Much better."

"Like I had a *choice*," Tristan mumbled, but then he clearly remembered himself. "It was an accident."

"Accidents are faults that can be rectified. Have you not learned to be more careful when sucking me off in the future?"

"Yeah, I learned." The boy spoke with so much venom, and when he added, "Professor," it sounded like an insult.

He knelt down to Tristan's level and fingered the straps locked around his throbbing cock. "Sacrifice. This is what happens when you displease me." He tugged at the straps, causing Tristan to cry out in pain. "Obey. This is what I will do should you defy me again." His hands cupped Tristan's balls and squeezed them. Tears rushed to his eyes, but Claude merely smirked at him. "Submit. Yielding to me will soon be all you can think about." Now, he caressed Tristan, so gently that a flush of pink claimed the boy's delicate skin. "Punishment. Even the pain will feel so good that you'll never want it to end." Tristan bucked into Claude's hand, stifling a moan. "Am I understood, boy?"

"Yes, *Sir*!" Either the boy was painfully stupid, or suicidal with his tone of voice. Both equally irked Claude. "Do what you want with me," Tristan mumbled through clenched teeth. "I don't care anymore."

"You don't care?" Claude pulled at one of the straps and tugged Tristan's dick forward. He hissed and arched his spine against the discomfort, the cuffs around his wrists scraping over the bedroom floorboards. "Not even for your own release?"

"Please," Tristan whimpered out, and Claude knew he had him right where he needed him to be.

"Please whom, Tristan?"

"Please, Professor!" he croaked out, clearly holding back a cry. Tears rolled down his face as Claude continued to tease his leaking cock. Such a delectable sight, indeed. Although Claude preferred his subjects to call him Master in these situations, Tristan's pitiful pleading had him turned on again. He grinned and patted the top of Tristan's head, and then leisurely stroked a finger down his tear-stained cheek.

"Good boy."

Tristan was finally allowed to come. He slouched over the edge of Claude's bed and pressed his forehead against the man's shirt, groaning as Claude unlocked the cage from his dick and nibbled the tip of his ear.

"You are to keep your legs open, or I'll edge you for another week," Claude whispered to him. "Now, lean back on the bed with me, and keep your eyes on the ceiling mirror. I want you to see your face when you finally submit to me."

They leant back on the bed, the plug still lodged deeply inside Tristan, but at least the cage around his cock had been removed. His balls were aching so badly that the cool, evening air spilling through the windows made Tristan's body twitch with anticipation.

He locked eyes on his reflection—tear-stained, green, bleary gaze staring back at him—and Claude's fingers gently brushed the side of Tristan's cock. He jerked forward involuntarily, and Claude tightened his grip around his chest.

"Be still," he murmured firmly. Another brush and Tristan remained still, letting a whimper escape his lips. "Better," Claude breathed out, then he gave a light tug, squeezing his shaft. "If you are still then I will reward you."

Tristan kept his gaze on his reflection while Claude

stroked his dick. He wanted to squirm and buck, but he knew better than to move. He couldn't go through another punishment again—especially not another edging. The thought of it was enough to make his cock wither.

The pace quickened, and he gritted his teeth together as his oversensitivity turned into pain. He was going to come any second; he could feel it rising, tingling in his balls. His breathing escalated and louder moans escaped him, nearly screams, but he kept his body still. He closed his eyes and turned his head.

"Eyes on your reflection!" Claude commanded, and Tristan's gaze tumbled back to the ceiling. "You are to watch your face when you come."

The play of desperation seized Tristan's features, moans impulsively turning into cries. He watched Claude's expression, which displayed hunger and desperation in its own way, drink Tristan in. Since Tristan wouldn't give his pleasure willingly, Claude was taking it by force, and either way, he would always win.

The sensation became too intense and Tristan wailed, relief flooding his cock and balls until he saw stars. He shot his load over Claude's large hand and white streams of it clung to Tristan's abs.

"My good boy," Claude whispered, slowing the strokes down as he nibbled the edge of his ear.

"Th-thank you, Master..." Tristan's eyes fluttered shut briefly until he realised what he had just said.

Master...

He'd never called Claude that or had any intention to. It had always been 'Professor' or 'Sir', but now he said 'Master' and it horrified him. It'd just slipped off his tongue, and he couldn't take it back. Had he truly submitted to this man? He'd thought his body was merely serving the results Claude wanted, but now... it had performed entirely on its own.

Claude's heartbeat pounded in Tristan's ears, drowning out the sound of his own. "Do you see the pleasure I give you, Tristan, as well as the pain? The joy as well as the torture? This is something you cannot possibly fight, for I always win. Is that not so?"

Tristan didn't want to call him Master again, but he knew better than to go back to Professor after dropping the bombshell. So, he answered with, "Yes, Sir."

"Now, because you've pleased me today, I will reward you with a gift."

Claude pushed Tristan off his chest, not harshly like he usually did, and stepped out of the bed. Then something terrifying happened. Claude held his hand out to him. Tentatively, Tristan placed his own into it, praying that no great horror was waiting for him next.

He just wanted to sleep. To eat and wash like a normal, living and breathing human being. His bones were in agony from being squashed in a wrought-iron cage for over a week, his body constantly re-angled to make himself appear as small as possible. And now, his aching mouth and relentless hunger, along with the need to brush his teeth, filled him.

Relief warped his senses when Claude led him into the

bathroom.

"Let's get you cleaned up," he said, making Tristan hiss out in pain when he suddenly yanked the plug out from his ass. It'd been in there for so long that when Claude ripped it away like a band aid, his hole was empty and gaping. Then he pulled the headband off and placed the items beside the sink. "I bet you miss having my cock deep inside you. Don't you, boy?"

Tristan flinched at the memory of how Claude nearly destroyed him in the theatre room, but there was no way in hell he was going to mess up again by protesting. *Say what he wants you to say.* "Yes, Sir."

Claude walked over to the huge, sunken bathtub and turned on the hot water. "I'm glad to see my obedient pet is back."

Tristan tensed at the words, but muttered a thank you and kept still, waiting for the next order.

Claude filled the bath with bubbles and warm water, and then he held out his hand again. But Tristan froze on the bathmat, unable to take that single step forward.

Claude craned his neck to look him over, and Tristan flinched, expecting pain to sear across his face. Although Claude had never physically struck him, except for those humiliating moments when he'd pointedly slapped Tristan on the face with his cock and then *raped* him, nothing with this man was truly for certain.

Tristan teetered on eggshells, and pain was just the beginning. He nudged his feet forward and let Claude take his hand again. With his spare one, Claude dipped a handtowel into the bath, squeezed it, and wiped all of the cum from Tristan's face and hair. Then he had him step inside the tub, and when Tristan sat down and stretched his legs, his eyes shot toward Claude, fear creeping over his hunched shoulders. He hadn't been told to sit down. But when Claude said nothing, Tristan breathed a sigh of relief.

"Wash yourself," Claude said, handing him a sponge. "And do not turn around. I'll be in the shower, so no funny business. If you try to drown yourself, I will be there to pull you out and punish you myself."

Although Claude had threatened Tristan before, he looked more anxious than anything. Did he really think Tristan wanted to kill himself? Sure, he had thought about it, but he'd rather see Claude die first than throw away his life like that. *He* deserved better, Claude didn't.

Tristan intended to escape from him at whatever cost, but to do that, he had to keep himself alive.

Claude walked around the bathtub, stepped into the monsoon shower beside the sink and began to hum. Tristan listened to the sound of the water rushing as he sank into the tub, allowing the steam and water to submerge him. He wasn't sure when he'd next be allowed to wash himself, so he savoured it, even if his mind told him that it was all a trick and that he should run again.

He moaned as the hot water massaged his muscles. His fingers played with the bubbles. He didn't know what Claude's plans were following the bath, but Tristan had a sinking suspicion he wouldn't be treated as well as he had prior to the theatre incident. Maybe, if he could truly get Claude to like him again, he'd let him go?

Tristan just had to act the complete opposite of his personality and be different in every way, shape, and form, and perhaps, Claude would treat him human again. And then he would escape.

Yeah, not difficult at all.

Even more difficult was the fact that Tristan hated this guy more than he'd hated anyone else in his life—including his parents, who couldn't cope with a gay kid.

He rested his head back and exhaled through his nose, sinking further down into the bubbly water. At the rate he was going, he'd never be free again. Fighting Claude was getting him nowhere, talking back and protesting had become a useless resolve, but he couldn't *pretend* to be obedient all the time. It was like telling his soul to simply no longer exist and say goodbye to his entire future—to Jake and Connie, his games and subscribers. Everything.

I just need to find another opening, or maybe the exits away from this stupid house.

Perhaps if Claude took Tristan outside, he could make another break for it, this time in the opposite direction.

"Cl—Master," Tristan called out, his small voice unsteady.

"What is it?" Claude's typical, inexpressive tone of voice, his English accent cutting through Tristan.

"May I learn how to cook like Oliver?"

He didn't respond, though Tristan heard him turn the water off and step out of the shower.

"Keep your eyes forward," Claude told him, and Tristan fixed his gaze on the shelves above the sink. After a moment, Claude approached the side of the bath, wrapped in a swan-white robe. "Oliver manages those kind of responsibilities," he said, startling Tristan's train of thought. "I have no need for you to cook, especially when you're already predisposed."

Tristan gulped, his eyes never moving from the shelves. "Maybe I can just help collect ingredients from the grocery store when you're off at work?" he suggested with a simple shrug. "Just so I'm of use to you, Sir."

From the corner of his eyes, Claude gave him a sharp glare. "I'll tell you of what use you can be to me, Tristan. You can hurry up washing and get back inside of your cage."

Tristan's heart sank and he turned his head around. "I-I didn't mean to offend you, Sir..."

Claude's face slowly softened. He bent down to Tristan's eye level, and droplets of water slid down his forehead and neck, catching a cluster of scars that had been laced into his skin. Tristan had never noticed the scars on his neck before, and for a moment, curiosity gripped him. Then he remembered that Claude was an irrevocable monster and he didn't deserve his pity.

But Tristan could see why he had been drawn to him before everything got destroyed. Claude mesmerised and intimidated you; he angered and aroused you. He took everything you loved in life and twisted it beyond repair. He broke and remade you and made it impossible to decipher which was worse.

"Why don't you finish washing your hair," Claude said, "and put on the pyjamas I had lain out for you on my bed?" He kissed Tristan on the forehead, turned, and veered toward the bathroom door. "And do not neglect your tail or ears, Tristan. Doing so will only displease me."

Tristan's heart squeezed at the prospect of being able to wear clothes again. He finished bathing as quickly as he could and washed the plug before gently placing it back inside. It slid in much easier than the first few times, with next to no resistance, and Tristan grabbed the headband and shoved it on, too, before he forgot.

Looking around for a towel, he saw one dumped next to the shower. He picked it up, hastily swept it across his body, and then placed it in the washing basket. He then walked toward the door, the fur of the tail tickling his ass cheeks and thighs, and took a deep breath.

Claude waited for him at the bed. He was fully dressed now, in an immaculately pressed, navy suit and a tie that was covered in silver moons. In one hand, he held the light green pyjamas, and in the other—Tristan's hope flummoxed—the leather cage and wands from before.

It felt like a test. Which one did Tristan *want* to use, and which one did Claude want him to pick? Obviously, he wanted to be clothed again, but he knew Claude had previously deemed that a luxury he was undeserving of. So, he walked over and tapped Claude's left hand.

A smile lit up the professor's completely shaven face. "Very good. Lie on the bed and spread your legs nice and wide for me."

Tristan lay on the bed, spread his legs open, and turned his gaze to look at Claude, who watched him from the edge of the bed, unmoving.

Then his lips parted, and his voice carried dangerously through the air. "Touch yourself."

Two words, and Tristan's circulation stopped flowing. *What?!* Claude must've sensed his reluctance, for he said, "Shame has no place in here, Tristan," and darkness glinted in his eyes; arousal had replaced itself with something sinister and obsessive. "I own you, and I am ordering you to get yourself off, or else I will fetch Oliver to do it for you."

"I'll...I'll do it," Tristan grumbled, grabbing his dick and tugging at it.

It felt impossible to get hard with Claude hovering over him like a vulture, but he sure as hell wasn't letting someone else do it for him, not the least of which was Oliver. The thought of the Irishman touching him—seeing him like this—it was incomprehensible.

Oliver seeing me like this… No, I… I can't! Ah… mmm… I won't!

Tristan stroked and stroked until his dick eventually began to harden. Claude's eyes never looked away from him, his posture unmoving from beside the bed. Once Tristan had fully hardened and was on the verge of ejaculating, Claude stepped forward and slipped the leather cage around Tristan's cock. Tristan whimpered a small protest, his climax leaving him.

"There we go. Don't you feel much better?" Claude asked him, cupping the base of his cock, and fondling it. Tristan's legs trembled.

"Yes, Sir." *Please let me go to bed*. His limbs trembled with overexertion, despite his twenty-minute-long bubble bath, and he wanted to punch that motherfucker in the face. "I've been good for you, Sir." *I just want to sleep… please.*

"Indeed, but not good enough."

Claude picked up the wand, and just like last time, he slipped it between the straps circling around Tristan's cock. It began to vibrate, as did the tail inside Tristan's clenching ass, and he whimpered as his entire body begged him for more release.

"*Now* you are ready for bed," Claude stated, stroking the side of Tristan's red-hot cheek. "You know, I wish I hadn't an engagement tonight. I would love to spend it fucking your gorgeous, tight ass 'til dawn." He brought his lips over Tristan's, and Tristan melted into his arms—but it wasn't because he wanted to. Claude practically forced him by covering his body with his.

Once he pulled away, he led Tristan over to the other side of the bed, and for a delicious, fleeting moment, he thought he'd earned the right to sleep in a bed again. But Claude unlocked the dog cage, pulled aside the metal door, and ushered Tristan inside.

"Be a good boy, Tristan," Claude said softly, locking the gate. "As I will be away all day tomorrow, Oliver will wake you in the morning, and you may eat your breakfast outside the cage. Until then, sweet dreams, my sweet boy."

He switched the lights off and left Tristan alone in the darkness.

Chapter 11

CLAUDE COULDN'T STOP thinking about his time with Tristan. The boy was perfect, even with his obstinate flaws, and he didn't know what else he *could* change. He wasn't sure he even wanted to. He loved to rip people apart and put them back together so he could better understand how they functioned. But with Tristan, it didn't seem possible. He had replicated Benjamin in every way, and Claude didn't want to lose him again.

Even if it meant keeping Tristan locked up for eternity, he would do it.

Nobody would take that right away from him.

"My dear boy!" Claude's father sauntered toward him and clasped him on the shoulder. He caught the attention of a nearby waiter at the prestigious venue in London and handed Claude a glass of champagne. "I'm glad to see you were able to take time off work to see your old man live another year. Birthday parties are such boorish, trivial things, but sometimes one must indulge in human sentiments if one wishes to make it in the world. Correct?"

Claude nodded at his slightly eccentric-looking father and took a sip of his drink. "I'm late." It wasn't an apology. "Flights to London at this time of year are never straightforward. I was delayed for at least an hour because of the snow."

The droplets still clung to his hair and shoulders.

"No matter," his father replied, patting the snowdrops away from Claude's suit. "You arrived, which is all that matters. I have you a seat next to Paisley, who'd like to discuss placing a new order. I'm to believe he'd already filled out a form and has his deposit to hand. Perhaps you can go over the terms and conditions with him, hmm?"

"Yes, Father. I left your gift with the hostess."

"Gift?" His father's equally dark brown eyes shot open, and his silver beard tilted into a cheap grin. "Let's see if you outdo last year's with your… parcel."

Claude nodded. "It's a mug."

"A mug? What in the blasted world am I to do with a *mug*?"

Claude smirked. His father was slightly smaller and leaner than Claude's build, but even at sixty years old, his father hadn't lost that daunting aura of his. He very much looked like an older, more refined version of Claude, except Tomus was hauntingly different from his son in a vast amount of twisted ways.

His father would make hell freeze over if ever given the chance. For decades, he'd been the most prominent scientist of all and had made a remarkable discovery in pathological science. It was because of his father's research that scientists were able to prove that the malleability theory could alter humanity's perspective and not just their behaviour. Particularly, he displayed how easily one could manipulate another's hyperarousal levels, which meant his father proved that it was possible to influence their decision to fight or flight and make them do what you *wanted* them to do.

With such influential knowledge that was later passed on to Claude, his father hadn't a need for a World's Best Dad mug. Still, it was an entertaining thought.

"That mug had better contain the drugs I need," his father said in his dark, threatening tone. "I didn't hand everything over to you just to be skimped out on my parcels. My clients will not be pleased."

"The drugs are inside the mug." Claude fought the urge to roll his eyes—such a Tristan thing to do. Was the boy beginning to rub off on him? "As if I would neglect your business partners' needs, father."

Business partners, being some of the most notorious organised crime leaders, were his father's largest clientele ever since the UK government stopped facilitating his research. Why? Because of fear. Modern-day human beings lacked the drive to seek what could go beyond human cognisance, all in fear of societal oppression. It was a pitiful, but expected downfall. One in which Claude strived to eliminate—to enlighten the public rather than frighten them.

"Good," he replied simply, and they walked over to the restaurant tables, already brimming with elite, VIP guests.

Claude sat down next to Paisley, and the balding, suited politician looked eager to speak with him, though he was going to regret that once Claude made his announcement.

"Twins," Paisley whispered into Claude's ear. "Male. Eighteen. I need them to be in pristine condition."

"Have you stated so in your application?" Claude didn't even bother whispering. It wasn't like the guests were unaware of his father's profession. Claude altered the subjects, his father sold them as slaves, just like his father taught him to do. It was no uncommon fact.

Paisley nodded grimly. Still whispering, he added, "Dmitry has it. I specified all of my requirements and sent you the five grand deposit. How soon can you have them altered, Professor?"

Claude shrugged his shoulders. He didn't want to be doing this, but he knew that to decline the offer, in his father's presence no less, was reckless.

To hell with it; he needed to be reckless at least once in his life. And if it went to hell, he would take Tristan with him. He rose from his seat and brought his champagne glass up.

"A toast to my father, who has taught me everything I know and has shaped me into the man I am today." He nodded toward his father, whose wrinkled, pinched gaze looked mildly intrigued by what Claude had to say. He swallowed hard, and the music playing in the background faded. "With a heavy heart, I would like to announce my retirement, ladies and gentlemen, and that I will be stopping all future applications from this moment on."

He shot Paisley a side glance, whose large, pink face looked as if it were going to burst with indignation.

"I have had an incredible journey," Claude resumed, "and wish my father and his future researcher the very best in their continued efforts. But as I have been researching for over twenty years, I believe it is time for me to step down and allow someone else to grasp control of the reins. Please, raise your glasses to Professor Tomus Galen, who is a remarkable man, father, and doctor. Happy Birthday, to my father."

The various, horribly confused attendees, raised their champagne glasses and wished his father a happy birthday. Claude, looking his father dead in the eye, raised his glass to him—but his father did, and said, nothing.

The party continued, just as Claude expected it to, but at the first chance he got, his father pulled him aside.

"What the *hell* was that all about?" he snapped, his eyes darkening and his white beard tightening into a grimace. It was the same, intimidating gaze that Claude had grown all too familiar with. But Claude stood his ground.

"My retirement notice, father." Claude smiled more smugly than he intended. The boy had *certainly* rubbed off on him. His father wasn't someone to idly make a fool out of, though, and Claude knew he would live to regret it.

"You are *not* retiring, and you *will* be giving Paisley his twins. Am I clear?"

"Father, for my entire life I have never disobeyed you. I have never disappointed you. I have always *served* you. But I have decided to retire, and I stand by that decision. I will, however, assist you in seeking a new researcher. If it helps you, I will even train them myself and have them secured in post by the summer."

"*If it helps me?!*" his father spat in a rushed whisper. Before Claude could react, his father backhanded him so hard that it split Claude's lower lip, sending his jaw snapping to the side. "Do not forget your place, *boy*! You are nothing more than a creation—*my* creation, and I will tell you what you can and cannot do." His eyes narrowed into thin slits. "I thought you learned your mistake of not obeying my orders after what happened to Benjamin, but it is obvious that you're just as foolish a boy as you were back then."

Claude ground his teeth together. "I have paid you back immensely since that day, father, and I will continue to do so, however, just not through researching."

"What has gotten into you?" His father took a step back and creased his thick, ash-grey eyebrows together. "Why are you defying my orders?"

"Perhaps it is a late rebellious streak, father." Claude straightened his sapphire tie and gazed at his father lazily. "Now, as I said, I will have a new researcher in place by the summer. Nothing will go wrong. You'll simply need to backdate the current applications and postpone any future ones. If needs must, then I will personally apologise to each and every one of them."

"I don't need your help getting a new *researcher*," he spat out. "I don't know how or why you're acting in such a… a… *barbaric* state, but I will find out, son, and I will destroy whatever is causing this sudden change in you." His father shoved into him, causing Claude to take a step back. "I think it would be better if you leave here before you cause any further embarrassments."

He watched his father stride away from him and mingle

with the superficial guests again before Claude took his moment to leave.

Well, he hadn't expected his announcement to go easy, that was for sure. Claude had spent the best part of a year contemplating retirement. Surprising himself, he'd even considered teaching full-time at Westside Charter. He actually enjoyed it, and he knew his studies could help alter people in other ways, too, not just sexually.

Moreover, if Claude Galen could spend the rest of his years with Tristan, then life would be a treasure worth seeking.

❦ ❦

Tristan's world had become a carousel of misery. He didn't know how long he'd been trapped in the cage for, or how long he'd endured the vibrations hitting his cock all over. He just knew that he wanted it to stop, but no matter how long he pleaded in the darkness for, nobody came.

The wands were programmed to produce pleasure whenever the clock struck an hour, which unfortunately for Tristan, felt like every damn minute. And dammit all to hell… a part of Tristan didn't *want* it to stop.

He begged for release every hour, but his pleas fell to deaf ears. Nobody was coming to release him. Nobody was coming to *save* him either.

Once Claude had left him alone, Tristan fantasised about all the ways he could murder him and get away with it. The longer he spent in the cage, the more gruesome and horrific those fantasies became.

He groaned and tried, yet again, to look at the digital clock that was in Claude's bedroom, but the cage was too low down for him to see around the bed. It wasn't like he could move around much anyway; it was barely big enough to fit a spaniel. The only reason Tristan played nice to that despicable bastard was because he didn't want any more punishments.

But here he was, in the cage again.

What did he do wrong this time? Claude didn't seem angry, but wasn't this a punishment? Hell if Tristan knew — the man was fucked up, and Tristan couldn't even begin to understand him.

Well, at least the vibrations were steady now. The only *good* thing to happen since Claude left for his business trip. Had it been another hour already? His body was drenched in sweat, and whenever he tried to rearrange himself, trying to *somehow* get comfortable in the cage, he'd scrape his body against the iron bars, or disturb the butt plug thrust up his ass. He'd discovered that any time he did move, the plug vibrated as if on cue. If he kept still, it stopped; it became bearable, but still impossible to resist the urge to move.

For the whole night Claude had left him alone, he didn't get a wink of sleep. All he wanted to do was come, then sleep, then come again. The desire for both was as extreme as the urge to slit the professor's throat from ear to ear, including each and every one of his henchmen, and then get the hell out of there.

He moaned against the metal bars, then the bedroom door slung open and a dark figure silhouetted the doorway. At first, he thought it was Claude, and he bit his lip so hard to stifle a protest that he drew blood.

It was only Oliver… who was seeing Tristan like *this.*

Humiliation heated his already-flushed cheeks, and there was nothing more he wanted than to disappear. The auburn-haired, middle-aged Viking walked over to the cage and bent down to unlock it. Tristan flinched away from him, though he remembered Claude had said Oliver would let him go to the bathroom and then give him some breakfast—not that Tristan had an appetite.

Food was the last thing on his mind. But this man was not sent here to hurt him. Even if he did look like he had just killed a guy. Tristan, now the prisoner, remembered from when he was a guest that Oliver had always looked like that.

Oliver yanked open the gate, and with unusual tenderness, pulled Tristan out of the cage. The guy didn't even bat an eyelid at him or glance at Tristan's throbbing cock. It looked like two beaten plums and an eggplant down there, but yet Oliver paid it no attention.

"Bathroom, food, then back inside."

Tristan was startled by the guy's thick accent. It was the first time he had heard Oliver speak, and his voice sounded familiar. Tristan's skin crawled, but he also fought the urge to moan as the butt plug vibrated with vengeance. Was it dawn already? Tristan glanced at the clock, then back to the sick fucker next to him.

"Let me come," Tristan begged, his voice close to cracking. "*Please*! We don't even have to tell Claude… Just please let me take this shit off me."

It's so painful! he almost cried, but he managed to bite his lips, and blood trickled between his teeth.

"Bathroom," Oliver growled, and his shovel-sized hands inched Tristan into the en-suite.

"Can you at least…wait outside?"

Maybe Tristan could do something to reduce his agony. Could he release himself in the bathroom? He'd never used this kind of thing before and had no fucking clue how a cock cage worked or how you removed it. But at least in the bathroom he had space to move around. Adjusting the cage and taking the plug out there might be possible.

Oliver grunted at him. "Keep that door open, or I'll knock it down meself."

Tristan kept the door open while he *just* managed to urinate. He hissed when the piss squirted out but denied the pleasure that gathered in his balls. When he came back out, there was a plate of food on the foot of the bed.

"Wow, this looks really good! Where did you learn how to make all this stuff?"

It was hard to keep a straight face and his voice steady while his cock and ass were repeatedly being stabbed with pleasure. Not to mention the fact that he was walking around with a tail hanging out of his ass and black cat ears on his head. Tristan really had been reduced to the size of an animal.

He shook his head. *Maybe this Viking guy will help me out.*

He had little hope of it, though, ever since the doctor refused him, and Oliver had pointed a gun at Tristan. But he couldn't give up on leaving this place. No matter what, he had to escape and get back to his life. Maybe Oliver despised Claude as much as he did. Maybe he was trapped here, too.

Oliver didn't respond to him.

He crossed his arms and nodded toward the food. Tristan tiptoed over, carefully sat down on the edge of the bed, and picked up a freshly baked croissant. There was a little jar of honey next to it, and Tristan smothered it over the pastry.

"This is delicious," he said over a mouthful. "So, how'd you come to meet Claude? You two friends or—" His eyes darted toward Oliver's left hand where his pinkie finger was missing. "I'm gonna guess not… Um, what's your family like?"

"No family left," Oliver rumbled, deep voice sending a shiver down Tristan's spine.

Tristan gulped. *No family left?* "How come?"

It was the most Oliver had spoken to him since they met over a month ago. Or perhaps it was longer. Time had no meaning here. All Tristan knew was that he needed help. He needed to get out of here!

He took another bite of his croissant and gulped it down with some orange juice. "Why are you helping Claude?" he asked once he'd swallowed, wiping his mouth with the side of his hand. "I really want to go home. I won't go to the cops or anything. You have my word."

"D'ya think yer the only one who's told me that? Eat up, kid, before I feed it to me mutt."

Tristan flushed, and despite the unwanted pleasure shooting up his back, he finished the rest of the food. "Thanks for the food," he said. "I've always wanted to learn how to cook, you know. Mainly baking. You know, pastries and stuff? I really like… I mean, I used to like apple pies." *Guess I'll never get to eat those again.* "My best friend's mom used to say I'd turn into one."

A ghost of a smile tugged at his lips, vanishing when Oliver picked up the tray and walked toward the door. Tristan stayed sitting on the bed, silent now as he watched the Viking leave. But then the guy stopped at the door, and he grumbled, "If ya wanna stretch yer legs, ye better hurry yer fluffy arse up."

Even with the tail in his ass, Tristan had never moved so fast in his life.

They left the bedroom and went downstairs into the gym, where they found Dmitry—another British asshat who had nearly killed him. Tristan's heart clenched still when he lay eyes on the man. He was the science rep who'd delivered the invitation letter. The British fucker who had led Tristan into this cold, merciless trap.

Tristan focused on his breathing, in and out through his nose. He refused to let these men break him. Butt plug thrust up his ass or not, Tristan stood his ground and looked Dmitry square in the eye. The fucker grinned at him. He just stood there and *grinned at him*, as if he hadn't been involved in this operation at all—as if Tristan was a friend of his who'd got lucky the night before.

"Time for exercise," Oliver said, pushing Tristan forward a step.

Dmitry eyed him coolly, and Tristan glared at him, desperate to smack that smug look off his face. He couldn't imagine doing exercise with the plug and wand still attached to him, not to mention he was *naked*. Then again, being naked in front of people was the least of Tristan's worries. Not after what he'd been through this past month.

Shame has no place in here, Tristan.

"Here's the thing," Dmitry said, crossing his arms, causing his black suit to tighten. "We don't always play by the boss's rules. Between you and me, we don't usually do this with the subjects, but you're a bit different, aren't you?"

Tristan was confused. Was he supposed to answer that? "What…?"

To his surprise, Dmitry laughed. "You're special to Boss. Not like the rest of his slaves. Anyway, here's what we're gonna do now. We're gonna take all this junk off you so you can work out, but it goes straight on once you're finished. We're also gonna keep this a secret, just the three of us, you hear? You blab to the boss about any of this, I'll shoot you with real bullets this time."

"What do you m-mean?" Tristan asked, and a spark of pleasure shot across his balls. It must've been nearing to seven a.m. *Shit!*

"When ya ran away that one night," Oliver replied with a shrug. "We were tryin' to hit ya with tranquillisers. Boss thought we were usin' real ammo, which was why he punished us for it."

"Yeah," Dmitry agreed. "We figured if we knocked you out and dragged your lame ass back before Boss noticed, you wouldn't have got punished for trying to run away."

"But...why didn't you just tell him that?"

"Have you *met* our boss?" Dmitry replied with a snort, but his husky voice still unsettled Tristan. Just standing near him caused anger to flood his veins. It was partly his fault that Tristan was here in the first place! And Oliver... Tristan bet he had been involved in his abduction, too. "He doesn't listen to anyone once his stubborn, old mind's made up."

"Anyway, ya listen here, laddie, ye've already cost me a finger, so ya better not try anythin' stupid. Put simply, if ya act like an eejit we'll fucking treat ya like one. All right?"

"All right," Tristan replied, then Oliver knelt down and removed the wand, plug, and cage—each movement like a huge weight lifted off Tristan's shoulders. It was strange to not have the vibrations anymore, and even stranger to have Oliver touching him. He tried to not cringe, but his mind was more focused on not coming—Oliver's hand would be enough to shoot his load all over the floor.

"Now go stretch your legs, and use whatever machines ya want as long as ya keep safe," Oliver said. "Boss only wants bruises on ya if he put them there."

"Well? What are you waiting for?" Dmitry huffed, his

shaven cheeks tilting into a grimace. "You've only got a few hours 'til Boss gets back. Better take advantage of it."

"Uhh…" Tristan glanced down at his cock and balls. They were in complete *agony*! Enough cum inside him to fill a jug. Oliver and Dmitry exchanged a glance.

The Viking nodded. "Fine, but ya will have to do it here."

Tristan looked at them as though they'd just said he had grown an extra head. "You want me to...do it...*here*?"

As if jerking off in front of two dudes was unthinkable, considering what he'd been through lately. Still… his cheeks turned crimson at the thought.

"Turn yer back, Dmitry, and give the lad some privacy," Oliver grinned, and twirled Dmitry around to face the door.

He didn't *want* to jerk himself off there, but he had no other choice. With the amount of spunk that'd gathered in the last hour, he'd fucking explode if he didn't come soon. He took a deep breath, then began stroking his shaft up and down, twirling his head gently at the end. He was unbearably sensitive, but he'd do anything just to get all that semen out of him. He yelped a little when the pressure became too intense, and then went back to work.

Finally, he shot out the first string of cum, followed by another, and then another, landing in the plastic bin. It was such a fucking relief when the pressure decreased, and by the time he was finished, his limbs twitched and his breath turned ragged.

The guys turned around, and their faces were uncomfortably neutral. "Finished, are we?" Dmitry quirked an eyebrow, and Tristan struggled not to grimace. His arms and legs were still shaking. He couldn't pick himself up from the floor. "I suggest your naked lil' butt takes advantage of his freedom, and workout while you can," Dmitry added, peeling Tristan from the floor as if he were a bag of bones.

Tristan didn't even bother to reply, or nod—as soon as his feet touched the floor and he felt steady again, he ran. There were so many pieces of equipment in the gym that he could use (not that he knew how), but running laps had been incredible after being locked up in that cage. And to be free of all the devices Claude had used to torment him with felt equally as amazing. If only he could use his legs to get the hell out of there.

Chapter 12

CLAUDE HAULED TRISTAN out of his cage, expecting the usual protests, but he was uncharacteristically quiet. He pushed him onto the bed, yanked out the plug while it still vibrated, then made short work of the cage and wands. Aside from the odd hitch in breath and a little whimper here and there, Tristan kept perfectly still. He normally said *something* by now — even if it was just a small yelp of protest.

Claude stroked Tristan's cock — much more aggressively this time — and he was pleased to see his body squirm underneath.

"Be still!" Claude snapped, though his anger wasn't because of Tristan. "Move again, and I will punish you."

"Yes, Sir," Tristan said breathlessly, keeping his body motionless.

Claude picked up the pace, and at first, it seemed like he couldn't get Tristan to ejaculate at all. The boy should be *screaming* for his release, but Claude knew it was because he'd recently shot his load out at the gym. Allowing his men to spare Tristan a kindness had simply been part of Claude's plan to regain Tristan's trust.

Still, it did not make his performance any less dissatisfying.

Claude made his strokes gentler, but he sped up the pace

when Tristan began to moan. Tristan arched his back against the white sheets, then he came… which was less than adequate.

Hardly anything.

Looking at the small patch of white on Tristan's abs, it'd barely fill a couple of teaspoons.

Would the boy confess the truth behind his lack of ejaculation? Or would he lie? *Time to find out.*

Claude grabbed Tristan by the throat, and he squeezed.

"I'm sorry, Sir!" Tristan pleaded, his eyes wet with tears.

"And what exactly are you apologising for?"

"For… for not doing well," he stammered out, emerald eyes glistening in the pale moonlight. "You were gone for so long… and I… I missed you, Sir!"

Claude loosened his grip, and his pulsating features slackened.

So you've chosen to lie, huh?

While pleasing Claude to avoid punishment was not necessarily a bad thing, it was still disappointing. He would've commended the boy's bravery if he'd spoken the truth.

No matter. It was time to show Tristan that good boys received rewards. And admittedly, Claude was in no mood to punish him. Not after the day he'd spent with his father constantly scolding him for retiring, and the longing to be with Tristan.

His lips assaulted the boy's violently, and they were lost for a moment in a deep, euphoric kiss. When Claude pulled back, Tristan was flushed and panting for air.

"Claude...?" he breathed out, his eyes now flushed with confusion.

He should have scolded the boy on his manners, but Claude didn't want to indulge any lectures that night; not when they were sharing such a unique and wonderful moment together.

Tristan's first attempt to openly please his master.

Splendid progress.

"It's all right, Tristan. You've made me very happy tonight."

It was time for him to begin Tristan's training again. They hadn't had sex since the theatre room incident, but this time, Claude would make sure to be gentle. He couldn't afford to lose control and hurt Tristan again. Not now—not when his boy could so soon become *his*.

Claude leant down and kissed him again, softer this time, and massaged Tristan's balls with his palm, making the poor boy wince beneath his kiss. He never pulled away, though, and never fought or clawed at Claude's chest. He rewarded Tristan's obedience with a quick nip at his lower lip, before darting his tongue back into Tristan's mouth.

For a researcher to desire his subject like this, it was categorically unheard of.

Forbidden.

And yet he couldn't stop himself.

Claude pulled away again and studied Tristan, taking in those beautiful, green eyes and bowed lips. Perhaps this boy had been sent to Claude for a particular reason. Perhaps there was more to life than carrying out his father's research—more to it than what his father had taught him since he was a child. Claude had never known life outside of his father's experiments, but perhaps this boy—this insignificant, beautiful creature—had been sent to Claude to be his salvation.

To show him that even monsters deserve a happy ending.

The question was—where to start? Claude was sailing uncharted waters here, and he didn't know the first thing about showing his affection, never mind to Tristan, one of his *subjects*.

He only knew that he wanted to.

Even if Tristan was intended to be his downfall—his darkness—then Claude Galen would never seek to see sunlight again.

Tristan continued to stare up at him, the prolonged fear twisting into dark confusion. Did he understand how compulsory he was in Claude's life? How crucial? Did he appreciate the sacrifices Claude had made for him so far—the disobeying of his father and retiring from his research?

There was only one way to find out.

"I'm going to hold you now," Claude said, his voice steady compared to the turmoil in his mind. "Give me your everything, Tristan." *Sacrifice for me as much as I have for you.*

Tristan gulped hard, his Adam's apple bobbing up and down nervously, but he nodded. When he started to turn around onto his stomach, Claude caught him by the arm, and pulled him onto his back again.

He had to see Tristan's eyes.

He had to see what he was giving everything up for.

Tristan's haunting, sea-green eyes that forever captured his pain as well as his pleasure.

It was about time he tested Tristan's submission.

Would the boy lie this time? Or would he accept his desires?

❦ ❦

Tristan's heart soared with abandon. He'd expected some kind of punishment for not performing as he should have—and lying, too—but the professor had soaked up his words like a sponge. At first, his reaction had been indistinct to Tristan, who was struck with so much exhaustion that he hardly moved when Claude rolled off the bed and toward the bedroom door.

Tristan didn't dare move. Although he'd only been a *prisoner* at the mountain home for over a month, he knew better than to displease the professor by acting of his own accord.

He heard the faint, whiffle movements of Claude rushing down the staircase, into the kitchen, and then back up the stairs again. The tall, muscular outline of his suited body framed his line of sight; he was holding onto a small hamper, filled with a bottle of chocolate sauce, a packet of strawberries, and a tub of honeycomb ice cream. He didn't say anything, but his dark stare commanded Tristan to rise, fully naked, from the bed.

"I unfortunately didn't get a chance to eat at yesterday's event," Claude said, his eyes glimmering with wicked amusement, "and I happen to be quite hungry. Into the bathroom. Now."

Tristan obeyed and tiptoed gingerly into the bathroom. The tiles were cold against his bare feet, but he was just glad to have been freed of the plug and cage. It was the longest he'd gone without it, except for his bath yesterday, and the relief was incredible.

Sunlight bled through the pristine bathroom. Claude entered with the chocolate sauce and tail in his hands. He placed them down next to the shower, switched the hot water on, and steam immediately engulfed the room. Tristan gulped. What game was Claude playing with him now? What kind of test? Dessert wasn't exactly something offered on the professor's menu, and Tristan knew better than to think he was just being nice to him.

"Step into the shower," Claude ordered.

When he did, Claude simply smiled, threw off his suit coat, and stepped in with him; carrying the bottle of chocolate sauce and still wearing his shirt, tie, pants, and socks.

The hot water felt amazing, as always, and he tried to ignore the fact that Claude was in there with him—and the bottle of chocolate sauce in his hands. However, all Tristan could think about was how could Claude use that bottle to hurt him. Unless the bottle was warmed up to boiling temperatures, Tristan couldn't think of many ways he could, unless Claude planned to rape him with the actual bottle.

With how sex went last time, a bottle was much better than Claude's cock.

He bit his lips, silencing the protests that ached to burst through him. He didn't want to be in pain anymore. He also didn't want to submit to this man. But hell, he wasn't sure his body could take the agony any longer: the lack of sunlight, kindness, and even silly, insignificant things like a cell phone again, or clothes and a bed. It had become too much. Too desirable. It had been over a week since he felt clothes against his skin—since he felt like a human being again.

Fuck, Tristan would give *anything* to get some normalcy back into his life and cease the constant agony of iron bars, cock cages, and darkness.

The waterfall shower gushed over Tristan's head and down Claude's shoulders as he towered over him. His white, plaid shirt was turning see-through the more he stood close to the water, and his black trousers tightened around his muscles. He couldn't have been comfortable, standing in the shower with his clothes still on, but he hardly seemed to care. His gaze was fixed on Tristan.

Squeezing an even amount of the sauce onto his middle fingers, Claude extended them to him. "Lick," he commanded, voice deceptively alluring.

Against his better judgement, Tristan hesitated. Words failed him and fear took up precedence. He couldn't even string a coherent sentence together, or whine in that stupid, bitchy way of his that said he was sorry.

"Tristan, I am not punishing you. This is your reward for pleasing me. A *reward*," Claude repeated, and he worked his finger gently between Tristan's lips.

A reward I don't even want?

But Claude wasn't giving him a choice. Tristan closed his eyes and lapped the sauce off his finger, all the way to the knuckle. He was still confused as to what was going on, but Claude wasn't hurting him, so he'd do whatever Claude asked of him.

Just don't hurt me.

Claude pulled his finger out, took the bottle and drizzled chocolate sauce over Tristan's chest. A cold contrast to the shower, Tristan's first thought was that he hoped Claude didn't expect him to lick his own chest, because it was physically impossible for him. He'd be punished for his impotence, and then thrown back into the cage.

But Claude didn't order him to lick himself clean. Instead, he pinned Tristan to the shower wall, lowered his head over his chest, and licked the sauce off slowly. Tristan stifled a moan when Claude's warm tongue flicked over his left nipple, then made its way to the other one. He was so sensitive now — the most sensitive his body had ever been — as though his flesh and bones had been trained to answer to this man, and this man only.

Tristan despised it.

And yet at that moment, he also craved it.

Betrayal sneered at him when his eyes closed, and his

head dipped back expectantly. His spine pressed against the wet tiles, and Claude teased harder at his nipples, the warm water gushing around them.

"Mmm…" A soft moan fled from Tristan's lips, and his eyes shot open in disgust.

Claude was gazing up at him, his watched hand pressed against Tristan's chest, pinning him still. "No shame," he murmured, his eyes and lips wet with droplets of water. "Especially when you are deserving of a reward."

In the back of his hazy mind, he tried to piece together what Claude had meant, but he was too lost in the pleasure shooting through him to make any sense of it. It was a different kind of pleasure this time. No pain, nor suppression or agony—just bursts of ecstasy shooting through his head and down to his toes.

What surprised Tristan the most was Claude bending down onto his knees, retrieving the bottle, and lathering Tristan's cock in chocolate sauce. The professor's expensive suit was now soaked to his bones, his black hair dripping wet and falling into his dark eyes, but he paid it no mind. His full attention was on Tristan, and lapping down his chest, his stomach, and to the edge of his cock.

Tristan bucked, bracing himself against the tiled wall. Claude's warm mouth wrapped around his cock, and he couldn't control his unwanted moans or heavy pants anymore. That wicked, terrifying tongue worked along Tristan's shaft, then pulled off just to lap over the slit, kissing the edge of his cock.

"Well done," Claude said in a breathy voice. "Keep getting hard for me, but do not cum in my mouth."

No more talking when Claude's mouth went back to work on Tristan's cock.

Just warm, wet pleasure devouring him again and again.

Tristan wished he had more to grab onto other than tiles, but he sure as hell wasn't touching Claude's hair—not when the man could bite his dick off at any moment.

How could it be possible for a man to inflict so much pain and misery, and yet arouse so much pleasure within him?

It made Tristan livid just thinking about it, and tears glazed his eyes. He was disgusting to want this—to feel like he needed this. Claude was his rapist, his captor, and yet Tristan wanted to cum in his fucking mouth!

What was *wrong* with him? Had he finally lost it? He hadn't been outside for so long, hadn't touched any of the real world, his games, or spoken to his loved ones. That alone was enough to make him psychotic.

Claude's hand gripped onto Tristan's clenching ass, and thrust his hips forward. He couldn't stop himself from bucking into Claude's mouth. His lips and expert tongue were so tantalising—and it was his first ever blow job. He couldn't stop… *so good… keep going…*

His orgasm gathered in his balls, his toes curled inward, back arched, and his cum flooded into Claude's mouth. His immediate thought was how good it had felt. But then he saw Claude's eyes gleaning up at him, and he knew he had done wrong.

"I'm sorry, Sir, it just—"

Claude's lips sought Tristan's before he could finish, and his tongue thrust forcefully into his mouth. But it wasn't just his tongue—something thick and bitter accompanied it, and it trickled down to the back of his throat, forcing him to swallow. The second he gulped and Claude pulled away, he knew he had been forgiven. Claude's eyes returned to their original, tempting chocolate, and his erection sandwiched between them.

Hunger heated Claude's gaze, raw with undulating need, and before Tristan could catch his breath, Claude turned him around and thrust his cock so deep inside him that Tristan gasped out an unexpected cry. His hole had long since been prepared, thanks to the plug, but it was still painful. Not to mention Claude thrusting evoked flashbacks to when he was raped, and his entire world had turned black.

The theatre room...

Claude continued to thrust into him, which was thankfully much gentler than the last time, even if Tristan still wanted it to stop. He wished he could forget that memory—forget this whole place entirely, and the fucked-up professor who funded it.

It didn't take long for Claude to groan and come in Tristan's ass, much to his relief. Thank God, it didn't go on and on like last time, and at least he didn't bleed or tear his ass again. This time, the pain and raw burning had been surprisingly manageable.

"We need your ass prepared every day for training,

Tristan, so I want you to wear this new plug I purchased for you. Tomorrow, you will carry my seed inside you until I say otherwise. It mustn't be removed. Am I understood, boy?"

"Yes, Sir."

Claude pulled out of him, and gave his ass a sharp spank. Tristan held himself tight against the wall, listening to Claude pick up and then insert a much colder, but smaller butt plug between Tristan's throbbing ass cheeks. He hissed when it slid inside, his ass still tender from overuse, and then waited for Claude to step away from him again. But he turned Tristan around to face him, and something unusual shone within those dark depths. His eyes had turned uncharacteristically soft.

"You're turning into such a good boy, Tristan. I am very pleased at your progress."

His lips claimed him again, gentler this time, then he steered them under the water and silently washed off the remaining sauce from Tristan's body with a soapy sponge. When Claude turned off the water, he handed him a thick, swan-white towel, and Tristan wrapped it around his waist gingerly.

"I have another gift for you back in the bedroom," he said, leaving the bathroom

After Tristan quickly towel dried his hair, he followed him, breath rapid as he prepared for something unpleasant. It seemed more accurate than another act of kindness from him.

"Sit on the bed," Claude rumbled, pointing to the king-sized mattress. He'd removed his shirt now—only his wet, black trousers sculpted his body,

Tristan did as he was told and kept his mouth closed the entire time. He watched Claude walk over to the hamper placed neatly on the bedside cabinet. He picked up the tub of honeycomb ice cream and fresh strawberries, then a glass bowl and silver spoon. He scooped out the ice cream and dusted a few strawberries on top before handing it to Tristan.

What was he supposed to do with *that*?

"It's for you to eat," Claude stated, when Tristan just sat there with the bowl limp in hands. "I think it's about time we stop treating you like a beast. You've pleased me greatly, and I want you to see that such an act will always elicit a reward." He nodded to the ice cream. "Now eat."

Dumbfounded, Tristan nibbled at the ice cream and was relieved to hear that he'd no longer be treated like an animal. Did that mean no more cage? Would he get his room back? Clothes again? Tristan couldn't get his hopes up; it could be like the pyjama pants. Maybe it was just another test. But he had already eaten the ice cream before he realised that. *Shit*!

What was he supposed to have done, offer Claude the ice cream instead? Yeah, maybe he should have. Why the fuck didn't he *think* beforehand? He was starving, that's why—but he hadn't realised that his mind had been starved of its rationality.

Claude didn't say anything, though; he just stood there and watched Tristan devour the dessert. He couldn't remember the last time he'd tasted ice cream and fruit. Way better than the bland crap they'd given him in the White Room, or the protein shit Oliver used to whip up for him when Tristan was a 'guest', and now, a prisoner.

When he finished, Claude took the empty bowl from him and placed it back inside the wooden hamper.

"How was it?"

"Delicious, thank you." He quickly remembered his manners, and his eyes blinked up at him. "Sir."

"Perfect." Claude replied with a tight, lopsided smile. "Good boys will always receive luxuries, Tristan, in place of punishments. I want you to remember that."

He nodded. "Yes, Sir. Have I made you feel good, Sir?"

Claude's face lit up like sunbeams. "Very. You do surprise me, boy."

"Then… then may I please, I mean... Could I have some clothes, Sir?" When Claude's eyebrows began to arch, Tristan hastily explained, "It's just, I'm so cold in the cage and sore and alone, and I can't take it anymore."

Not a lie.

In fact, it was the third, most honest thing he'd ever said to Claude.

"The cabin's temperatures are always set on high, Tristan. When you've pleased me more, I may consider the possibility of returning your clothes. Until then…" Claude pulled back the bedcovers, took Tristan's towel from him, and said softly, "you can sleep with me. Go on inside before you catch a cold."

Tristan almost shook his head. But he couldn't stop his

eyes from straying toward the cage and then to the bed again.

Is this another test?

"Unless you would rather sleep in the cage than with me. If so, then by all means, go right ahead."

Claude turned toward the bathroom, then he added over his shoulder, "I'll expect you to have made the correct decision by the time I return."

Tristan didn't have to think twice about it then.

He crawled straight into the bed.

The next morning, Tristan woke to pure and utter bliss. No pain, no overstimulation, and no cramped muscles tightening against a cage.

Sleeping in Claude's arms wasn't as bad as Tristan had expected it to be, although it'd come as a shock initially. There were times during the night when Claude's hands wanted to play with Tristan's cock and balls, and sometimes his nipples, pinching and twisting them. It wasn't too painful, but Tristan would arch into Claude's body as the teasing continued, and a groan escaped him.

It granted him a small chuckle from Claude, who would then stop, or continue if he wanted to hear Tristan moan and whimper more. The strangest thing, though, was Claude waking up in a good mood—the best Tristan had seen him in so far. He didn't know what he did right, but he wished he knew so he could keep on doing it. A happy Claude meant little to no pain. If only Tristan could repeat everything he did the night before, so Claude would be happy all the time, and he'd have a greater chance to escape.

"Good morning," Claude said, rising from the bed with a bright smile. "Did you sleep well?"

"Yes, Sir." Well, aside from the teasing, and the fact that Tristan was trapped in hell. "Thank you."

"I must do some work this morning in my lab," Claude said, no longer smiling. "You may go to the kitchen and ask Oliver to prepare your breakfast for you. You may also wear one of my shirts and pyjama bottoms, but only when it is around other people. When you are with me, I expect nothing to be hidden. Understood?"

Tristan nodded and got dressed in the clothes Claude had laid out for him, relieved to be wearing something again, regardless if they were too big for him. He waited until Claude left the bedroom and disappeared down the hallway before he felt safe to venture outside.

It was a beautiful relief to walk beyond the bedroom, though his visit to the gym had been unexpectedly welcome.

Above all, it was such a luxury to not be confined in that barbaric cage again.

He made his way down to the kitchen, where Oliver was peering into the refrigerator.

"Hey," Tristan said, voice chipper compared to what crushed his insides. "Thanks for helping me the—"

Oliver quickly faced him, and his sapphire eyes blinked to the small camera in the corner of the room. Tristan took that as *he needed to shut the hell up*. They were being watched. *Of course* they were. How could he have forgotten about the cameras? He hadn't noticed to begin with, but since he realised he was imprisoned, they were *everywhere*.

"Claude wants me to ask about breakfast," Tristan said instead, slowly pulling out a stool and sitting at the breakfast table. "He said I can have something to eat. Whatever I want. And I'd like pancakes, please, if that's okay."

They used to be his favourite thing to eat. He'd tried not to dwell on the fact that Connie whipped up the best pancakes in all of Montana, and it'd been his, Connie, and Jake's Sunday meal together.

Oliver nodded, turned toward the stainless steel countertops, and began cooking. He looked much angrier than the other day and way more flushed in the face than normal. Maybe he'd just finished working out. At any rate, Tristan enjoyed sitting in the kitchen with him. He enjoyed being able to communicate with another human being—even if he didn't talk back.

Whilst Oliver busied himself making pancakes, Tristan's eyes roamed around the cabin. It seemed like weeks since he'd been down here and not stuck in the cage. He took in his surroundings as if he were seeing them clearly for the first time—the perfectly varnished floorboards, the luxurious, ivory furniture, marble countertops, wooden canvases, and the main feature, the opulent fireplace, which divided the kitchen from the living room.

Tristan noticed that it was lit, and he craned his neck to watch the embers crackling.

A glimmer of normalcy...

The window overhead held Tristan's attention. Snowdrops splashed against the windowpane, framing the snow-capped mountains outside.

It's always snowing here.

He found himself welling up just looking at the scenic view. He wanted to be out there. His entire body, his *soul*, was aching to be freed—to just stretch his wings and fly again. But he knew it wouldn't be happening any time soon. If it would ever happen again.

Oliver set a plate of blueberry pancakes down in front of him. He turned his broad back toward the camera and kept his voice so low that Tristan was sure the camera wouldn't be able to hear him. Tristan quickly wiped the tears from his eyes. "Look kid, I need your help in bakin' a cake for the boss since Dmitry sucks at doin' it."

"A cake?" Tristan asked, matching the volume of Oliver's voice. He tried to keep his head ducked, so he was hidden out of the camera's view. "Why? Is it the professor's birthday or something?" Not that Tristan cared, but this was his henchman, after all.

"Boss is retiring," Oliver replied with a ghost of a grin. "Announced it at yesterday's party, apparently. Looks like you're the last subject. Isn't that something?"

"But... why?" Tristan repeated, as he took a mouthful of pancakes. If the announcement was true, then it explained his mood yesterday.

Oliver shrugged nonchalantly. "Suppose the boss grew tired of this kind of lifestyle. Personally, I say good riddance.

It ain't an easy or a pleasant lifestyle to lead."

"You mean, you don't like your job either?"

He frowned, and then folded over his arms, his emerald sweater tightening around his biceps. "Eat your pancakes."

Tristan cut into his pancakes, munched, and stewed on his question hanging in the air. He realised after his third bite that Claude hadn't stated where Tristan was to eat his breakfast. If it was part of a test and Tristan was meant to sit with Claude, he'd blown it by the time he realised. Just like the ice cream. He tried not to dwell on the punishment,

Just enjoy this food while it lasts, man…

"I can help you with the cake," Tristan offered, stuffing the rest of his pancake. Still eating, he added, "but I can't bake for shit."

Oliver nodded and scratched at his ginger, Viking-length beard. The man needed some serious flowers braided in there. Tristan could try to help with that, too, anything to keep himself occupied, and more importantly, away from Claude. The only way he'd manage to stay sane.

"Yer a good kid," Oliver said, his smile fading. "I'm sorry ya got thrown into this mess."

Finally, somebody who *cared* about him! Tristan reached over the table and touched Oliver's hand, squeezing it gently. Had this man always cared for Tristan but couldn't voice it in fear of his boss overhearing? Was Oliver perhaps a slave here, too? Thinking about the things Claude had done, and reduced Tristan to, made those ideas entirely possible.

The warm moment between prisoner and servant was

ripped away when Claude stormed into the kitchen. He pushed Tristan out of the way and onto the kitchen floor, and then grabbed Oliver by the throat.

"Did I say you could talk to him?" he ground out, and even though Tristan couldn't see Claude's face, he knew those threatening eyes too well to have them send shivers down his spine. "Did I say you could *touch* him?"

"I meant no harm from it, Boss!" Oliver protested, and Tristan could see the fear surface in his sapphire eyes. "Honest, ya know am not *that* much an eejit."

"It's my fault!" Tristan cried out, rising to his feet. He couldn't let Oliver get hurt because of his mistake. "I'm the one who touched him! I was just saying thank you, Sir, I'm—"

"Stay out of this, Tristan," Claude snapped. "He knows better. You don't."

"He wanted my help baking a cake," Tristan stammered out hastily, "for your retirement party. He asked for my help since Dmitry can't bake, and I wanted to do it... to... to... help celebrate! You're just so important to me, Sir, and I wanted to help make you happy."

Claude released Oliver's throat. He didn't say a damn word, though; he just stormed out of the kitchen, leaving both Tristan and Oliver dumbfounded.

What had *that* been about

Anger boiled in Claude's veins, so powerful that he could not recall entering his lab again. One moment, he'd been watching Tristan eating his breakfast through the security feeds in his lab room, and then the next, he was strangling one of his subordinates. His most trusted one, at that rate. What had come over him?

Claude brought a hand to his mouth, and it trembled against his dry lips. How was that even possible? How could he be distressed by this? He wanted to punish Oliver for touching the boy, but he'd told him to gain the boy's trust. He'd thrown the ball into Oliver's court, not Tristan's.

Oliver was simply following orders.

And then the fear in Tristan's voice... it had unsettled Claude. *Why*? He'd heard that fear multiple times before, but now it was like some horrible drug that constricted his muscles and clouded his better judgment. It made him want to lash out. To break something. To *destroy*.

He returned his attention to the footage again, and replayed his boy questioning Oliver. His subordinate, of course, had refused to answer the boy. He'd done exactly as he was ordered to do: abstain from physical contact with Tristan, for only verbal was permitted.

Claude had been the one to lose control. *The second time in twenty years.* First, in the theatre room, and then just moments ago... *This boy will certainly be the death of me.*

He swirled the alcohol in his whisky glass, one leg perched on an ivory desk, and the other dangling by his side. The room was wrapped in faint glows of pale lamplight, shining over the countless equipment, hospital beds, and plastic chairs that were spread over the tiled floor. His gaze fixed on the camera again, onto Tristan reaching over the breakfast table and caressing Oliver's hand.

That was when the unchecked fury had consumed Claude. An invisible, red-hot knife stabbed into his chest and twisted until it cut through his heart and into his throat. An irrational part of him had actually wanted to kill Oliver. It must've been the alcohol or the argument he had with his father or the conflicting feelings he had toward his retirement. There had to be *some* logical explanation for Claude's emotions rioting inside, destroying years of his father's hard work.

There was always an explanation—a solution—to why something was the way it was.

Claude just needed to figure it out, and destroy it.

Perhaps his neurological status had been compromised due to his retirement. His father certainly hadn't taken it well. Claude might've been a man who had it all, but beneath the surface, he was still only human. Neurosis abnormalities were not impossible. It happened even to the best of medical experts or scientific geniuses, and as Claude understood well, a slight adjustment to one's mindset could alter them indefinitely.

He would arrange for an MRI scan in the morning, and perhaps Munro would examine him, just to be on the safe side. A mental impairment was the only logical explanation Claude had to excuse his behaviour. Not his retirement, but his reactions to all things concerning his boy and the people who'd dare snatch him away.

His mobile vibrated against the steel desk, and Claude picked it up to connect the call. "Hello, Father. Had you a pleasant birthday?"

It had only been one day since Claude saw his father, but he knew he wasn't calling for idle chit-chat or to enquire how his son was.

"I'll ask you again to reconsider your retirement," his father replied, voice clipped and straight to the point. "I will not accept insolence as a probable cause."

Claude exhaled a sigh. "Father, I wish you would understand. Everything I have done up until now has been in repayment for what happened to Benjamin. Please do not make me regret having announced my retirement in such a respectful way, Father, because I can change it."

Dead silence for a moment, and then his father's low voice cut through it, carrying through Claude's ears like an unpleasant wail. "I will not be threatened by one of my subjects! You are nothing without me, Claude. Who was the one to put you back together once Benjamin had broken you?"

"Because of your experiments, Father. Do not forget that I was not the one who tortured Benjamin."

He really did not want to be arguing with his father, but Claude would not back down. He deserved more than a life of servitude and torture. Perhaps he *could* have more, if he just kept going…

"He died because of you, foolish boy," his father spat. "You made him soft. You were the one to make him weak and disobey me. Never forget that."

Claude's jaw snapped shut, and he threw his whisky glass down onto his desk; it slid off the edge and smashed over the floor. "'The merits of emotion do not appeal to me, Claude', is that not what you once told me, Father? I have served you well since Benjamin's death, and before then. I have done everything to make you the man you are today. You cannot revoke my decision because the announcement has already been made public."

"I could have kept my reputation, despite the incident with Benjamin," he shot back, voice artificially calm now. "I could have given my client *you*, but I didn't, because I saw your potential. Now, I realise I have made a grave error in judgement, and I will now have to live with the consequences. At least, if you were sold to the Triad, you would have been worth something."

Claude felt nothing at his father's clear abandonment. He only ever felt anger and resentment, as if he'd been drained of every other emotion when he was a child—thanks to his father.

But even at that moment, he couldn't find it in himself to feel anything. He suspected he would feel pity. As remarkable and intimidating as his father was, he pitied the scientist who had conceived a child as a means to break other people apart. He pitied him for the monster who had held his son against the White Room mirror while he ordered his men to defile him over and over again. He pitied Tomus Galen for the old, lonely fool he had turned himself into. He pitied him because, in the end, his theory simply did not work.

After years of careful conditioning, Claude had disobeyed his creator.

"I am sorry to have become such a disappointment to you, but I must be off now. I have an appointment with one of my own clients. As you used to say to me, Father, time is precious when the world turns so swiftly. Goodbye."

"Benjamin never loved you," his father squeezed in, clearly needing to have the last word. Had his father always been this pitiful, or was Claude just now seeing it? "You were nothing but an escape to him. Even after his death, the boy's venom still manipulates and tortures you." His father sighed, his anger escalating into obvious irritation. "I saw the wickedness in him the moment I looked into those murderous, green eyes. If I had known they would soon ensnare and hold you prisoner for the rest of your life, I would've destroyed him sooner."

"I really must go now, Father," Claude managed calmly, his jaw almost snapping with the force he was using to clamp it down. He knew his father was merely attempting to manipulate him through the guilt of Benjamin's death. A predictable fall back. But his father had forgotten that he taught Claude to become the master of his emotions—the master of his mind—and he was not a man easily exploited.

His father had finally realised that his son, his precious experiment, had at long last failed him. He was human after all, and he could no longer be brainwashed into submission. He wanted to change. He had to *be* the change.

"Then go, but be warned, Claude—you will *not* be retiring." His father's voice was so calm, so controlled and familiar that Claude could picture him pacing around his London office, hands scolding the speakerphone on his desk, face purple with rage. "Even if I must reprogram you myself, as old as I am, I will do it, and do it to such a degree that you won't be able to recall your old life let alone rebuild it. Do not displease me, boy, and remember what I taught you. You were created to train, and train you shall until your last subject's breath. Understood?"

Claude ended the call. He then sat back into his chair and stared at the blank wall until his eyes stung, and his breathing calmed down. The White Room lay across from him, separated by a thin, glass window that showed nothing but darkness inside. Vengeful tears gathered into his black eyes as he stared at it. He couldn't go back to training, not anymore. He'd been researching and training these helpless kids since he was nineteen years old. *Twenty years...* He'd had enough of it. Enough of his father wielding him like a puppet and enough of destroying people like insignificant dolls.

It was moments such as these, when Claude had been stripped back of his everything, that he felt most human of all.

Most vulnerable of all.

What had once been Claude's biggest fault had become

his ultimate strength. Anger was the one thing that neither corrupted nor abandoned him. He'd used it to pay back his father's debt—to make amends for the subject (and subsequent money) he'd lost him. But nothing he did was ever good enough. No matter how many lives he ruined, how many hearts and minds he damaged, it was not enough to make up for Benjamin's death.

Now, his anger had turned into vengeance. Picking up a shard of glass from the whisky-covered floor, Claude gathered the rest of the scattered pieces into his palm, and then walked over to the waste bin. His hand deliberately tightened until blood trickled between his fingers and down his wrist. It was time to put an end to his father's theory once and for all.

Chapter 13

"DO YOU TRUST me?" Claude asked him, and Tristan hesitated.

No. Never. He hadn't seen Claude since his freak-out in the kitchen an hour ago, but now, in his bedroom again, Claude had cornered him in the en-suite when Tristan started brushing his teeth.

"Do you trust me, Tristan?" Claude repeated, and his gentle eyes glinted as he waited patiently for an answer.

After what happened with the pancakes and Oliver, if Tristan wasn't careful, then the bastard would probably chop his balls off in another fit of rage.

"Yes…" he answered, lowering his gaze.

The word felt like razors on his tongue.

"Then close your eyes. I'd like to show you something."

Tristan's breath hitched as Claude put on a blindfold, and then they started walking with Tristan still naked. What if Oliver or Dmitry saw him? They'd seen him naked before, but that didn't mean Tristan wanted to show off the twig and berries again. Then again, the guys had also seen him jerk off and come inside the gym room, so did it really matter?

Yes!

Once he escaped from here, he wanted to leave with some kind of dignity.

Slim chance of that happening. Now he was being

paraded around the log cabin like he actually had something to show off.

They continued to walk, and the distinctive aroma of bleach and chemicals hit Tristan's nostrils. Were they in the lab room again? The equipment lacing the colourless walls, the hospital bed, the computer screens, and medical carts littering the floor, were as clear to Tristan's mind as they were in his nightmares. Not even a blindfold could conceal their existence from him.

Why do I have to be here? Was it because I touched Oliver? Is he going to kill me?

Oh, God, what if he *was* being punished? Claude said he had just wanted to show him something. *Yeah, show, my ass.* Another sound of a door opening, and Tristan walked through it, feeling the familiar, padded flooring underneath his feet. A sharp gust of air swept over his naked body, causing him to shiver and goosebumps to travel the length of his limbs.

"Tristan, it is all right. Calm down. I am not going to hurt you."

Tristan hadn't realised he'd been freaking out until Claude's arms wrapped around him, shushing him gently, and telling him everything would be okay. Tristan grabbed tightly onto Claude's shoulders, burying his face into the solid chest.

Why am I here? Why won't Claude just stop?

His whole body was shaking as Claude attempted to calm him down. "This is not a punishment," he said firmly. "We'll keep the blindfold on, but you will not feel that kind of pain. Not again."

What choice do I really have?

Tristan finally nodded and loosened his grip. He couldn't anger Claude, not when they were in the White Room, and he was at Claude's mercy. He could leave him in here to rot for all he cared.

Claude guided Tristan deeper into the room until they pressed into a cushioned object—most likely a table. Of course it was the table, Tristan knew that. He knew this room all too well.

"Lie down on the table," Claude commanded. "Arms up and legs apart."

Tristan did as he was told, numb throughout the process.

He moved more mechanically than anything, pressing his back against the table. Once he got into position, Claude restrained his wrists and ankles with soft leather binds. Ghostly fingers snaked up Tristan's left arm, over his chest, and then down his other arm and to the edge of his shaking fingertips. Footfalls padded to the other side of the table, and Tristan's heartbeat throbbed like a train spiralling off the tracks.

He gasped when something hard and wet slipped between his lips.

"You are to recognise only my touch," Claude said, and Tristan squirmed, wrapping his lips around the ice cube. "You need to prove you'll surrender everything to me, so I've set up a little test. We're going to examine your senses by having you familiarised with our elements. Expect no real pain, Tristan. The first will be water."

The melted ice cube rolled down Tristan's tongue and lips. Claude slipped another cube into his mouth, and he swallowed the water dripping from it.

He spent a few moments sucking on the ice cube, but he gasped when another touched his right nipple. His body was beyond responsive to Claude's touch now, and he couldn't conceal his reaction. He gasped and writhed at the coldness.

Claude moved the ice cube in rhythmic circles around his hardened nipple. Then the ice cube disappeared from his mouth, and God, Tristan actually *moaned* a protest. Claude returned it a moment later, rested it against his lips, and then withdrew again. Darkness, and the cold, wet ice cubes were all he had to rely on.

And the sound of Claude moaning his approval as he watched Tristan suck the ice between his swollen lips.

Teasing him.

Dragging him to such wanton depths of ridicule that he could scarcely recognise himself. Did he even want to?

Tristan's cock jolted. The ice cube left his nipple and trailed down his chest, stomach, and then rested on his hipbones. Another was placed directly opposite it, one more on the cusp of his abdomen. Water trickled down to his slowly hardening cock, emitting a sharp gasp from the captive.

Claude's tongue slid down the panes of Tristan's neck, following the watery trails of the ice cubes. He couldn't believe Claude's tongue was on his skin—lapping him up as if he were, well, covered in chocolate sauce again.

When his tongue reached Tristan's groin, Claude pulled back.

"Well done. So far, your body has answered to my touch nicely. Hasn't it, Tristan?"

"Yes, Sir," he managed over a gasp of air. "I—it has. A lot."

"Next, we have fire."

Tristan counted his breaths, painfully aware of Claude being close, yet so distant to him. Silent and yet deafening at the same time. He heard the snick-snick of a lighter, and Claude sighing.

"Such a beautiful thing," he murmured, still no signs of where or what he was doing, just that he was dangerously close. "It can inflict so much, and yet requires so little. Beautiful... truly beautiful."

What's beautiful, Sir?

But then he *felt* it. Three droplets of scalding hot wax splashing down his rib cage.

Tristan hissed and arched his spine against the pain. "Please, stop! You said it wouldn't hurt!"

Claude merely chuckled, his deep voice carrying through the inky darkness. "If you think this is painful, Tristan, then you have already failed my test. I thought you *liked* to be tested? *Liked* to suss out the greater, more elusive methodologies of physiological science? That's why I had invited you to join my program. Let me teach you. Let me show you how it is possible to alter a person entirely." Another droplet, and this time Tristan tried to dodge it. Futile with his hands and feet bound to the table. "All you have to do is trust me."

The wax cooled, and Tristan sighed with relief. It was odd to have the wax hardening on his skin, but at least the pain was beginning to subside. Then the wax hit his cock and balls, and he fucking yelped, jerking more fiercely at his restraints. He hissed through clenched teeth as more wax dripped down, and then more; each droplet became hotter than the last. "No more! Please, Sir."

"Hush, Tristan. Your body is answering to me quite well."

He bit down hard and whimpered when hot wax hit his chest and nipples, silencing his protests. The worst part of all was that Claude was right; Tristan's cock was painfully erect in spite of his protests.

He wanted to scream when more hot wax painted his abs, but there was no way in hell he was going to give Claude the satisfaction. Finally, the wax stopped dripping, and the cold remains sticking to his flesh hardened. Claude peeled every droplet off his body; the strange sensation making his skin crawl. Somehow, though, Tristan *liked* it, regardless of how alien it had been for him. Almost like a snake shedding its skin and leaving the remains of his old life behind, Tristan knew he wanted this.

Was he really being conditioned into somebody else? He didn't know anymore.

But he'd be damned if he were going to surrender his old

life without a fight.

This sonuva-psychotic-bitch of a professor doesn't deserve the victory.

"Impressive resistance, Tristan, but futile. Doesn't it feel good? Don't you enjoy the pain I give you as well as the pleasure, boy?"

"No." It wasn't a lie, even if he did enjoy it a little. "I'm not a fan of pain, Sir."

"Nor is anyone when it's out of their control. But I'm trying to show you that it is what your body desires, Tristan. What it *craves*. In this instance, balance."

"B-balance, Sir?"

"Yes—balance. Light and darkness, fire and water, pain and pleasure. All aspects, which allow you, over time, to explore your innermost desires. Without balance, there is nothing, and without nothing, there is no malleability theory."

Tristan's body stiffened, even after the hot wax had been removed from his skin. He didn't burn as much as he did, but his temperature was still sickeningly overheated. He was sure he'd throw up or faint if he wasn't so worried about punishment.

The urge to spit at Claude overwhelmed him, but with the blindfold, Tristan would most likely miss. Besides, he wanted Claude to like him enough to drop his guard. If Tristan could just get Claude to act like he did *prior* to the theatre incident, then Tristan could try to escape. He was getting so close.

He just needed to wait this out. Claude was only human, a simple man like everyone else. Sooner or later, he'd crack and make a mistake. And when that moment arrived, Tristan had to be strong enough to never stop running.

Tristan's restraints were loosened, and then Claude guided him off the table. As he led him a couple of feet forward, Tristan fought the urge to scream out for help. The padded floor took him back to those awful moments when he was left in here to rot—to be forgotten about like he'd meant nothing. *Because of this man!* His heart pounded, and more leather straps were latched around him.

He was going to be suspended again—he was sure of it. The colour drained from his face while Claude busied himself with the straps. It reminded him so much of when he was placed into the White Room and forbidden to sleep. They'd drag his ass up from the floor and hang him from the ceiling as though he were a slab of meat.

"Do you recall what I once said about honesty?" Claude breathed against his skin, his breath hot against Tristan's ear. His hands were drawn to the ceiling, and Claude slung his chains onto the hook. "That honesty is something to be taught? Just like honesty can be taught, Tristan, dishonesty can be rectified. I suggest you always choose wisely."

Was Claude planning to whip him? After the wax, Tristan supposed it was possible. It might've been one of those cases where Tristan did nothing wrong, and Claude just wanted to be a sadistic son of a bitch. If that were the case, he wouldn't beg or cry. He'd take the lashes and keep that fake smile of his painted on his face. At least, Claude couldn't get off on his weakness. He couldn't let Claude know that he'd broken him.

When he sensed that Claude had moved closer, Tristan's muscles tensed. He nearly yelped when something light trailed down his stomach but smouldered it to a quiet whimper.

It's just a feather… only a feather. Breathe, Tristan, breathe!

He relaxed his muscles and the feather trailed up his abs and to his nipples. He wasn't all that ticklish, but the sensation felt incredible compared to the wax. His skin prickled under the light caresses of the feather, then sweat gathered and dripped down his forehead and into the blindfold.

His skin felt as though it were on fire, but the feather somehow cooled it. How was that even feasible? The feather trailed down to his cock and balls, and Tristan jolted. Okay, maybe he was a *little* bit ticklish down there.

"Keep still," Claude chided coldly. "Take what you are given."

The feather tickled his balls, and he wanted to squirm and he wanted to laugh. *I want to scream!* Then, it trailed up his shaft and over his oversensitive slit, and this time, Tristan *did* squirm.

"Don't make me turn this into a punishment," Claude threatened, still teasing his wet slit. "We can stop right now, and I will get the whip out."

"I'll stop," Tristan said, forcing himself to act still as the feather continued to tease him. "It's just… It feels good, Sir."

Finally, the feather trailed to his thighs, followed by his legs and knees. It made its way to Tristan's toes, and thankfully, his feet weren't a ticklish area for him. However, it was still strange since he hated having his feet touched; at least, he managed to keep from squirming.

"Too bad you can't see how hard you are." Claude's voice was thick with arousal as the feather went back to Tristan's shaft. "Already leaking with pre-cum—just for me. Good little boy you are, Tristan."

Yeah, well, it was kind of hard not to be leaking when his dick was being teased in such a callous manner. Claude couldn't possibly think Tristan enjoyed his presence? Not unless he truly were all kinds of fucked up in the head and didn't know right from wrong.

Cool breath hit Tristan's swollen balls as the feather circled over his navel. Either Claude had been chewing something with cool mint in it, or he placed an ice cube into his mouth. Either way, his breath was torturous against Tristan's erogenous zones. So much, in fact, that he was worried he'd come without Claude's permission.

He'd had water, fire, earth, and now air… Tristan gulped.

The feather slid to his slit again, followed by the cool, minty breath. He wanted to yell out that he was close to coming—the pressure kept building with every soft blow of air, every flick of the feather, but Tristan couldn't let Claude realise he was enjoying it. It was humiliating enough that he was hard; he couldn't come, too.

"Give in to me, Tristan," Claude whispered against his searing skin, blowing another cool breath around the tip of his cock. He moaned. "Give in to me once and for all; you know you want to. The pain will stop and I will only ever give you pleasure. Anything you desire, it will become yours. My heart, my soul, my world. Anything. Just let yourself go."

Like he'd ever let *that* happen. But he couldn't keep on fighting under those circumstances. He tried to relax again and relied on the straps to keep himself upright. The sensation of the breath trailing up his abs, his chest, and then to the back of his ear—his most sensitive spot—sent shivers down his spine, curling his toes again and again... *Fuck...*

"That's it, Tristan," he whispered again. "Give into the sensations. Let your beautiful voice moan for me, and tell me you want more."

Tristan groaned and tilted his head back as the feather trailed across his throat, the spearmint breath following soon after. He knew better than to enjoy this. Knew better than to give in. He bit his lip again, stifling another moan.

"Tell me how much you want this, Tristan."

"I want it more than anything, Master," he cried out, words breathless against his wet lips.

Master. He'd used that word again. It didn't horrify him as much as the first time, but that alone gave him more reason to feel utterly betrayed by himself.

By that point, Tristan would take whatever the hell was given to him, so long as Claude never stopped touching his body like that... *Never stopped, period... Mmm, yeah...*

The relentless tickling continued, and Tristan sank further into boundless pleasure by the second. This could go on forever, and Tristan would not run away from it. At that moment, he'd forgotten how painful the wax had been, the rape, the abduction, and the torture. All that mattered was *this*.

Then everything stopped.

Tristan protested as Claude unsuspended him, his body sensitive with undying need—need for Claude's touch. He only held his hand this time and steered Tristan forward gently; darkness still coating his senses.

The most painful revelation of all was not that Tristan had forgotten everything Claude had done to him but that he *wanted* this. He wanted Claude to keep on touching him, to never stop, and keep roaming his body like he was someone to be loved and adored and appreciated and acknowledged. For the first time in his life, he felt alive, and it was because of *Claude fucking Galen!* The man who started all of this—who had done so many unforgivable things to him.

But now he was doing something entirely different.

He was breaking Tristan.

And his good boy actually *wanted* it.

If this is what it feels like to be alive, then I never want to be whole again.

"Place your arms against the glass," Claude breathed in Tristan's ear, steering his elbows to the glass. "And be a good boy for me. Yes, like that. Well done."

Tristan could only assume he was leaning against the

mirror. There were no other windows or visible doors inside the White Room; not from what he could remember.

He let Claude position him exactly as he wanted and held his breath. His wrists were still bound, so he couldn't move them anyway. Claude nibbled at his left earlobe, and then trailed his tongue to the nape of his neck, every touch sending ghostly shivers down his spine.

"Relax. Let yourself go, and I will give you everything."

Claude's hard dick pressed against Tristan's hole, rousing an unexpected squirm from him. Claude's dislike for impromptu movements caused himself to still. He throbbed from head to foot, so sensitive against the glass wall, and now his ass clenched as Claude carefully massaged it. And then he slapped one of his ass cheeks, and red-hot pain seared through his body.

But it feels so good!

Blood spilled onto Tristan's tongue—he was biting his lips so hard that his teeth left puncture wounds. He wouldn't submit. Couldn't submit. *It's all I have left!*

A soft kiss grazed the side of Tristan's shoulder, echoed by another on his neck and then the back of his head. After the last kiss, Claude spat into his hand and smothered his saliva around Tristan's hole. It wasn't as unbearably tight as it had been before, thanks to the daily use of his plug, but— just spit? Wouldn't he tear again?

"I'm going to enter now, Tristan," Claude whispered, so angelically that a shudder crept down Tristan's spine. His legs were trembling, lips swollen and tinted with blood.

Please, God, let me get through this! I don't want to surrender!
"And you're going to enjoy it," he added before he plunged deeply into Tristan's ass.

He didn't tear apart. *Thank God!* Claude's thrusts didn't rip him asunder, but something worse happened the second his cock touched Tristan's body. Tristan didn't fight him. Because he didn't *want* to. Instead, he wanted to feel his cock pounding into his ass, wanted to feel Claude panting against his ear, whispering to him in that godawful, foul way of his, telling him that he was a good boy and that he wanted this.

Because he *did*.

This man had once been Tristan's nothing, and yet now he'd become his everything.

And it petrified him.

"A-a-*aaahh…* It feels... so good, Sir!"

Claude grunted his approval, a distant echo that felt suffocating in the White Room. He pulled out of Tristan again, paused, and then rammed in so hard that Tristan's head almost spun. "Tell me this is what you want, Tristan, and I'll always give you it. Please me, and you'll always feel this pleasure. Tell me!"

"I want to...please you, Sir... *Master…*please...don't stop!"

Fuck, he was breathless, but he couldn't stop himself. He wanted this so badly that it burned in his core, which had never existed until this man had broken and reshaped him.

Tears streamed down Tristan's cheeks. "I want to come, Master... Please!"

"What an obedient pet you are, Tristan."

The professor wasn't nearly as breathless as Tristan, though he could feel how scalding his body was against his. Claude's hand slithered around Tristan's waist and began stroking his cock in time with his fucking. It didn't even take long for Tristan to cum—without the cage and butt plug, his load poured out of him after only the fourth tug.

"Mmmm, yes!" Tristan groaned, relief tingling through him. His mind saw stars, his legs trembled and twitched with exhaustion, but the feeling of shame quickly resurfaced—and he couldn't stop himself from sliding down the mirror.

Claude grabbed onto Tristan's waist and pinned him harder against the glass. He pounded into Tristan, rocking back and forth until his body stiffened, and his spunk filled Tristan's clenching ass. A few moments later, he pulled his cock out and ripped the blindfold off.

Pale light—not blinding as it had been—poured into Tristan's watery eyes. Claude whipped him around, and Tristan saw that the professor's face was unusually flushed and sweaty. But a certain level of pride shone within those sparkling, black depths, and it weathered a strange look of fascination that Tristan hadn't seen before.

His eyes roamed down the professor's fully clothed body, and landed firmly on his bandaged hand. Still panting, Tristan found himself gawking at it as though it were a pig flying through the sky. More injuries? Scars? Had somebody attacked the professor?

"Nothing to worry about," Claude concluded, waving his bandaged hand dismissively—but he hid it behind his half-buttoned shirt all the same.

Tristan wasn't convinced. He pushed his back against the glass and gazed up at him. "Were you attacked, Sir?"

"*Attacked*?" Claude chuckled. "Oh, no. Just a cut. Even monsters have demons, Tristan. But you…" He touched Tristan's sidearm, a caress, and smiled at him. "You have made me incredibly happy."

"H…happy, Sir?" he croaked out, already knowing what was coming next.

"Do you not feel relieved now that you surrendered to me, Tristan? Gave me your everything?"

That sweet, soothing voice was like music to his ears now—music that poisoned his soul like a septic perfume snatching away his senses.

Tristan nodded, too exhausted to care.

"Yes, Master."

If he wanted to survive, then he had to keep making Claude happy.

Otherwise, he was a goner.

Chapter 14

Twenty years prior...

THE FIRST THING Claude had noticed were those beautiful, green eyes. They'd been filled with so much hatred that merely talking to him had felt like hunting a wild animal.

The subject's name had been Benjamin, and his father wanted Claude to observe how he handled their subjects—a first for nineteen-year-old Claude Galen. Up until that point, Claude had never spoken to anyone who wasn't his father or a researcher. All the subjects had been locked away from Claude, leaving him in solitude for the most part of nineteen years.

But his father had thought it was time for Claude to see how to train a subject on his own. After all, he'd be carrying out the research for the rest of his life. It was his only purpose. His *calling*. To serve, and then to break.

Claude's duties were to ensure the subjects did not try to escape or kill themselves, which was not an easy task. His father particularly fretted over *this* subject's safety—Benjamin Lockhart. The boy had been wild compared to the others, filled with aimless rage and recklessness and seemed hell bent on escaping by any means necessary.

Something about that kind of determination had

fascinated Claude.

About two weeks into observing his father, Claude was ready to take hold of the reins. He'd grown to understand that the boy's recklessness was merely to mask his humiliation. The dark room had been hellish for the boy, which Claude understood completely. He'd been trapped in that room many times before, begging for an ounce of sunlight or physical contact.

In total, there had been three rooms—one white, one black, and the other the lab room. The white and black rooms were designed to create a void of sensation: to drown out every ounce of one's humanity and leave nothing but dark silence and mental agony behind. Claude knew both experimentation rooms well enough. How there had been nothing but emptiness to comfort you—to the point where Claude had assumed he'd either gone crazy or had died.

Like most subjects, Benjamin didn't speak after being released from the dark room—he only sat in the corner of the White Room, and he whimpered. The light in his green eyes had momentarily faded, and Claude knew the will to fight was slowly being drained from him. That was what the Dark Room accomplished after all. It drained you until you became absolutely nothing. Until you *remembered* absolutely nothing.

"Here," Claude said, kneeling down and extending Benjamin an apple pastry. "You like these, don't you?"

Benjamin, the scrawny, dark-haired Londoner said nothing at first. But eventually his soulful, green eyes turned upward, and he grabbed the oval-shaped pastry with ravenous speed. Hesitant at first, he brought it to his pink lips, sniffed, checked it was safe to eat, and then devoured it in four bites. It probably made a change from the boiled crap he was used to. Though much smaller and lighter haired than Claude, Benjamin, at eighteen, was like a poorer reflection of himself.

Alone and desperate for normalcy.

A pity neither would help.

"My name's Claude," he said with a gentle smile, sitting down on the padded floor next to him. "You have such beautiful eyes."

To his surprise, Benjamin laughed weakly, and when he spoke, his accent was distinctly English, too. "Out of all the fucked-up shit I've gone through, *that* has to be the creepiest thing."

Claude was a little affronted, but amused all the same. "I don't want to cut them out or anything. I just meant that I like looking into them."

They were so green and innocent, and yet filled with such a staggering amount of hatred, it was no wonder the staff were anxious around him. If the eyes were the window to one's soul, then Claude was looking right at his.

Benjamin laughed again, then bit his lower lip. A sad smile crept over his young, obstinate features. "Name's Ben. Don't know why I'm telling you since I'll probably be dead soon anyway."

"Why do you think you're going to be killed?" Claude

asked him, tone unaltered.

Benjamin's pale face turned into a grimace, and tears stood in his eyes. He glanced down at Claude's body, noticed he was wearing the same colourless clothes, and then looked up again. "Because they...they brought me here. Did all those things to me. Tortured me and raped me—that man, the scientist, he comes to me every night and he—he—"

Claude touched Benjamin's shoulder; a caress. "Calm down, Ben. I've been like you, too. I've been in that room." Claude glanced over Ben's shoulder, as if he were seeing something in the distance. "I know what they do to you. But there's nothing we can do about it." His eyes returned to Benjamin and sank so deeply into those sorrowful depths that he struggled to remain focused. Everything seemed to slip away from him the longer he gazed into Benjamin's eyes like some hypnotic dream that he never wanted to wake from. "All we can do is obey them, and hopefully, we live to see another day."

If only Ben would understand that resisting his father was futile. Claude did.

Benjamin looked at him for a moment, his lips parting. "You're... you're like me, aren't you? The clothes... the scared eyes... Is he doing this shit to you, too?"

Claude nodded and scratched a hand over his young, hairless face. "You're the first other one I've met... It actually feels a little less lonely in a way."

"We need to get out of here," Benjamin argued, his sweet voice now desperate. "If we can get more people on our side,

I reckon we can escape. Outnumber them, you know. Run the fuck away together. Are you with me?"

Claude's heart squeezed. Together? Could they really be together? Oh, how terribly naive, but it was a beautiful notion. Where could they possibly run to? His father had always spoken of how cruel and unclean the world was and that Claude wasn't like the other human beings. The concept of love didn't exist for special people like him, though he desired it. Yet, when he looked into Benjamin's hopeful, green eyes, it almost seemed plausible.

"We need to stay here," Claude said finally. "We'll get punished if we disobey. I know it hurts now, but once you submit to him, it stops hurting. I promise. The doctor has done this many times, and you'll never miss your old life."

"That isn't a life to live," Benjamin growled at him, his lip bearing into a snarl.

"My father—"

"If a father can do this much to his child, I would rather he killed me."

"Please don't talk like that." Claude couldn't stand the thought of losing Benjamin, even though they'd only spoken today. Truthfully, Benjamin was the first person Claude had spoken to in *months*, besides his father during their...training. "You have so much potential, Ben, and you're going to one of the best clients—father's biggest Triad leader, apparently. He says you're going to be one of his greatest works." Claude couldn't help but smile at that, a strange sense of pride flooding through him. At least Benjamin would be safe.

"Well, aside from me of course. I'm a…I'm a different kind of subject."

Yes, that was what his father had said to him—*intended to train, not obey, Claude.*

"Don't you want a better life?" Benjamin whispered, his voice still hoarse from disuse. He glanced around the room, making sure none of the medical staff were entering the White Room. "This isn't all there is to it." He straightened his posture and grabbed Claude's hand. "We can still…still get out of here, and live!"

He held onto it, mirroring the boy's posture with those same itchy, white scrubs clinging to his body. He understood full well that it was hopeless to dream of new beginnings, but he couldn't help but indulge Benjamin's fantasy. A new life with someone who shared his pain didn't sound all that bad.

Take what you are given, Claude.

Yes, Father…

"Help me escape," Benjamin pleaded again, squeezing Claude's hand with a new level of desperation, "and we can have a life together. We… we can see the world, and I promise never to leave you. I just need someone… to help me!"

Claude sighed. Negotiating was to be expected of the subjects. There was shock to begin with, and then denial, aggression, bargaining, isolation and suffering, and lastly, acceptance. Submission was the final step in the subjects' rehabilitation, but that was still a long ways off.

Benjamin had stuck himself into the fruitless bargaining

stage, which was why Claude had been sent to the White Room in the first place.

To put an end to it. His father planned to sell Benjamin in three weeks' time. *He must be ready.*

"That would be perfect, wouldn't it?" Claude smiled, and half of him really meant it—really *wanted* it. But he knew once his father latched onto you, there was no way back to your old life. Claude was living proof of that. He had simply been born to be a test subject and nothing more—conceived to obey his father for eternity. All of the subjects were. And soon, Benjamin would, too.

"Perhaps it'll happen someday," Claude said, squeezing Benjamin's shoulder. "Right now, though, you need to do everything the doctors tell you to, okay? It's the only way to survive. I know you can't see it now, but something amazing is happening to us. Something you'd never have thought possible—not even in your wildest of dreams."

"L-like what?" Benjamin's eyes briefly lit up, and his bottom lip trembled into an uneasy smile.

"Transformation," Claude said, "into a new human being."

A few days swept by, and Claude brought Benjamin a gift.

After spending the last twenty-four hours in the White Room again, Benjamin needed something to keep him going. Claude knew the extent of the room's pain—the aftershocks it had on your body, which could last for several days if done right.

If Benjamin was anything like Claude, he needed something to keep him sane.

None of them were ever allowed to leave the facility grounds. Claude had been born into his father's lab room, and he had never left it. Never met his surrogate mother. In a way, he didn't know what he was missing from the outside world because he had never experienced it. Just TV, books, and radio to keep him in the loop—and even then, the TV was a luxury for his sixteenth birthday, and the rest of his facilities were restricted.

Claude had lived in the shadows of his father's mountain home for his entire life. It was in the middle of nowhere, north of Scotland, so communication had always been limited. So far, Benjamin had been Claude's only source of outside contact, apart from the staff.

But the guards and doctors hired at the cabin only knew how to hurt Claude physically, and his father to torture him mentally. It was hardly what someone could call a *friend*. Even his tutor, who had been hired to homeschool Claude, hadn't discussed anything with him other than his studies. When Claude reached the age of twenty-four, he had obtained his Masters of Science at Cambridge University, and then later, his Doctorate of Psychology. He'd been under his father's strict surveillance the whole time.

But now, Claude was free of that life. In return, he had to work with his father's subjects, and soon, he'd take over from him so that he could retire.

The only reason I am hurting you so, Claude, is because to inflict this measure of pain, you have to receive it. How else can you exercise it?

Claude handed Benjamin the colouring book. At first, Claude was the only one to be seen colouring, but with gentle coaxing, he managed to convince Benjamin to join in. Tentatively, he'd picked up a yellow pencil and started to fill in the spaces, never going out of the lines.

Claude couldn't help but smile and study Benjamin colouring away, pleased that he'd accepted the gift. There were no windows inside the White Room, but Claude wondered how Benjamin would look bathed in sunlight.

"We could get a small apartment together," Benjamin whispered, breaking the calm silence. "It'd just be the two of us, and you wouldn't have to be stuck here anymore."

"Could we buy a pet?"

"Well, I'm more of a dog person, so…" A goofy smile shot over Ben's youthful features. "Maybe a cat first, and then a dog. The cat would be the boss, I think."

"But the wolf does not perform in the circus," Claude retorted, absently quoting from the book he had been reading in his cell room.

"As if!" Benjamin snorted, throwing Claude a handful of daggers.

He looked up and shot Benjamin a small smile. He could see why his sponsor had submitted an application for him. Benjamin was a beautiful boy to look at, strong and adamant, eighteen years old, and so full of life.

So *young*.

In an ideal world, Claude would take Benjamin away with him. His sponsor didn't deserve a boy so special. The other subjects were less than mediocre to break, but Benjamin's nature had been a whirlwind of change and impressive endurance. First, he would be so sweet and submissive that he'd do anything to end his pain, but as soon as you did, he was back to square one. Looking for escapes, disobeying, and trying to kill himself were a daily occurrence for Benjamin, and he'd been in the White Room more times than Claude could recall.

"Yeah, we can get one of both," Claude grinned at him, crossing over his legs on the cushioned floor. He'd grown so used to these floors that chairs compromised him. "We could rent a cottage in the countryside. Norfolk? Northumberland? Yorkshire?"

"I'd—I'd love that, Claude. I...I can't go much longer in here... The Dark Room's so quiet, but the White Room....that noise…!"

He threw his crayons away, and his hands instinctively shot to his ears, shielding them.

Claude reached over and clasped them both. "I know... Trust me, I know." He really did, and he wished that he could save Benjamin. Stop him from ever stepping foot in those rooms again—but it was a futile notion. There was no escape. There could be no escape. His father had made damn sure of that. He'd track them both down to the ends of the earth should they ever run from him. Was one moment of freedom worth the exchange of a lifetime of safety and love? Of being cared for by their sponsor forever?

"But I'm here for you, and I'm not leaving. We're in this together. The pain will end soon, and the pleasure will begin, and then your freedom. I promise. Just please hold on a little longer."

"Freedom?" Benjamin choked, tears streaming down his cheeks.

"Of the White and Dark Rooms," Claude explained. "After our time there ceases, my father told me, then the two of us will be sent elsewhere. You'll go to your new home, and I'll continue working here. I may even come to visit you if father allows me to."

Claude knew his father wouldn't let him visit an ex-subject, but he knew after Benjamin had been altered and sent to his sponsor, he'd live a happier and less painful life. His sponsor didn't want a brute as a slave—he wanted someone soft and forgiving, according to his application, and Benjamin was exactly that.

If Benjamin lived up to those standards, then he'd always be safe. Safe from men like his father and from boys like Claude.

Benjamin picked up the crayons again and resumed colouring. He seemed fascinated by the colours pouring across the book, and Claude watched him hard at work.

His heart ached for this dear boy, but there was no other solution. Claude was almost twenty, and his father had trained him to quench any human emotion that would hinder his decisions. He'd gone through exactly what

Benjamin had: the long, excruciating hours of darkness and silence, encroached by their ever-present hunger and fear of isolation. Not even touching on the humiliation of the sexual torment his father's servants seemed obliged to fulfil. Their caresses still plagued Claude's memories at times; he could not escape from them.

The malleable theory had happened to Claude Galen just like it did to every other subject at the facility. The fact that he was his father's son had meant nothing, for if Claude was to one day inherit his research, he had to experience it for himself. It didn't matter that he'd only been a child at the time. Age was irrelevant to a system that sold your soul to the devil.

But Benjamin… he was special.

Claude almost didn't want to tamper with his mind, but he knew it was foolish, and he knew his father was watching his every interaction with Benjamin. He had to be careful of the ever-watchful cameras.

Then the most surprising thing happened. Benjamin grabbed Claude's face with both hands, and he kissed him.

Chapter 15

"YOU HAVE NOT been successful so far, Claude. I had hoped for better. You *must* convince Benjamin that you are on his side, for to alter one's mind, we must first obtain it. Do you follow me?"

His father's sharp, inky eyes looked almost reptilian as he waited for an answer.

"Yes, Father," Claude managed, holding his gaze long enough to not appear weak.

"And so you understand the importance of explaining to Subject Two that *this* is his home now? His salvation? That there is no escape?"

"Of course I do, Father. I'm ready for this."

His father touched Claude's shoulder gently, nothing more than customary acknowledgement, and then whisked around the laboratory's steel countertops; his wispy hair falling over his broad shoulders and white cloak wrapping around his ankles.

Through the one-way mirror, they saw Benjamin rocking back and forth inside the White Room. He hadn't even touched any of his cereal that morning or yesterday evening. He must've been ravenous beneath that stubborn, impressive exterior of his.

"Yes, Claude. I think you are, too." His father's slender

fingertips picked up a pair of metal tongs from the countertop, retrieved a silver bullet from one of the plastic containers, and hovered the instruments over a crucible filled with white-hot liquid. "That is why I am giving you this opportunity. To prove to me that you are worthy enough to become a researcher. The ultimate sacrifice."

He released the tongs, and the bullet disintegrated as soon as it hit the surface of the acid.

"Yes, Father."

"Good." His father smiled at him, sweeping a hand down his cloak and then slapped on a pair of latex gloves. "Now, go tend to your subject. He is waiting on you."

Claude nodded mechanically, exited through the double doors, and then emerged into the White Room. He'd been visiting Benjamin for a couple of weeks now — ever since his father allowed him to partake in the case study. It'd been a joyous moment when his father announced Claude ready to begin his actual training.

No more White or Dark Room.

No more torture.

Now, Claude could become a true researcher, and he could show the subjects how great human life could really be.

Unfortunately, there was one thing that was not going according to plan. Benjamin was not submitting. Claude had ruminated all of the logical possibilities as to why he refused to yield. Why Subject Two, his father's prized and soon to be most expensive subject, was refusing to surrender himself.

At this late in the stage, subjects normally succumbed to the treatments by the fourth week. But Claude had observed Benjamin for a month now, ever since he'd given him the pastry, and he'd saw exactly what his father had seen in him.

Unyielding potential.

But in order to ensnare that potential, they had to make sacrifices. His father had sacrificed two recent application forms because Subject Two was taking up so much of his time. That meant two unsatisfied sponsors who wouldn't be pleased the next time, if and when, they submitted a new application.

At any rate, that was nothing to do with Claude—his father handled the transactions. All Claude existed for was to observe, to research, and to train. He'd come to the conclusion that Benjamin was holding out because of him. He really believed they could have a life together, which was partly Claude's fault. Every day he visited Benjamin, and every day they had the same discussion of breaking free. While Benjamin lived in the hopes of that truly happening, Claude had known from the beginning that it was futile.

Claude closed the White Room door and slipped his pass into his pocket before Benjamin looked up from his corner of the room.

"Claude..." he croaked out, lifting his gaze up from the floor.

His bottom lip had been split open and dried bits of blood flaked his pale, left cheek. New bruising on his neck, too, though it looked more like a love mark than anything.

Whatever Benjamin had done to anger Claude's father, he'd been punished and then rewarded for it afterward. Hopefully, Claude could get Benjamin to listen to him, and it'd put an end to his misery. He could show him how his life would be outside of the cage… if he only obeyed.

Was his resistance truly because of Claude, or something else? He'd have to do his father proud and force Benjamin to believe that his old life had never existed, and soon, he wouldn't even question that. This was their life now.

This is both our lives now.

"What happened this time, Ben? I thought you said you'd stop fighting back."

Claude nodded to Benjamin's lip, and then sat down on the floor and leant his back against the cushioned wall. He was so close to Benjamin that his plimsolls nearly touched his folded-over legs.

Benjamin absently touched his split lip, eyes glazed over as if in a daze. "Yeah. He…the man…scientist…he…" He was unable to finish, choosing instead to press his forehead against his knees and sob.

Claude gazed at him softly, trying his best not to squint his eyes against the brightness of the white lights. "You can trust me, Ben. I'm your friend, remember? I'm here for you." He took Benjamin's hand and caressed it. Benjamin looked up, and took a sharp, shuddering intake of breath. "We're in this together."

"He made me do things and I… Claude, I don't know what's happening to me. My body… It's changing, and I fucking *hate* it! We need to get out of here fast," he added with fixed determination, his voice lowering. "Please, I—I don't want to be here anymore. I can't take it. I don't know what to do, who I am..."

Benjamin's behaviour had been different that day. His hard, determined voice turned desperate and his body more lethargic. But those eyes were incinerated with that usual sense of unforgiving hatred, bringing to Claude a sense of relief. At least Benjamin was still here. Indeed, he hadn't submitted yet, and by the looks of things, he'd have to suffer more of his father's wrath before he would. While Claude was fascinated by Benjamin's endurance, disobeying his father would only result in greater pain and misery for him.

"I feel the change, too," Claude whispered, sympathising with him. He was still holding Benjamin's hand, so soft and warm and trembling in his palms. "My body eventually started to answer to him and—"

"I can't control it!"

The sudden outburst took Claude off guard, and he flinched, staring at Benjamin in disbelief. That was *not* like him.

"That your body wants to be touched, you mean? That you actually want it?"

Admitting would do Benjamin wonders right about now. *Just accept it, Ben... admit it, and the pain will stop.*

"I... I...don't know!"

Benjamin tried to yank his hand back, but Claude reached over and cradled him close to his chest. Emotionally, he felt numb and unsympathetic. But somewhere hidden among the deepest parts of his core, pain unhinged itself, and Claude's heart shattered for him. Trapped in the mirror that so frequently stormed Claude's nightmares, he could see his younger self, tortured and alone in the White Room, and the agony he had felt—the thirst for survival, hunger, and freedom. But his father was a remarkable man, and he had broken that side of his son.

Empathy was of no use to a researcher who would soon extract it from one's humanity.

Claude had to extract it from Benjamin's, otherwise, he would suffer.

They both would.

"It's okay," Claude soothed him, holding Benjamin's trembling body in his arms. "It's okay. I'm here for you. I'm not going anywhere. I… I don't know when we'll ever escape from this place, but I know that if we really wanna get out of here alive, then we've gotta listen to them. There's no shame in survival, Ben, and to survive in a place like this we need to adapt to the shadows. Even if we still see sunlight. You get me?"

Benjamin shook his head.

"We need to stay alive," Claude stated, matter-of-factly. "This place, for now, is our only home." He pulled away and fixed his eyes on Benjamin's bright green ones, where tears stood triumphant, ready to fall. "I surrendered. It took me years, but I gave in. The pain stopped, but more importantly, I managed to stay alive. If you kill yourself now, how will we ever get out of here alive? How will we get that house, or the dog and cat? How will we ever do anything?"

He sounded sincere because, when he thought about it, he was telling the goddamn truth. He knew the idea was useless, but deep down the hope still burned vibrantly. The want for a normal, loving life.

His father would never allow that. Claude had no mother, brothers, or sisters. No other family members other than his father, who trained him to receive orders, and in return, deliver them—to break and then reprogram subjects. Not to make them *whole*. Was he a fool? Feeling remorse for one's subject was the ultimate sin, because that's all the subjects were—lab rats.

Benjamin lay his head against Claude's pounding chest, and he wept. "S-so I've to kill my soul...if...if I want to stay alive... But *why*?"

"Because in the end, you'll be cleansed of every human weakness. Of the pain and sadness, of the instability and isolation, and the constant fear of being alone or suppressed by society. Everything that makes you *you* will be stored someplace else, and a better, stronger person will be born. That is what my father's malleability theory is all about. Adaptability. Reprogramming. Rebirth. Can't you accept that?"

"I might not have finished high school, dude"—Benjamin had stopped crying now, but his voice and hands were no less shaky—"but even I know what brainwashing means. Your... that beast... he did this to us. To you, his own son...

I'm not an idiot. The man's a *monster* and you, we *both* deserve better. I'll get us out of here. You wait and see... I'll get us out."

He kissed Benjamin on the forehead and whispered, "You're the only bit of happiness I've ever had."

In my entire life, he nearly added. Benjamin had been Claude's only source of human contact beside his father. And in some selfish, perverse part of his brain, Claude took advantage of that.

I don't want to be alone anymore! Please! Help me!

"I promise to get us both out of here," Benjamin said, curled up against Claude chest.

Claude said nothing, but his contented sigh carried through the air and exhaled against the mirrored wall.

To be free is a lovely, agonising thought...

❦ ❦

Benjamin's situation only worsened later that night. Claude had finally convinced Benjamin to eat some of his meal—the same, colourless rubbish that Claude had been all too familiar with. After they'd played a long game of chess, and Claude won, he had kissed Benjamin on the cheek, his nose, and then lastly his lips, before leaving him alone in the White Room.

He did as he always did afterward—he never left Benjamin right away. He watched him from opposite the mirror and marvelled how the boy had scrutinised every piece of the chessboard, and then each cushion on the floors and walls.

Once or twice, Claude's head nearly smacked against the mirror, and he had to pinch himself awake. He'd only retire to bed once his subject had fallen asleep, once Claude was certain the boy was safe and out of harm's way.

With the amount of pacing Benjamin had been doing that evening, Claude was surprised he finally curled up on his futon and went to sleep. As soon as he did, Claude switched the lab room lights off, retired to the guest bedroom upstairs, and thought of how he could ease Benjamin's suffering more and more with each day.

The only solution to eradicate it permanently was for Benjamin to submit to Claude's father, but that wasn't going to be anytime soon. Benjamin might not have looked like much, but the boy had impressive endurance, and he refused to obey.

Lying in his single bed — a luxury compared to the futon he'd been used to — Claude pondered about taking Benjamin outside the next morning. He'd like that. Perhaps a walk through the forest, breathe in the cold, autumnal air, and then sit by the lake Claude had only ever seen in the photos that hung next to the front door. Its beautiful view overshadowing Aviemore's renowned ski resort and village would surely lift his spirits. The fresh air would hopefully drive some sense into him, too. Into them *both*.

But that day never came. The fresh air, the walk through the forest, picnic on the lake with rustic red leaves covering the surface—none of Claude's attempts to befriend Benjamin ever arose.

After he'd left Benjamin and fallen asleep himself, Claude had woken with a start during the night. As soon as his eyes shot open, he felt himself drowning in an all-too-familiar puddle of sweat; his heartbeat pounding, his eyes wide with fear as his nightmare of the cloaked figures and syringes slowly faded, and he returned to reality.

He straightened up in the bed and forced his legs over the edge. The ceramic tiles of his new bedroom floor were cold against his bare feet. He veered toward the mahogany door, gently stepped over the threshold and into darkness.

A gust of wind permeated the hallway on the other side. Was his father returning earlier than expected from his business trip? Or was a nurse on night duty? Claude couldn't see anything. There was nothing but darkness and silence in the hallway; no sound of anything scuttling in the shadows, or a rodent circling the walls under the scant slithers of moonlight that bled through the windows.

Nothing.

Claude strained his ears, but he could only articulate the sound of his breathing and heartbeat hammering against his ribs. Something had definitely woken him from his sleep, but the evidence so far had been lacking. Perhaps Claude's useless pleading for him to wake up from his nightmare had finally worked.

He crept farther down the hallway, gripped the wooden railing of the staircase and descended them on his tiptoes.

When he reached the bottom and emerged into the open-planned living room, his entire world froze.

Benjamin. Out of his cell. Escaping.

In a series of blurred movements, Benjamin scrambled through the shadows like a deer skating on thin ice, clawing and tumbling his way toward the bolted-up front door. Before Claude could even register what he was doing—how Benjamin had escaped from the White Room—his body pounced after him. He ran across the living room, careful not to scream and wake the servants, but Benjamin's white, gowned body kept missing his grasp by a hair.

Pain stabbed at Claude's ribcage, his breath short and ragged, but he kept going. He had to reach Benjamin before he touched the door. He could see his whole life flashing before him—could see Benjamin's life rushing through his mind as he darted in his steps.

"Benjamin…" Claude managed to whisper. "Stop…! *Please!*"

If either of them were caught escaping, it'd be the end of them both. His father would make sure of that; he didn't believe in second chances. Benjamin halted at the door, his eyes darting around the room in search of the key. He tried the handle three times before violently kicking at its solid, wooden frame. It was locked, as were the windows, which he'd soon figure out. Everything in the cabin had been locked in order to keep them here.

Prisoner, slave, creature, beast. You are nothing more than an animal to me, Claude, do you comprehend?

Yes, Father. I am your creation. I am your subject.

"Dammit!" Benjamin sobbed, punching at the bolts latched on the door. "Motherfuckers!"

Claude approached him cautiously, his heartbeat rocketing in his ears. The room was dark, but faint slithers of moonlight slashed through the wide, living room windows and bathed Benjamin in a silver hue. Claude caressed his shoulder, and Benjamin wept, pressing his forehead against the door.

"Locked," he choked out, his fingers curling against the door. "I was so close... I was going to get us outta here, Claude... Free us."

Claude could hear Benjamin's nails scratching at the wood, his body puddling on the floor in defeat. All Claude could think about was getting Benjamin away from the door and back into the White Room... before his father found them.

He prayed his father wouldn't return early and catch him like this. He prayed he could pretend that everything had gone smoothly in his father's absence no matter how close Benjamin had come to escaping. How Benjamin had managed it was beyond him, but he knew why he'd attempted it.

Freedom.

Benjamin wanted to be a free man again.

Don't I, too?

"They've locked *everything*! I thought....I thought I could've gotten us help... I even took your pass... I'm sorry,

Claude, I'm so sorry! I tried...!"

Violent sobs rose from Benjamin's lungs, and pity invaded Claude's senses. He bent down to take Benjamin into his arms, and then he did something unexpected. He claimed Benjamin's mouth, and his sobs shuddered against Claude's lips, growing weaker by the second.

They were lost for a moment, wrapped up in each other's arms with the darkness and moonlight bleeding all around them. And then alarm kicked back in, and Claude pulled away.

"You could've put yourself in danger," Claude whispered, holding Benjamin at arm's length. At least, he had stopped crying and clawing at the door now. "It's not safe out there, Ben. We're in the middle of nowhere." Anger laced his tone, but likewise, there was a deep sense of hurt that was impossible to hide. "Are you trying to get yourself killed?"

Benjamin's green eyes, wet with tears, bore weakly into Claude's. "But don't you see? They're going to kill us anyway... They're turning us into *slaves*! We've gotta get outta here, man, before it's too late." He lowered his voice, eyes darting quickly toward the ceiling and then back again. "We could really do it, Claude. Everyone's gone for the night or they're asleep... I was going to come back for you, but then you chased me and—"

"Shh, shh, ssh." Claude rocked Benjamin back and forth, tucking his dark hair underneath his chin. "I know you would've come back for me. I know that you're strong and want to find a way out, but please listen to me when I say there *is* none. I've looked for it. I've tried. Submission was the only thing that ever kept me alive here, Ben. I...I let them take me. I let them do all those horrible, monstrous things to my body and mind, and you know what I realised? That it doesn't matter how we survive here, Ben, as long as we just do."

"Oh, but it does matter."

The deep, resonating voice didn't belong to Benjamin.

"F-Father, I was..." Claude didn't even have time to release Benjamin or peel them up from the floor, for the next instant saw his father driving the wind from Claude's lungs, and he went scraping across the living room floorboards.

"Thought you could escape from me, boy!" His father's hands grabbed Benjamin's hair and dragged him backwards with an effortless heave. Benjamin grabbed onto his hands, face contorting in pain, but his father merely tightened his grip until his knuckles blanched white, and he heaved him toward the hallway that led to the lab. "Thought you could make a fool out of me. Then let me show you just how far I can *really* go."

"No!" Benjamin's legs scrambled futilely against his father's grip, but Claude knew it was only angering his father even more. "Get fucking off me!"

"Such a pity," his father sneered, however, Claude could hear that he was panting with rage. "I thought you were progressing splendidly, but instead of yielding to me, you have manipulated my son into assisting you to escape!"

"Father, he did not—"

"*Enough*! I will deal with you *later*."

His father bent down, grabbed Benjamin by the scruff of his neck, and though it was dark, Claude could see the fear crippling his only friend's features. But it was nothing compared to the look of insanity that consumed his father. If not for the familiar, white cloak that was draped over his shoulders, and his nearly equally as white hair and beard, Claude would never have recognised him.

He was supposed to be gone... away on business.

Claude wasn't sure if it was desperation or blatant stupidity that sprung him forward. Before he knew it, he was scrambling after his father and down the hallway that led to the lab room Claude knew all too well. His hands guided him in the darkness, and once they located the White Room door, he twisted the door handle. But his father had locked it from the inside, sealing him and Benjamin from the rest of the world.

Desperation clung to him now, catching around his throat until his lungs heaved and begged for help. Claude clambered into the Dark Room next door, switched on the lights, and saw his father beating Benjamin in the middle of the White Room. It was just as he'd feared. His father had tied Benjamin to an iron hook in the ceiling, and his body swung forward with every stroke of his father's whip.

"Please *stop*!" Benjamin wailed, fruitlessly trying to swing his body away from the whip.

But the more he did so, the harder his father struck his

leather whip. Again and again, it came crashing down and latched around Benjamin's skin like a sheet of tarp around wet stone.

Benjamin shot forward, screaming out against the agony, but the more he begged him to stop, the more Claude's father increased the force. This was the first time Claude had ever seen his father lose control and beat Benjamin... Benjamin who, for the most part, was so sweet and gentle that it was impossible to ever stay mad at him.

Yes, he refused to admit that he wanted to be broken—to be altered and remade—but he was a pleasurable subject to research, from what Claude had been able to articulate. He did not deserve this. He was not a slab of meat to be left hanging dry out in the sun. He was special, and he deserved to be treated like a normal human being.

Crack!

Blood spurted out from Benjamin's lacerations, his limbs now tied together like a cruelly discarded marionette, and yet... his father kept going. Even with the irrevocable symptoms of his father having crossed over the line, his hands kept moving, and the whip kept falling.

Another strike... two... six... twenty-three... *forty*.

"Father, stop this!"

Claude's hands pounded against the glass mirror in a desperate plea for silence, but he knew his father would be unable to hear him from the other side. Still, Claude fought the soundproof barrier, begging his father to see reason again. He'd always taught Claude to never break his composure. Never show emotion. And yet, everything his father was doing defied that very logic. He had claimed that the malleability theory would rid a human of its emotional leeches and that they could become the epitome of self-control.

His father was supposed to be the *prime example* of that study, and yet…

What his father exuded was not standard protocol for punishment. It was not scolding a naughty dog, or slapping a mischievous child on the hand. It was years and years of suppressed anger finally unleashing itself; it was frissons of red-hot fury pulsing through his body and out the ends of a merciless, leather whip; it was his *humanity* pouring out from him at long last, cracking like a viper, sinking its teeth into its bloodied prey.

Claude's arms grew tired of beating pointlessly against the glass and soon his limbs trembled with exertion. By the time his father had stopped flogging, Benjamin's body no longer moved, and Claude knew he had died. He didn't need to watch his father unclip Benjamin from the hooks, drop him to the floor, and check his pulse rate to know that. He'd seen the life fade from Benjamin's eyes, and for a fleeting, sickening moment, Benjamin had looked pleased to die.

The White Room lights switched off, and Claude, breathing heavily against the glass with his eyes clamped shut, didn't turn to face his father.

"*Kneel.*"

It was all his father said, and within a heartbeat, Claude

had collapsed onto the floor, his palms still pressed against the cold, frictionless glass.

"You will kneel in your place rightfully, boy, or I will put you there myself."

Tilting his trembling body around, Claude crawled his way over to his father's side. He didn't even have to look up to see the condition of his father—the droplets of blood trickling down from the seams of his white cloak were enough to garner an image.

His father bent inward and grasped Claude's chin so that he was forced to look up at him. He looked like a madman— bathed from head-to-toe in Benjamin's blood. It was even splashed in his dark eyes, and Claude could see his reflection gazing back at him the longer he stared, and he could still hear Benjamin screaming, his pleading, his apologising.

His father squeezed Claude's cheeks together. "Tonight, you have cost me what was intended to be my greatest alteration yet, and you will pay dearly for it."

"Yes, Father."

"Until I say otherwise, you are to spend the rest of your life repaying me for what I have now lost."

Claude nodded again, his neck stiffening in his father's tightening grasp.

"You are never to escape this fate. You are never to defy me again. Never question or go against my orders. To your last breath, you are my creation—an object in which I control and can annihilate at any second. Am I perfectly well understood?"

"Yes, Father."

He watched his father unhook the belt from his black jeans and snake the leather between his bloodied fingertips. "Now, boy, let us restart your training."

❦ ❦

Present day

Claude's shadow swelled around the lab room. It was peculiar how nothing had changed since Claude became his father's sole researcher. The White Room, the lab room... Even the Dark Room still existed as his father intended it to, though Claude had it locked numerous years ago.

A strange sense of foreboding washed over him. Claude had defied his father by making that announcement. He had gone against his father's orders and publicly expressed that he'd no longer be training his subjects, without first consulting his *creator*. At thirty-nine years old, Claude had grown exhausted of his father's attempts to keep him shackled down, and instead of obeying him, he had overpowered him.

Something that he never contemplated until the day he met Benjamin. That boy had given him hope in a world that never experienced it. Those bright, green eyes, dark hair, and pale, stubborn expression were by no means a coincidence to exist within Tristan.

He had been reincarnated as Benjamin, it was as simple as

that. He offered Claude the one thing so little had ever done: he offered him redemption. And this time, Claude would not destroy it.

Chapter 16

TRISTAN HAD BEEN in the log cabin for four months. Four solid months he'd been fighting Claude Galen; acting as his submissive, and even befriending his henchmen, all in the hopes to see another day. Or make it back to his loved ones. The agonising longing to see Jake and Connie slammed into him every night, and he wept—he wept so hard that he thought he'd dried himself out. But each night the weeping continued, and Tristan vowed to escape from this hell and return to them.

He'd once dared to venture around the cabin and look for a hidden way out. He found touching the windows to be a huge mistake, though. Not only were the doors and windows locked, but Oliver checked them every night to ensure they were secure.

He'd never get out of this prison.

Tristan eyed Claude's tablet on the king-sized bed and strode over toward it. Claude was still in the lab, but maybe Tristan could get the tablet open and message someone for help—there were no phones after all.

He picked up the tablet and turned it on, and his heart sank to his stomach when he saw the password protect screen. Tristan could be punching in numbers for days and still not get the correct combination! And he doubted Claude wrote it down somewhere—probably a code he had memorised.

"Don't bother," Dmitry said from the doorway. "Boss makes damn sure everything he owns is protected."

"I just wanted to play some games," Tristan grumbled, tossing the tablet back on the bed. "I'm bored as fuck around here."

Well, it wasn't a lie. Tristan *was* bored.

The only plus side to his situation, so far, was that he was allowed to venture around the cabin freely again… as long as he didn't try to go outside or get too close to the front door.

Fresh air? Wind against his skin? Grass and snow under his boots?

Not necessary now, apparently.

If he ever tried to escape, Claude would be there to remind him that if he so much as touched the doorknob, he was going back into the cage.

Tristan shuddered at the thought. He'd do *anything* to avoid going back in there with those horrible, relentless vibrators torturing him and the butt plug thrust up his ass. Not to mention the cold wrought iron constantly pressed against his tender skin.

Tristan would obey Claude even more to have the chance to go outside again. To actually feel the wind rush through his hair, sunlight on his face, and leaves crunching around him…

"Come on," Dmitry said. "We can hang out in the living room."

Tristan followed him, going down the stairs to the large

living space. They walked over toward the couch and Dmitry sat down, picking up a newspaper.

Tristan stood there awkwardly, then stuck his hand inside his jeans pocket. He pulled out an empty gum wrapper and walked over to the rubbish bin between the living room and kitchen, eyes glancing every so often at the front door.

He threw the wrapper away and slowly walked back to the living room, body gravitating toward the front door.

"Away from the door," Dmitry called out when Tristan neared it again. He flipped a page in the newspaper he was reading and took a sip of his tea before going back to reading; his light brown eyes never moved from the paper, and his legs folded on the fabric sofa. "Last thing I want is for Boss to chop my balls off because you decided to make a run for it."

"I'm not going to run away," Tristan protested. "I was just throwing away some trash."

"You don't need to be that close to the door to throw away a wrapper." Dmitry narrowed his eyes in a way that said *I got my eye on you, boy* as he went back to his paper. "If you can't behave yourself, I'm sending you back to your room."

"You mean *Claude's* room." Tristan crossed his arms and huffed out a sigh.

It was stupid that, of all things, he missed having his own room. He missed not being fondled in the middle of the night or commanded to please Claude and spread his legs so he could please *him* in return.

But he kept reminding himself that anything was better than the cage.

"Can't I just take a short walk through the woods? My legs are killing me." Not to mention that his brain felt starved of oxygen. "Claude doesn't have to know."

"I'm the one babysitting you," Dmitry said, and a loose strand of light brown, slicked-back hair fell into his almond-shaped eyes. "If anything happens to you, it's on my ass. You're attracted to that damn door like a fly to shit."

"I just want to go outside for five minutes." Tristan hated how whiny his voice sounded, but he knew Dmitry well enough now that it wasn't too humiliating. And he might actually persuade the guy to let him go out for a walk. "You can walk with me so you know I won't escape. Please? We don't have to tell Claude—I'm going crazy in here!"

"Sorry, kiddo, but this is one rule I can't break."

Tristan stomped over to the sofa and collapsed down next to him. "This is fucking bullshit," he grumbled, crossing over his arms. "When will I get my own room back?"

"I doubt you ever will. Boss seems pretty taken to you, and I doubt he wants you out of his sight. Just be glad you have the freedom to walk around on two legs again."

Tristan wanted to snap at that, but warmth swelled in his chest at the thought of Claude seeing Tristan as someone or something special again. *It just means that I can escape. Doesn't mean I'm changing. And if I* am *special, then I can use it against this sadistic motherfucker to run away!*

Because the idea that he might be falling for the man—no, *monster*—who had done this to him was simply unacceptable.

There was no fucking way he'd fall for a crazy bastard like Claude Galen. No matter how much his body craved him during the night.

Claude couldn't have asked for a better morning. The snow had let up, and his boy might not have been the most obedient subject, but seeing his smile at last had made Claude forgive him with only a mild scolding; meanwhile, he'd hide his own smile behind the pages of his book.

Over the last two weeks, the snow storm had begun to fade, and with it, Tristan's insolence melted away. The boy was beginning to settle in the cabin, but more importantly, around Claude. No more attempts to escape. No more foul-mouthed protests. There had been moments when Claude suspected the boy was taking Claude for a fool, but there absolutely was no way he could conceal his lust. It burned on his face every night, and deep down, Claude knew it was because of him.

Tristan *wanted* Claude.

Just as much as he needed Tristan.

Those moments at twilight, when Claude would hold Tristan in his arms, and the boy would lay his head against his heartbeat, proved exactly that. Slowly but surely, the boy had learned to obey.

"Can we go outside?" Tristan asked, plopping down onto the sofa next to Claude.

He'd clearly spoken too soon. "You know my answer, Tristan. You've yet to be trusted."

He didn't glance up from his book, but he could see the boy sulking in his peripheral vision.

"But I promise to not do anything wrong. I just want some fresh air, is all?"

"It is not your behaviour that worries me," Claude gritted.

No, it certainly was not—it was *his*. Tristan had been glued to his side for the most part of a fortnight, since he'd returned from his father's birthday in London, and it wasn't that he was overly complaining about Tristan's displays of affection. He wanted Tristan to desire his master's attention—almost as much as he desired his touch every single night. It was the only time he ever felt alive.

Felt hope.

But he'd been waiting on Tristan, testing which boundary of Claude's he could begin to push. Two weeks of uninterrupted bliss was unrealistic even to the most foolish of beings. "The snow is nearly six foot deep outside, Tristan," Claude explained to him softly. "You are not going outside."

Not to mention the last time Tristan had ventured outside he'd gotten snared by the hunting trap and shot at by Oliver and Dmitry.

"I'll stay by your side," Tristan protested, lightly grabbing hold of Claude's thigh and caressing it. "I won't wander off— I swear! You can come with me."

"No, Tristan," Claude said, voice stern and eyes narrowing. He folded his book over and turned to Tristan.

"It's not safe. End of discussion."

He saw the hope drain from Tristan's eyes, who averted his gaze the moment Claude put an end to his useless pleading. Overhead, in the kitchen, Oliver whisked chocolate cake mix into a ceramic bowl. Claude scrutinised the Irishman bending around the refrigerator, peering at them on the sofa with a smidgen of batter on his left cheek.

Against Claude's better wishes, Oliver was preparing a cake for his retirement, which had been in full swing for two weeks now.

"Four months in here would drive anybody crazy, Boss. Just sayin'."

He disappeared again, and Claude blew an irritated sigh. He tossed his book aside. "Get your coat and scarf."

The light came back to Tristan eyes, and a wide smile blossomed on his face. "Really?"

Claude's heart clenched. He looked like Benjamin when they talked about getting a house and cat together.

Together…

"Hurry up before I change my mind. Oliver, you and Dmitry will come with us." He glanced at Tristan, whose face had lit up like sunbeams. "Wouldn't want any accidents like last time," he said, but there was an edge of foreboding in his voice.

A warning.

If Tristan tried to run, he'd only be throwing himself into the White Room again. But if he didn't try to escape, and he passed Claude's test by obeying him, then things could truly become different.

While Claude no longer worked to break Tristan, he prayed for the latter. To gain Tristan's trust would be to slowly start their lives together.

Let this be the final test of all, Tristan… Can you be trusted?

They walked out into the garden where the snow had piled on thick. Claude had already wanted to go back inside, but Tristan was rolling around in the snow along with Oliver's dog, Fionn, who seemed to enjoy the fresh, brittle air as much as the humans. Astonishingly, Claude couldn't bring himself to destroy the boy's one moment of happiness. After such amicable behaviour lately, Tristan deserved a reward. And as much as Claude hated to admit it, Oliver was right—four months, while not intentional, was a long time for someone to be caged inside.

Unless he wanted to drive Tristan crazy, as this had happened once before with a previous subject; he had no choice but to let him outside.

Tristan galloped through the snow with Fionn, interlacing Claude and Dmitry, and then chasing the dog again. It was strange to see Oliver interacting with Tristan—strange because he'd never really communicated with the subjects unless Claude permitted him to.

But Tristan's not a subject!

Things were different now. Claude was giving everything away for this one. Tristan was not a subject. Claude had proved that the theory was ineffective anyway. Now he just had to fly away.

Claude traipsed through the knee-high snow, lost in one of his contemplations, when suddenly something wet slid down the back of his head. Lumps of snow peppered his shoulders, soaking his grey duffle coat and thick, woollen scarf. He turned around in time to see Tristan laughing—such a beautiful sound—while pointing at the dopey-looking dog.

"It wasn't me, it was Fionn!" He fell backwards into the snow, encouraging Fionn to jump all over him. Claude let it slide and continued to walk—not before catching the hint of a smirk crossing Dmitry's features.

"There's no traps 'round here, Boss. I checked meself," Oliver stated, walking next to Claude.

"There should better not be after last time," Claude growled, and the Irishman lowered his head; if he'd scouted out the area in fear of Tristan's safety or Claude's vengeance, it was unclear. Claude sighed, his breath swimming away from them. "But well done, Oliver. We must keep him safe."

Oliver nodded firmly, his sapphire eyes glistening with happiness. "Yes, Boss."

After a moment, he fell back into step with Tristan and his dog, and Claude walked down the snow-ploughed forest lane, leading toward the loch. He owned every acre of this secluded land, and while Aviemore had been popular in his youth as a skiing resort, the village was truly breathtaking to behold.

When his father had let Claude out of the lab room for the

first time, he'd thought he had just strolled into a nineteenth century novel; the moors, the buildings, the sidewalks, prairies, and animals were all so breathtaking and real. It'd been a shock to his system when he visited London soon after, following his father across the world to promote his research. Claude had spent nineteen years in that forsaken lab room, knowing nothing of what luxuries awaited him in the outside world.

Aviemore would forever have a place in Claude's heart. There was just something...familiar about it, and he guessed it reminded him of Benjamin; the only true happiness he'd ever had.

Until now.

Tristan stopped laughing behind them, which caused Claude to freeze in his tracks. Panic squeezed his heart, but then he saw a wide grin spread over Tristan's face.

"What the fuck is *that*?" he demanded, his eyes widening into two large, emerald saucers.

Claude looked ahead and saw a monstrous Highland cow in the far distance. He grinned at him. "You've never seen one before?"

"No... But I am going to pet it."

Claude grabbed Tristan's shoulder when he tried to trudge by him and pulled him back. "You're not petting anything, boy. It could hurt you."

Fionn chased after the cow, though he wouldn't be able to reach it, and Oliver and Dmitry stood dumbfounded next to them. As pleasurable as the moment was, seeing Tristan alive again, if Claude wasn't careful then it would cause all sorts of chaos. He could be lenient, but he couldn't be foolish to give Tristan a too-long leash. That was a route he had no desire in taking.

Tristan gazed at Claude with a lopsided grin. "I pet you all the time, and I managed to survive."

This time, Claude did not find the boy amusing. He narrowed his eyes, reminding himself not to punish the boy for talking out of turn.

This is his reward for being good.

Oliver spoke up, slinging a gun into his back pocket and then flinging his auburn scarf over his broad shoulders. "We better hurry, Boss, or else hell will start to freeze over."

Tristan picked up a wad of snow, throwing it at Oliver. "Like that?"

Oliver patted the chunks of snow from his beard, walked over to Tristan, and put it down the back of his shirt, making him yelp out. "No, like *that,* you feckin' eejit!"

Tristan danced around him, knocking the snow from under his shirt, and then shivered. "Fine, I get the point. I give in! I surrender—leave me alone already!"

Claude gulped, and beads of perspiration painted his upper lip. The further the four of them walked through the trees blanketed in snow, bypassing the numerous highland cattle perched on the snow-capped hills, the more Claude felt eager to step back and claim Tristan in front of his men.

Mine!

An unusual sense of jealousy carried his thoughts, and

when he caught Tristan talking with Oliver and Dmitry, it grew more violent and desperate to be freed. The dog received more affection from Tristan than he did. And he knew deep down, it was because none of them had ever hurt Tristan the way he did.

He wanted to have a future with Tristan, but he knew his chances of obtaining that were slim. He wanted to prove himself—prove to Benjamin—that he was worthy of human sentiments and normalcy, but… he glanced at Tristan… he just wasn't sure he was capable of it. He'd hurt Tristan in so many ways, and nearly shattered his soul to pieces. He wasn't certain a future together was possible when you faced the facts.

The boy did not love Claude.

He was simply afraid of him.

Claude had seen it before. He was afraid of angering Claude, of stepping over the line and being punished, thus he had resorted to feigned submission. He'd already tried escaping, bargaining, everything all of his subjects usually did, and had realised they were all futile. But with Claude being so uncharacteristically lenient with him, what else had the boy to lose other than his dignity?

Claude was a master of minds and breaking people apart. But when such a boy had rooted himself so deeply within his soul, was it possible to still be the master of his heart?

"That's us here, Boss," Dmitry said, lighting a cigarette. "The loch hasn't changed a bit."

Claude lit one, too, and watched Tristan come barrelling

through the trees with Fionn, stopping opposite them to gaze at the beautiful, nearly frozen loch. He had always wanted to share this place with Tristan.

"Here you go, Boss. It's still roastin' hot." Oliver extended a flask of tea, and the smell of peppermint fumes filled the nippy air. "Figured it'd help warm you up."

He was about to take a drink, but then he noticed how cold Tristan must've been from playing in all that snow with the dog. His face was completely flushed, and his ears and nose were an even darker shade of red.

Claude sighed and walked over to where Tristan stood and handed him the flask.

"Drink this before you catch a cold," he said, forcing the flask into Tristan's crimson-tipped hands.

Tristan looked at him with hesitant eyes for a moment, then opened the lid. There was a new look that crossed his face, almost like he was *touched* by the gesture. "Thanks," he mumbled, taking a small sip. "Sir."

Claude didn't even register that he was taking his scarf off and putting it around Tristan's shoulders. "We should have dressed you warmer. I wasn't expecting you to be rolling around in the snow with a dog."

Tristan's flush deepened, but this time it wasn't from the cold. "Sorry, Sir. I guess I got a little carried away."

Claude gently tousled his hair. "Drink up," he said. "There's a bench over there, by the water. Come sit with me when you are finished."

Tristan closed his eyes and pretended he was on the edge of a cliff.

It wasn't the kind of dream where you stood on the precipice, and your body jolted awake as a reaction from the fall. Tristan was seeing over the cliff, across the sea, and to the birds that flew over troubled water. He watched their wings expand out in formation, flying against the wind.

For a brief, satisfying moment, he saw himself flying with them and revelled in the depth of freedom that consumed him. When his eyes shot open, a wet nose brushed the side of his leg, and he looked down to see Fionn on his hind legs, staring up at him. His mismatched eyes gazed at Tristan hopefully, and he realised at that second, he was more like Fionn than any of the birds.

He'd never be able to fly away from here.

Come sit with me when you are finished.

Tristan moved toward the bench and sat down next to the professor, whose eyes were rooted on him. He would've preferred staying back with Dmitry and Oliver, where it was safe, but he had a sinking feeling that if he didn't follow Claude's order, there would be some sort of punishment later.

Even Fionn wouldn't come near Claude, and instead, he trotted back toward Oliver, who was skimming rocks across the semi-frozen water. At least the lake was beautiful, and he was outside again. A family of swans skirted the farthest surface, and Tristan wanted nothing more than to be there with them—far away and out of reach.

The sun glittering off the lake beamed against the flask gripped in Tristan's hand. He handed it back to Claude. "Thank you, Sir," he said, his voice low. "I... I've missed this kind of thing, you know."

Missed was an understatement.

Hot drinks, video games, working on *GamerOn*, and spending hours on his laptop with Jake were only some of the things that had kept Tristan going in life. Now more than ever, he craved the things that he'd always taken for granted. His bottom lip trembled just thinking about Jake, Connie, and his *GamerOn* subscribers. Would he ever get back to them? He'd give anything to be sitting in a café somewhere, sipping a hot cocoa and scrolling through his *GamerOn* while Connie complained about the length of Jake's hair. He hadn't posted to his channel in... God, he didn't even know. Had it been about four months, or four years?

Is the channel even active anymore? Is Jake still uploading vlogs and reviewing the new releases?

He wished he could be normal again, even if it was just for one day.

But he might as well have been asking to walk on the moon.

Claude chuckled beside him. "I thought you preferred hot chocolate if I am not mistaken."

He wrapped an arm around Tristan's shoulders and watched his breath exhale as though his lungs were filled with smoke. Tristan's neck stiffened, and he could feel his shoulders tensing in Claude's hold. Then, taking a sharp breath, he allowed his body to relax and be brought forward; the body heat was useful anyway.

But Claude's comment surprised him. He remembered Tristan's favourite drink?

"Oh… Yeah," he murmured, losing himself in Claude's rich scent that was thick around him. Honey and peppermint, stale cigarette smoke and vanilla-scented aftershave. The smell was hypnotic, subconsciously making Tristan hungry for it. "Hot cocoa *is* my favourite. But Jake's mom used to make me drink tea with her on Sundays. She used to get me to hang her laundry in the yard, then sit with her and drink fruit tea while she read some stupid weekly, OAP magazine. Sort of like a religion to her."

Fuck. Tears were in his eyes now, and his voice cracked against his will. He tried not to think about them, but it was impossible. Jake and Connie kept him fighting and fumbling his way through the darkness. They were all Tristan had to hold on to.

A warm hand rubbed Tristan's lower back. "I can make you happy, Tristan. Tell me one thing you would like."

Tristan was going to open his mouth and answer freedom, but that would only irritate Claude.

"I miss playing video games," he said instead, cuddling closer to Claude for the sake of warmth. That, and he told himself that Claude wanted him to.

"I'll have Dmitry find some for you," Claude replied

casually. "He knows more about that stuff anyway. You deserve it for being a good boy."

A strange sensation washed over Tristan. It was warm and fuzzy, but he was not certain if it was Claude's body heat. "Thank you, Sir... I'd like that."

His eyes strayed to the swans again. They were so close to the edge of the lake that Oliver was trying to coax them to come onto land. But Fionn, running backward and forth, kept on scaring them away with his barking. Dmitry surveyed the area next to them, smoking a cigarette as per usual. With the snow surrounding them, and the breathtaking view of utter seclusion and tranquillity, Tristan couldn't help but feel a slight glimmer of happiness rouse inside of him.

Even with Claude touching him—those hands that had inflicted so much pain and suffering, he felt bizarrely at peace.

What's happening to me?

Chapter 17

THE SMELL OF vanilla aftershave and peppermint tea had vanished. Now, the sharp tang of mango was on Tristan's tongue. The steam from the monstrous bathtub was hot against Tristan's flushed cheeks, and he swished a hand through the water to check the temperature.

"Nice and warm," he said to himself, pushing himself up from the edge of the tub.

He'd used nearly half a bottle of citrus bubble bath, and so a lot of it had brimmed over the side and onto the floor. No matter. He figured Claude would still appreciate the gesture, and hopefully, if Tristan's bath pleased him once he woke up, he'd be allowed outside again.

Yesterday, while walking to the lake, he'd spotted signs leading to a ski resort only three miles away. Three miles away, and Tristan's freedom could potentially be within his reach! As if he'd let an opportunity to scout out his imprisonment slip by. He wasn't stupid. Last time, he'd learned the hard way where *not* to run to—into the woods—and instead, he'd focus next time on reaching the resort before he eventually died in this fucking hell hole.

His body shuddered at the thought of escaping, but a small part of him sank. Although Tristan tried to block out the notion, he knew it was because he didn't want to leave.

He'd become mates with Dmitry and Oliver, who always let him work out whenever Claude wasn't around, and they gave him whatever food he asked for. Even Claude... Tristan's body shivered again, quenching the thought of Claude being anything but a monster.

However, Tristan had realised that by staying on Claude's good side, he avoided pain. He wanted to avoid that son of a bitch like the plague. So, he kept on being a good boy. He kept obeying. He kept *pretending* so that Claude would let his guard down, and every day Tristan would grow closer to his freedom. It was only a matter of time before Claude cracked.

Claude emerged into his en-suite bathroom, wearing a black pair of pyjamas and slippers. Tristan remained partly crouched over the bath, his eyes cast downward.

"I, uhh, thought you'd like a bath, Sir."

He heard his footsteps coming closer toward the tub, and Tristan flinched when they stopped in front of him. A splash of water. "It smells nice. Where did you get these from?"

Claude held one of the pig bath toys in his hand and inspected it.

"I asked Dmitry to pick them up," Tristan answered. "I asked for ducks, but he went with the piggies instead."

To his surprise, a throaty chuckle rose from Claude's chest. "You never cease to surprise me, Tristan."

Tristan's entire body relaxed, and a small smile crept onto his face. "Should I leave you in peace, Sir? I can help Oliver make breakfast."

"No." Claude's eyes darkened. "I want you to join me."

What? Tristan swallowed the lump in his throat, nodded, and then stood up.

"Y—yes, Sir."

He shouldn't feel shy about bathing together, but something about it seemed *too* intimate. At least with the sex, Tristan could believe it was just a primal need Claude had to get out of his system, but with a bath... well, wasn't that something *couples* did?

Surely Claude didn't think he and his hostage could be a couple? Tristan certainly didn't, although his dick seemed to think so, jolting at the thought of sharing something so intimate. He'd never bathed with someone before.

You're really asking that, you dumbass? He kidnapped you and tortured you! He's just trying to manipulate you again.

"You're already hard," Claude noted with his eyes pressed on Tristan's crotch. Clothes were forbidden whenever he was alone with Claude.

Damn it, Tristan!

Of course his dick would betray him when he was at his most vulnerable. Tristan's face heated but he kept his head down low, refusing to meet those penetrating eyes. If only he was allowed to wear clothes when they were together, then maybe he would've hidden his erection.

"Get into the tub," Claude ordered, his voice now deep and predatory-like. "You know the drill, boy: keep your eyes forward."

Tristan's dick jerked when he carefully lowered himself into the warm water, gluing his eyes onto the shelves again.

At least the bubbles hid his embarrassing erection, and he could try to relax as the citrus smells surrounded him.

While Claude stripped out of his pyjamas, Tristan did everything to not glance at his tantalising body. Once he dropped in the bath behind him, he pulled Tristan closer, and his muscles pressed against the small of Tristan's back.

Motherfucker!

He tried not to acknowledge the two legs draped at either side of him, and he *especially* tried not to think about Claude's hard on sliding against his ass cheeks. But dammit, everything about Claude Galen consumed him.

He almost jumped out of his skin when Claude's arms splashed through the water and picked up one of the sponges floating in the bubbles. He rinsed out the water, and then ran the sponge up and down Tristan's arms.

"You're…" Tristan stopped, and bit his lip. *Hard*. He hadn't meant to speak, but he wanted to know why Claude was bathing him and not himself. Wasn't Tristan just his prisoner?

"Tell me what you are thinking," Claude murmured against his ear. "I want you to."

Tristan closed his eyes, a chill sweeping through his overheated body. "You're…you're supposed to be washing yourself, Sir, and not me."

Claude squeezed more water from the sponge, and let it trickle down Tristan's spine. "I can do whatever I want, and right now, what I want is to make you happy." He leant in closer to Tristan's ear, the hot breath tickling it. "To take care of you forever."

Tristan let out a sharp breath. He hadn't noticed that he'd been holding it. "Forever?" he breathed.

"Yes. Now, tilt your head back for me, and close your eyes."

He tilted his head back, the warm water dragging him closer to Claude's chest, and the sponge soaked through his hair. Claude's hand running through it caused a groan to escape Tristan's lips.

It feels so good…

More than he wanted it to.

"You're mine now, Tristan," Claude whispered, then a warm kiss touched his neck, followed by a nibble that made Tristan gasp. "And I'll kill anyone who tries to take you from me."

"Why?" Tristan breathed out. "Why do I mean *anything* to you?"

He'd always wanted to ask that. What had constituted for Tristan to be ripped away from his life and thrown into a world he'd scarcely known existed? A world of darkness and pain and misery? What did Tristan ever do to deserve such a life?

Claude paused, and Tristan could feel his heartbeat pounding against his back. "Because you're special to me, Tristan, and all I want to do now is make you happy."

Then why did you do all those things to me?
Why did you kidnap and rape me?
Torture me like I meant nothing to you?

Just a bag of meat for you to devour...

Tristan held his tongue and let Claude wash his hair with the coconut shampoo. When he dipped his head back again, Claude washed the soap from his scalp and gently massaged his head. He dotted a soft kiss on his temple as an afterthought.

Tristan hadn't meant to, but his body moved on its own, and he reached up and kissed Claude in return. He pulled back with a flinch, though, and waited for the punishment to commence. He'd been told to keep his eyes forward. He couldn't make any sense of why he'd kissed him. It had felt right. As if Claude *wanted* him to do it.

"You're not like any of the others," Claude continued, sending chills down Tristan's body. "You give me hope, Tristan, and it terrifies me. I've never had hope in my life before." He traced a warm hand down Tristan's forearm, caressing his tattoos. His fingers paused on the raven skull. "Sometimes, I don't know what to do with it. With myself. And I do things I'd never thought myself capable of."

Tristan knew he should've kept quiet after that, but it was an opportunity that tore his logic asunder. "We don't have to live like this," he said, voice catching in his throat. "We can... we can move to the States together. Live like a *real* couple, you know, and maybe rent an apartment somewhere in the city. Staying here doesn't have to be everything as long as we're together." He gulped hard and almost choked on the reluctance catching in his throat. *Say it.* "We could have the world, Sir, if you'd only trust me. Just the two of us...

Forever."

Tristan froze, and a sea of piglets sailed by him. Claude's fingertips had ceased tickling Tristan's arms, and his heartbeat throbbed like a drum. Tristan closed his eyes, shoulders bulking up instinctively. But the reprimand never came.

"In an ideal world… yes," Claude replied, and then he started scrubbing Tristan's chest; every feather-like touch light against his skin, every word soft in his ear. "What is it you miss the most about home?"

Tristan almost blurted out his friends and family, but he somehow knew that was the wrong answer. Even he was smart enough to know that only Claude could now be in his life. So, instead, he said, "I miss gaming, and I miss going to the mall. Working on the channel with Jake—he was really big on that. You know, just chilling out with my best friend and his mom. Simple things, you know?" Unless Claude could put an entire mall in his house, Tristan knew he couldn't provide any of those things.

"Perhaps one day, I can take you to the mall."

"I'd like that, Sir. I'd like to go outside again."

The mall would be crowded, and if Tristan ran off, Claude couldn't catch him unless he wanted the cops on his ass. That one day wasn't soon enough. He couldn't spend another six months here. He just *couldn't*.

"I know," Claude breathed, and he dropped the sponge into the water. His hands gently grasped Tristan's biceps and pulled him backwards so he was on his lap. Tristan yelped at

Claude's erection poking at him, sliding between his ass cheeks and prodding his hole; it was always so sensitive. Claude had taken the butt plug away some days ago—another reward, apparently. "But you understand how it is difficult for me to do that. I do not want to lose you, Tristan. Your life's far too precious."

"I'm not going to run away," he replied, sounding more defiant than he wanted to. "I promise. I just want to take Fionn out on a walk, and he knows where all the animal traps are." Another good reason to have Fionn there when Tristan escaped. He couldn't risk a repeat of last time. He'd learned that the hard way.

Claude sighed, and Tristan waited for an answer. "Perhaps today, after breakfast. As you know, I've retired from being a researcher, which means the majority of my time will be spent here with you." He snaked a finger down Tristan's neck, circling it underneath his ear. "I'd like us to start again."

As if I'd forget, you sick fuck!

But Tristan nodded, knowing better than to mess up a chance of freedom. "I'd like that, Sir." In some perverse part of his brain, he... sort of meant it. "I love you."

He felt Claude's body tense, and then loosen against his back. His finger slid down Tristan's spine and into his hole with a sharp prod. "In time, you will, and it will be all you can think about."

Tristan clenched around Claude's finger and grabbed onto the edge of the bath for support.

The most terrifying thing of all, for the first time, Tristan actually wanted it.

He wanted Claude Galen.

As he made his way to the bedroom door, Tristan spared the bathroom a glance. Claude was still in there, straightening his tie and then combing his hair to the side, his elbows pointed toward the mirror.

"There's a gift for you downstairs," Claude said to him, not bothering to look away from his reflection. "It should keep you occupied at the very least… I hope you enjoy it."

Tristan nodded. Now fully dressed in a baggy rock T-shirt, jeans, and brand-new sneakers, he made his way toward the stairs.

Judging by Claude's ash-grey business suit, he hoped he was going away for a few days. Whenever he did, Oliver let Tristan use the gym as much as he wanted, and sometimes they walked Fionn together—against Dmitry's wishes. He'd been out a few days ago, but he was itching to get outside again.

Tristan ran a hand through his semi-wet hair. It smelled like coconut and mangoes. He could still feel Claude's lips on his skin, on his back, his arms, and his ears. Shit. He had to get downstairs quickly, or else he'd do something stupid again.

Like kiss Claude fucking Galen.

"Oliver has your gift," he heard Claude say, though Tristan was already at the staircase. "I'll be down shortly."

Tristan didn't bother with a "yes, Sir," he was too busy running down the stairs like a child on Christmas morning, barrelling toward the mountain of presents. When he arrived downstairs, he saw Oliver hooking up a game console, and Tristan's eyes lit up.

"You got me a game?" Tristan said, hopping down the stairs, skipping the last two steps. "Are you going to play with me?"

"I have to cook breakfast," Oliver said, a little resentment in his tone. "And it's the boss who bought it for ya, not me. I'm just hookin' it up since he doesn't know a thing about consoles. The last time we let him hook something up himself, the toaster caught on fire."

Dmitry sniggered in the background, sliding through the back door. "Yeah, he ain't kidding. So, whose ass am I beating on *Solar Predator*?"

Tristan raced toward the sofa, sprawled over the fabric and sank into the cushions. He didn't know how long he was allowed to play video games for, so he didn't want to waste a minute of it.

Dmitry tossed Tristan a controller and sat down next to him. "All the games are in the cupboard underneath the TV. Exclusive limited editions, so you better show the boss some appreciation."

"Of course I will. Will I start first?"

Dmitry grunted, and Tristan hit play. He crossed his legs on the sofa. His hands were trembling with excitement — he could literally feel the adrenalin settling in his gut and giving him butterflies. He'd waited so long for this... so long, and finally, he was now doing something he genuinely loved and missed.

The question was *why* Claude had done this for him. Did he truly want to make Tristan happy, or was it just another mind game? Another test? He was too excited to dwell on it. Too happy in that moment to care.

"Did you already set it up?" Claude asked, descending the stairs with his laptop folded under his arm. He passed by Oliver who was busy cooking eggs in a frying pan.

"Yes, Boss," Dmitry said over his shoulder.

Claude narrowed his eyes, and Tristan could tell by the look on Claude's face that he was trying his best to keep his composure. Trying, but somewhat failing. No matter what Claude did, he still delivered that same intimidating aura, merely intensified by how regal he looked in that perfectly tailored suit of his, and the Rolex flashing on his left wrist.

Tristan gulped, and offered Claude a smile. "Thanks, Claude."

It was the first time in months where he hadn't addressed him as Sir, and he regretted it. He was about to correct himself when Claude gave him a sharp nod as he entered the kitchen.

Dmitry burst out laughing, and Tristan wondered if the man had a death wish.

"You'll get used to Dmitry," Oliver replied, appearing in the living room to collect his apron from the coffee table. "He's the boss's cousin. Sooner or later, though, he's gonna get his nuts ripped off."

"Nah," Dmitry replied, still grinning. "I'm too adorable to have that happen. Plus, me and the boss go way back, even before..." Dmitry trailed off, and Oliver shot him a glare as he swept by the sofa and back to the kitchen.

"Before what?" Tristan asked, but Dmitry shrugged his shoulder.

"Forget about it. I should warn you that I've completed this game twice already."

"But it's only just been released! The first volume, Solar Prey, sold out on the first day. How did you get this?"

"Boss has contacts all over the world, kid. He can easily dip his hands into the right pockets depending on who's asking."

Contacts all over the world? Yeah, he'd said that to Tristan once before, when he'd lied to him and said he could work shadow someone who studied lizards. Total bullshit, now that he thought about it. Just like everything else has been.

He resumed the game before he put himself into a bad mood, and then grumbled, "I wish one of those contacts would put a bullet through his head."

He immediately froze, hoping to God that Dmitry didn't hear that.

Or worse, *Claude*.

What the fuck was he thinking? It just sort of... slipped out, like that kiss in the bathtub; like the time he called Claude Master or stopped resisting his advances in the middle of the night.

A horrible, gut-wrenching feeling settled in Tristan's stomach. That, and something much worse roused between his legs.

Tristan squirmed.

❤️ ❤️

Claude planned to work in the kitchen that afternoon. Not only did he receive a better Wi-Fi signal downstairs when Skyping his research associates in various countries, but he wanted to watch over Tristan as he played one of his favourite past times.

And the boy was ecstatic. So much so that, give or take a few minutes, Claude expected Tristan to burst into tears with excitement. It was remarkable, if not slightly terrifying, how much the boy's presence altered his mood. A simple smile from Tristan's lips, and his entire world lit up. He no longer sought to see him suffering or in pain like his father had trained him to seek. Claude was beginning to think that after all these years *he* was the one being altered.

The researcher who altered people for a living was finally changing.

And it was all thanks to Benjamin—the boy who had convinced Claude that the light was still worth seeking in a world full of darkness. True that his hope had lain dormant for thirty-nine years, but thanks to Tristan, it had woken. This time, it would not be silenced.

A knock on the front door shocked Claude from his

reverie. His eyebrows scrunched together, and his muscles writhed underneath his jaw.

He was not expecting any visitors that day.

Going by the look flitting over Oliver's bewildered face nor were they waiting on any last minute deliveries.

Claude closed his laptop and watched Oliver reach for the door handle.

"Sir...?" Oliver said, confusion lacing his voice as he stepped away from the entrance to reveal Claude's father. "We were not expecting you today, Sir Tomus."

"Indeed. But I see Claude has still kept you around," Tomus said with a dismissive once-over. "Such a pity. I would've thought he'd killed you and that damn mutt of yours years ago."

Claude sighed under his breath.

Ever trying to get a reaction out of people, Father.

From where Claude was sitting, he could see Tristan rising up from the sofa; his knuckles blanched around the controller. Dmitry had the sense to drag him back down before he was seen, much to Claude's relief. The longer Tristan stayed out of his father's sight, the better for them all.

Claude stood up from the kitchen table and extended a hand to his father—who shook it briefly. In the back of his mind, he'd hoped Dmitry was meanwhile sliding Tristan out of the room.

Taking a sharp breath, Claude straightened his suit jacket and offered his father a seat at the kitchen table.

"Oliver, prepare some refreshments," Claude ordered,

then looking at his father, he asked, "Sir, would you like a drink? Whisky? White wine?" But his father wasn't looking at Claude.

His eyes were fixed on Tristan.

Claude had seen that look many times before.

His father had spotted his prey.

He was making a point of staring the boy out, who thankfully looked away after a few seconds. Dmitry pulled him up from the sofa and shoved him through the back door without a further sound, and momentarily relief flushed through Claude.

They'd all learned to acknowledge how dangerous his father's scrutiny could be.

"What's brought you here, father?" Claude probed subtly.

"I was in the country and thought I'd stop by for a visit. After all, Aviemore is only an hour's drive from the capital. My assistant is waiting in the car. You, boy, will take her some refreshments, too. No peanuts; the woman is allergic."

Tomus snapped his fingers at Oliver, who merely inclined his head and made short work of the refrigerator's ingredients. Tomus said nothing until Oliver disappeared with a tray of organic food, and then he turned his attention to Claude, his snake-like eyes locked on him.

"You've found yourself a pretty boy, Claude," he noted casually. "So beautiful, in fact, that I bet Paisley would be thrilled to have him over some measly twins."

"He's not for sale," Claude ground out.

Tomus only smirked. "Such striking green eyes. I can't

say I'm surprised you found a replacement for Benjamin. Tell me, Claude, has this one offered to love you, too? Promised you a happy life if you let him go?" When he said nothing, Tomus chuckled. "I thought as much. No wonder the boy is uncouth. Do you really think by treating your subject as an equal, you can gain its respect, Claude? I thought I'd taught you better than that. How are you to master the subject's mind when you cannot even master your own baser instincts?"

Claude's neck stiffened, and it took all his strength to stop his eyes from pinching together. That was what his father wanted from him. A reaction. Instead, Claude feigned disinterest and pointed towards the sofa next to the fireplace. "Would you like to sit down? You must be tired from your journey."

"Believe me, as old as I am, I'm still capable of scolding a disobedient dog. Do not test me."

His father swept to the living room anyway, and flattened out his ash-grey travelling cloak before he sat down on the armchair. Claude followed by extension, but he was no less inclined to sit with him. It was *his* home now, and he had to stand his ground.

Claude remained poised beside the fireplace, his silk suit tightening around his biceps when he folded his arms. "Might I ask why you are visiting so unexpectedly?"

"Mind your place, boy, or I shall put you in it," his father growled at him, thin lips shaping into a snarl. "Within these four walls you call me Master or Sir. That rule has never changed."

Claude unfolded his arms, but kept his head held high. "Yes, Sir. But need I remind you that I am not a child anymore and that this is my home? Not yours. Not anymore."

His father snorted a contemptuous laugh. "I vowed to find out what made you defy my orders and that I would soon destroy it." He spared a lazy glance around the room, and a loose strand of his white hair fell into his menacing, ebony eyes. A tight grin lit up his eccentric features. "And now I see that it was all for a boy. A slave. A subject, no more and no less. How very disappointing."

"He's more than that," Claude said, not even meaning to sound as sincere. "If you haven't noticed, *Father*, I'm retired, therefore whatever I do with my life has nothing to do with you. As long as my decisions do not affect your affairs, then my private life is none of your concern. The same applies with my men. They are not your problem."

His father slowly unfolded his legs and swept a wrinkled hand down his tartan trousers. "Oh? Then tell me, who afforded you this private life? The luxuries? Who created you, you foolish little boy? Throwing your life's worth of research away for a slave. Do not make me laugh!" His father was standing now, nose just inches from Claude's, his dark eyes boring into equally colourless depths. "I created you, yes, but I can easily take it all away."

Claude didn't even flinch. He found himself not caring if his father destroyed him so long as Tristan remained safe.

Claude had already made sure that if something were ever to happen to him, Oliver and Dmitry would be the ones to take care of the boy. They'd all be taken care of. It was the least he could do.

"Your words cannot control me as they once did," Claude spat through gritted teeth. "You can't use Benjamin against me this time. I repaid my debt. Now it is time to repay yours to me."

"Debt?" His father scoffed, lips bearing into a snarl. "And what debt would a creator owe its invention?"

Anger coursed through Claude's veins impulsively, and he stepped forward. It was like a beta stepping up to its alpha, sizing the wolf up and calculating its next move. Claude believed he could overpower his father. It was as though he were seeing clearly for the first time in his life.

At that moment, he saw himself as not the young boy his father had tortured into submission, but rather the man worthy of a life greater than what his father had afforded him.

He was no longer blind, and he would not be silenced or brainwashed like the countless times before. Claude would not back down. Enough was enough.

"Any man who tortures his son into doing his dirty work for him deserves to *rot*." Claude pushed by his father, but Tomus grabbed onto his arm and swung him back around. He didn't say anything, though he didn't need to—the look of murderous fury did him just fine. "I think it's about time you leave, Father, before you cause any further embarrassment."

He snatched his arm back and shot his father one final glare before he swept away from him. He didn't walk far enough, though—for he still heard his father's last words.

"You're a fool if you think that... *subject*... loves you. All his words are lies, Claude. He'll say anything to lower your guard so that he can escape. I have seen it many a-times, and the moment you turn your back on him, he's gone."

Claude screamed inwardly to walk away. But he couldn't bring himself to do it. He felt rooted on the spot, destined to hear his father convey Claude's deepest fear.

"Benjamin planned the same thing," he snarled, "and I did what I had to in order to protect my research. Even if that meant soiling my reputation, I did it because I had no other choice."

Claude kept his back to him and made for the kitchen. But as he walked by the fireplace, he saw Tristan standing in the back doorway, Oliver and Dmitry at his heels. All of them were silent and wide-eyed, their jaws nearly licking the ground.

"See to it that my father is escorted off the premises," he told Oliver, who nodded his head and stepped over the threshold.

Meanwhile, Claude climbed the staircase and entered his bedroom. Closing the door behind, he collapsed onto the wooden floor, and his entire body went numb.

The front door was open. It was *open*, and Oliver and Dmitry were nowhere in sight. Tristan could make a run for it, and he might actually escape this place.

But after what he heard Claude say to his own *father*... His eyes darted to the stairs where Claude had staggered up. He looked so defeated from his father's visit that he'd eloped to his room before anyone could suggest to help him. His hands and legs were visibly shaking when he walked by Tristan, not meeting his gaze, and his face appeared as though he'd just seen a ghost.

Tristan had never seen Claude like that. So vulnerable. He began to wonder if Claude was injured. What if he'd hurt himself? What if he needed help? He didn't look at all steady on his feet.

No. Tristan *had* to get out of there. This was the best — probably his *only* — chance to escape. Everyone was too distracted to be focused on him, which meant he could make a break for the ski resort before Claude came to his senses.

What if Claude *couldn't* come to his senses? From what Tristan had seen at the back entrance, Claude was just that creepy old fuck's puppet... He wasn't the one running the twisted operation like Tristan had thought. He wasn't the monster, but rather somebody who'd been trained to fear them — fear his father — and follow his orders at all times. Even if that meant breaking people apart in the long run.

It didn't excuse what Claude had committed, but it at least began to make sense.

He looked back at the opened door and took a deep breath. He had to choose. Help Claude or fight for his freedom one last time?

Chapter 18

TRISTAN GENTLY PUSHED open Claude's bedroom door, and when he stepped inside, he couldn't see the floor with the amount of clothes, books, and furniture that had been thrown across it.

Steam misted his vision as he traipsed over them and toward the bathroom door. He'd chosen to stay—to help the man who had broken him. Why? Because even monsters have demons. It made sense now!

"Claude...?"

He knocked on the bathroom door and waited for an answer. He didn't bother with "Sir" or even a "Professor" this time. Despite everything the man had put Tristan through—which was *hell*—he needed to know that there was more to life. More to it than the years of abuse his father had evidently forced him to endure.

Claude had once been a slave? A subject for his father's own experiment? Tristan couldn't comprehend it, but then again, he didn't have time to. He slid his fingers around the bathroom doorknob, twisted, and then slipped inside.

Claude hunched underneath the shower, his writhing hands pressed against the wet tiles, head bent low, and chest breathing rapidly.

"Claude!"

Tristan raced over to him, and grabbed hold of Claude's

arms. The water was scalding hot against his skin. He glanced at the shower dial and noticed it was on high.

"Are you trying to burn yourself alive?!"

He turned the dial ninety degrees, the water instantly cooling, but Claude didn't answer him. He was still half-dressed, breathing heavily against the cracked tiles, his shoulders and neck burnt from the boiling water. Tristan tried his best to pull him away, but he wouldn't budge. He felt like he was glued to the tiles, but his body, despite the sauna-like atmosphere, trembled.

"Just tell me what you need, and I'll get it for you. Claude, speak to me, please!"

"Out..." Claude's head drooped further down. He'd managed that one word before his hand grabbed Tristan by the shoulder and shoved him away. "Get...out...*now*!"

Tristan stayed put. He couldn't leave him there like that. "I'm not leaving you," he said, voice firm and unyielding. "I'll be quiet if that's what you want, but I'm not going to leave you."

Clearly, he needed all the help he could get. Sometimes, just having someone beside you helped.

Where's Oliver? Where's Dmitry? What the fuck is happening here?

He felt as though he were in a dream, watching the scene unfold like a distant memory. He didn't feel a part of the world anymore, not when his hands swung Claude around and gazed into those fathomless, deep black eyes. That cold, calculating gaze, which had accomplished so many unforgiving things, had never yielded, never broke, and yet at the moment, they had never appeared so human.

It was as if the void suppressing his every emotion had been ripped from him, leaving Claude naked in the backdrop of a distant firelight, so vulnerable and broken, barely clinging to the last of the embers.

Tristan lifted Claude's head up, but the second he let go, it lolled forward, hanging between his arms. Water gushed down and around them, blinding Tristan's line of sight and soaked every inch of Claude's suit.

Tristan reached over again, and this time he switched the water off. He could hear more clearly now, but nevertheless his dream-like movements did not fade. His legs and fingers had turned completely numb, crippled with pins and needles; however, he tried grasping more fiercely at Claude's slippery body.

Claude slid down onto the floor and averted his gaze, his arms drooping listlessly by his sides. Why wasn't he saying anything? Why was he acting as if the world had ripped his heart out and crushed it?

It occurred to Tristan, as he bent down eye to eye, that Claude did have a heart. That after everything he'd done, the professor was really only human. And right now, it was his turn to be broken.

Whoever Benjamin was, his father had known to use him as a weapon against his son. Was he perhaps someone Claude had once loved? Or was Benjamin a cruel and elusive tool of manipulation and had simply been a fodder his father had used against him—to keep him shackled for all of his life?

"Claude, please speak to me… I just want to help you."

Still no coherent words. But he was hyperventilating now, arching his back and choking intelligible words through the air. Tristan swept the plastered, wet hair away from Claude's eyes. It'd been a while since Tristan had a panic attack. He remembered hazily that Connie always said to place your head between your knees.

Tristan gently touched Claude's head and tried to bring it forward to meet his knees. But before he knew it, Claude had managed to sputter another incoherent word, and then grabbed Tristan by the throat.

Now his entire world became all too real again, and stars assailed his weakening vision.

"Cl—Claude…I…just…wanted…to…*help*."

"I. Don't. Need. Your. *Help*!" Claude bellowed, pulling Tristan forward by the scruff of his neck. "This is all because of *you*!"

The raw, undiluted anger had returned to Claude's eyes now, and instead of pity, Tristan found himself breathless and confused.

"Claude…" he choked out, but whatever kind of beseeching he tried in his tone, it fell to deaf ears.

Rising up from the floor, Claude dragged Tristan with him, and in a series of rough movements, he hauled him through the bedroom door. Tristan dangled listlessly in an iron-tight grasp, his feet barely touching the floor until they reached the steps outside. There, he grasped desperately at Claude's hands, but he wouldn't let him go.

If anything, Claude merely tightened his grip and dragged him down the stairs and onto the living room floor.

Oliver and Dmitry were already standing there, clearing away the game console and games.

"*Get him out of my sight!*" Claude roared while Tristan wheezed on the living room floor, panting for breath.

"Boss…?" Oliver exchanged a bewildered glance between Dmitry and Tristan.

Through his watery vision, Tristan saw Oliver walk towards him and help him up. "I—I just tried to help him," he explained hastily, still gasping for a single breath. "Oliver, I didn't do...*anything*...wrong...I—I only—"

"*Now!*" Claude thundered. "And you'd better do it quickly or else you will fucking join him!"

Dmitry was beside them now, circling a firm hand around Tristan's quivering shoulders. Oliver didn't move. He just stared into Tristan's eyes, and something lost shone within their blue depths. Neither of them wanted to follow Claude's instructions, but whatever they were about to do next, they made sure it would be done effortlessly.

Tristan screamed and fought them the entire way to the lab room. He clawed at every door they passed in the hallway, he grasped at the White Room entrance, digging his fingernails until they bled into its steel hinges, and he kicked and he flailed and he swore he'd never forgive them for taking him back there.

For doing this to him again.

"I was trying to help him!" He wept at them, but Dmitry, undressing Tristan with rigid, quick movements, paid him no attention.

They said nothing to him.

Could say nothing to him.

They simply dressed Tristan in those familiar, sickening white clothes and then locked him into the White Room as if he'd never meant anything to them. Just another slave to be locked away and forgotten.

"I should've run when I had the chance, you fucking *psychopaths!*"

It was the last thing Tristan managed, before the lights were switched on and the noise smashed through his skull like a million, red-hot needles, and he screamed.

❦ ❦

The scalding hot water poured over Claude's body. He rested his forehead against the bathroom's grey tiles that trailed up toward the window.

All his words are lies, Claude. He'll say anything to lower your guard so that he can escape. I have seen it many a-times, and the moment you turn your back on him, he's gone.

His father's words polluted Claude's mind, mixed with the sound of Benjamin's screaming. Or were they Tristan's? He couldn't tell anymore—he just wanted them to stop.

His body tensed under the water, secretly hoping it'd melt

his flesh clean off. At least, then he'd be focused on the pain instead of hearing his father's voice telling Claude what he already knew.

He needed to hurt the boy. No, *destroy* him. It was the only way out of this, and Claude would prove to his father that he was still the same man. Still his perfect researcher. He couldn't come out of retirement, but he'd show his father that some damned *brat* didn't break Professor Claude Galen.

He'd prove that once and for all Benjamin had meant little to him. He'd just been a subject. Nothing more, nothing less.

Claude turned off the water and stepped onto the bath mat. His neck and shoulders throbbed with pain, yet it was a pleasant kind of pain. After drying himself in the bathroom, he pulled on a new, dry suit and combed a hand through his wet hair.

He'd punish the boy for getting his favourite suit wet, too.

Once Claude was through with the string of punishments he had planned, Tristan Kade would learn to miss that precious White Room. His father had been right—Claude's purpose in the world was to punish, not desire; to obey, not defy. It was all he knew.

He looked in the mirror and carefully combed his soaking-wet hair back. Droplets of water fell from the edges of his hair and onto his shoulders; staining the fabric of his navy blazer. He almost laughed at how his hands trembled as he gripped the comb.

No one but Tristan had ever seen Claude at his most vulnerable, and soon, there would be nothing left of the boy to divulge any secrets.

Claude took a look in the mirror one last time and straightened his posture. He supposed it was time to check on the little rat, who meant nothing to him.

Absolutely nothing!

His father's voice kept telling him that over and over again. Punish, not desire. Punish, not desire. He left the bedroom and emerged into his lab, though Dmitry and Oliver were already inside, watching the boy through the one-way mirror, their faces expressionless.

"I'm surprised he hasn't thrown out his voice yet," Claude stated, his own voice oddly calm compared to the mess of emotions forming inside him.

He stood in the middle of his men, their reflections swelling against the glass, and gazed at Tristan. His stomach lurched. Tristan lay underneath the White Room mirror, curled up into a tiny ball, barely moving. It was as if he knew they watched him from the other side. The voice was in full swing, though the men couldn't hear it from in the lab room. How could that be possible when Claude felt Tristan's every mute scream cut down his back, every useless plea construct in his throat?

When the torture ended, Dmitry switched on the intercom, and Tristan's mouth hurled out loud, shuddering sobs that seemed to be dragged from the depths of his being. He begged Oliver to let him out, begged Dmitry to help him, and begged Claude to go fuck himself for eternity.

"I only w-w-wanted t-to *help*…please, Oliver…help me!"

If Oliver wanted to rip Claude's throat out right there and then, he knew better than to express it.

The three of them fixed their eyes on Tristan and said nothing.

Chapter 19

FORTY-EIGHT HOURS had gone the next time Claude entered the lab room. He was surprised to have found it empty; Dmitry often kept a watchful eye on the boy.

Claude switched on the lights, and his eyes sought Tristan. Panic threatened to squeeze his body when he didn't immediately locate the boy. He strode toward the telecom system next to his computer, tapped it, and he heard Tristan's low, shuddering breaths within the White Room walls. He rotated the camera and saw Tristan had curled into a ball underneath the mirror. Claude zoomed the camera in, and Tristan's once vibrant eyes had turned a startling shade of pale.

Colourless, lifeless, broken…

Claude had seen that look before. It was the defeat of his prey; a sign that his victim had surrendered at last. It was Benjamin's expression the moment he had died, when he had given up everything and yielded to his father. Not the kind of submission that spoke of promising servitude, but admittance to a life he no longer wished to endure. It was death, darkness, and nothingness all wrapped up into one.

Tristan's eyes were a replica of Benjamin's suffering, and it tore at Claude's twisted heart all over again. Had he pushed Tristan too far? His father had snaked his way into

Claude's mind again, gripped his only weakness, and forced him to act as he once did: to be the perfect slave he was intended to be. He had contorted Claude to the point of unrecognition, broken him again and again, always digging those claws so deeply into Claude's chest that his soul was irreparable.

Claude had wanted things to be different. Yes, he had wanted Tristan to submit to him, to give Claude his all, but he did not want this. He had retired from that forsaken lifestyle. Claude wanted Benjamin: his spirit and endurance, his courage and his love.

He had wanted to test such boundaries within Tristan and see what the boy was capable of. He did *not* want to turn Tristan into a hollow creature, without feeling or desire or lust or even that sweet, reckless naivety of his.

Claude felt as though he had been forced to relive Benjamin's death, to witness the light fading from those beautiful, green depths, and see the soul removed far from his body.

Claude grabbed the keys hanging outside of the White Room and pushed open the door. Had Tristan even moved at all in the two days? He was still in that same spot beneath the mirror, no longer moving or pleading. Claude wanted to race over to him, but his legs felt weighed down by a ton of bricks. The best he could do was creep toward Tristan's hunched figure and lower himself to the boy.

Tristan didn't even flinch when Claude put a hand on his shoulder.

"Your punishment is over, Tristan," he said, trying to keep his voice low, but there was an edge of desperation to it. "Look at me."

Tristan didn't move. If it weren't for the staggered, wheezing breaths coming from his lungs, Claude would have thought the boy had died. He was sweaty and pale, heavy dark circles underlined his eyes, and his lips were covered in leftover froth.

Claude grabbed the boy's chin and forced their eyes to meet. The light within those depths had truly been extinguished. And it was all because of Claude.

To be capable of such destruction... The subjects weren't the monsters needing to be altered, it was he and his father. Claude had trained and remade their subjects into greater human beings, but he had never shattered them as his father had Benjamin. But now Claude was no less a monster than his father.

Claude held Tristan in his arms and carried him out of the room. The boy didn't even cling to him for support as they walked down the hallway and up the living room stairs. It was like Claude was carrying a doll with all the stuffing ripped out of it. It wasn't much of a stretch, at all—Tristan felt light and frail.

He took the boy to his guest bedroom again, and laid Tristan down on the bed. Maybe a bath would help him, but Tristan looked far too exhausted. Claude wanted him to rest. After what he'd done to him again, a bath would be of no use to him now.

He left the bedroom with the door open an inch to allow in the light, and then he entered the kitchen.

"I took Tristan out of the White Room," Claude said to Oliver's back; he refused to stop washing the dishes. "I want you to fix him some pancakes and hot chocolate. Plenty of sugar. He needs it."

"You said he was the last one." Oliver didn't even look at him; up until now, he had never disrespected Claude in such an impertinent manner. "Ya wanted to put all that shit behind ya, and Tristan was to be treated differently. That's why we *cared* for him. *Looked out* for him. Ya put him into the White Room even when it wasn't necessary!"

Guilt gnawed at Claude's insides; however, he could not show it, even if Oliver had been right in what he said. The Irishman whipped his body around, and Claude could see the hurt flashing in those sapphire depths. It was the same expression he had the day his father brought him to the cabin.

Utter betrayal.

"The feckin' kid only tried to help you," Oliver snarled, his freckled cheeks burning with indignation, "and yet yer doin' the—"

"Mind who you are talking to!" Claude's own voice had risen, and he straightened his posture so that it shadowed Oliver. "As far back as we go, I still will not tolerate disrespect. At the end of the day, Oliver, you are still just an employee. Now, prepare the boy something to eat, plenty of sugar and colour, and then take it upstairs to his bedroom. You may install the game console there for when he comes to. Get to it."

"What about a doctor?" Oliver managed, his voice lower as the blood drained from his face. "Doesn't he need one after all the shit he's been through?"

"The boy is alive; that's all there is to it. It will not happen again."

Furthermore, Claude swore, the White Room was no longer operational. Such a device was no longer necessary. It had *never* been necessary. He'd terminate its existence at once.

If only Claude had done so the day he met Benjamin. Things would've turned out quite differently if he had.

A few hours passed by, and though Tristan had awoken, he was still unresponsive. He wouldn't eat or drink, hardly moved, and refused to utter a word to anyone. Claude had even brought Fionn inside the bedroom (and that beast was never allowed further than the attic), but nothing roused Tristan's interest.

Fionn licked at Tristan's face, but the lack of response caused him to whimper and jump down from the bed.

Claude had grown increasingly anxious. "Enough with this," he told him sternly. "You are to speak to me right now, or I will be forced to punish you."

He had no intention of punishing the boy, but he hoped it would gain a reaction from him.

Nothing.

"Dmitry," Claude called out, and his henchman came in

without a word. "Make the boy speak."

Dmitry shot Claude what he suspected was an uncertain glance, but he approached the bed all the same. His hand shot out and grasped Tristan's shoulder. Still no response. Leaning into the boy's mouth, Dmitry listened for a breath. He sighed with relief when he heard the faint, whisper of a breath trickle out Tristan's mouth.

They'd never seen a subject—*Tristan* like this. Or perhaps they had and Claude had always been blind to it. Now that he'd cracked through his father's madness, he could see the theory in its natural form, and he despised it.

Dmitry left after Claude gave him a curt nod. Oliver was sent in next, although this time, he sat on the side of the bed and caressed Tristan's face; seconds after Claude gave him permission.

"Hey, eejit head. I've brought you some more pancakes. Yer favourite, right?"

Claude remained perched on the bottom of the bed, watching in agony for a ghost of a response. Oliver cut off a thin slither of blueberry pancake and offered it to Tristan's lips. Claude could feel himself peering forward with anticipation, and his heart thudded when he saw Tristan tilt his head away.

Claude sank back into the mattress. Oliver pulled the pancake away and sat the plate down on the nightstand.

"Ya know, if ya don't eat anything, am gonna have to feed ya meself. And I ain't gonna tankya for that." He touched Tristan's hair again, and Claude hated the instant jealousy that rose in him. "Especially not when I've got a lil' kitten to look after. Yeh, I found him at the side of the road yesterday mornin'. He's a tiny nipper, too, about the size of me hand. Was wondering if ya had any names I could give him. Dmitry likes Peanuts, but meself likes… Little Nipper. He reminds me of ye. Tough and stubborn as fuck. Ya wanna come and see him? He's in the attic with Fionn. Would ya believe that? They actually like each other, and you know Fionn's the funny type when it comes to other animals. He still tries to hunt the highland cows 'round here."

Stroking Tristan's head, Oliver glanced at Claude, seeking some kind of approval. He nodded, and watched Oliver lean forward and press his lips against Tristan's forehead.

"I never really liked ya to begin with, kid. But ya sort of grow on me, like this cat. I hate seeing ya like this… Ach, speak to me, buddy?"

Just then, Tristan tilted his head back and tears raced down his cheeks. "It hurts, Oliver…" he croaked out, voice broken. "Everywhere hurts… I just wanna go home. Please… take me home? Don't let him hurt me again!"

He closed his tear-stained eyes again, and let out a loud sob.

If Tristan knew Claude was in the room with him, he didn't acknowledge it. Oliver kept his head bent low, but Claude could see his ears were flushed pink with anger.

Claude wanted to tell Tristan that he'd never hurt him again, but he knew no words of comfort would ever measure up to the pain he'd caused. They wouldn't erase all of the hurt. The fact that Claude was *seeing clearly* for the first time meant absolutely nothing.

He had hurt this boy, and now, he'd finally broken him.

For what? His father's theory of how simplistic it was to alter one's mind with punishment and pleasure? None of it mattered anymore. Claude stood up from the bed and left them alone. As much as he didn't want to leave Tristan, he knew in his heart that he was the last person Tristan wanted to be around.

❦ ❦

Emptiness. That was all Tristan felt—if emptiness was a feeling at all. Not even Oliver helped ease the numbness that had crept into him. He no longer had the desire to live or die; nothing mattered to him anymore. Claude would always own him. Always destroy him. Always remake and then break him again. That was what monsters did, right? They devoured and destroyed people until there was nothing of them left.

There was certainly nothing of Tristan Kade left. The last parts of him had finally died in that White Room.

Oliver held a bite-sized piece of pancake up to his lips. "Just a small bite?"

Tristan's lips stayed clamped shut. He could not eat it. Didn't deserve it; because somehow, he'd done something awful in his life to warrant the future he had now. For some reason, fate or coincidences, or even the big man upstairs, had decided Tristan deserved to be with a man like Claude. Maybe all the petty crimes and childhood misdemeanours added up, and maybe Tristan wasn't a good person when it came down to it. Maybe he deserved to get thrown out at thirteen, abducted at twenty-one, and now imprisoned for the rest of his life.

He deserved everything.

So he turned his head away, which felt like jogging fifteen miles in the hot summer heat. His entire body was aching and his temperature felt hot—too hot, and yet it was also frigid cold. Every muscle resisted his attempts to move, even though he did little of it. Just existing had become too painful.

Please get me out of here…

He opened his mouth to beg Oliver for his help. Nothing came out. His body felt dehydrated of any happiness he'd ever had in life and starved of any desire to fight and protect himself at all times. He'd always learned to look out for himself. But now, he just felt numb, and he wanted to die.

Oliver sighed with defeat and turned the room lights off when he left. Claude hadn't the brains to keep them switched off when he took him to the old guest room. As if Tristan's retinas hadn't suffered enough brightness in the White Room.

It was funny… Tristan had been aware of everything that went on around him—being dragged from the White Room, carried down the hallway and laid down on the spare bed, but he couldn't respond to them. Whenever he tried, his body shut down.

Listen to me, you sonuvabitch! You better move your ass and get outta here, because nobody else is gonna do it for you!

He lifted his arms up, noticed he was wearing the same white clothes, and then dropped his limbs. He couldn't convince them to function properly. Moreover, he knew there was no escape. Somewhere in that White Room, Tristan had given up. Claude Galen was everything he couldn't control, and not even his survival could drown that out.

Is this it? Is this all part of the fucked-up theory? To convince me that Claude wasn't the monster, for me to choose him over my freedom, and then to be broken by his own hands?

If it was, then Claude had won.

He'd broken Tristan once and for all.

Chapter 20

"WHY EVEN BOTHER was all the lad said."

"He really said that?" Dmitry asked outside Tristan's bedroom door.

"Yeh. It's been three weeks," Oliver sighed, "and he's eating a little, but he doesn't want to. He only ate soup today because I said the boss'll use an IV on him."

"And he hasn't spoken since?"

"Not a word."

Tristan rolled around in the bed, turning away from their voices. He could still hear them, hear the worry lacing the tones of the only humans he'd met since this nightmare began.

But it's not a nightmare.

No matter what I do, I can't seem to wake up from it.

I'm not asleep!

He was simply dead inside a body that still drew breath.

"Boss won't be back for another few days," Oliver added, and a glimmer of hope glimmered in Tristan. "Ain't we feckin' delighted."

"Is he still in New York?"

"Yeh. Something about repairing a relationship with one of his father's business partners. His old man's taken the retirement pretty hard. Boss is trying to settle the waters, apparently."

Dmitry didn't respond. After a moment, Tristan heard them leave the hallway, and he was alone again. He turned his head toward the large window, the blinding light searing across his eyes. He blinked against it and thought of gathering enough willpower to throw himself through it. Maybe it'd be enough force to break his neck and finally release him from Claude's imprisonment.

But Claude wouldn't be the one to find him: Dmitry and Oliver would.

Why do I feel guilty about that? Dmitry brought me here!

Tristan rolled off the bed and trailed into the bathroom. He didn't know what he was going to do in there, but somehow, it felt safe. He managed to hold on tight to the sink and turn the cold water on. The entire bathroom felt uncomfortably warm, his sweaty skin did little to cool his rising temperature. Had he always felt hot after the White Room?

Tristan pulled off his T-shirt and shakily splashed some water over himself. It wasn't a shower, but in his state, it was enough.

If only he killed Claude that time he had the scalpel. Why was he so fucking weak and pathetic? He'd had a weapon… he could've stabbed Claude right in the artery and ended this suffering. He'd probably save Claude's next victim a shit load of misery.

A small smile crept onto his face at the prospect of a deceased Claude. But then something sharp stabbed at his chest, and watery images gushed through his mind like a grey day noir sequence. Tail, ears, mouth prop, cage, ripped clothes, rape, whiteness, noise, animal trap. The memories seemed to siphon through Tristan's brain as if on cue, and the more they invaded his thoughts, the heavier his breathing became.

He tried shutting his eyes, but they wouldn't stop.

Stop!

He tried to scream, but the words wouldn't come out. The floor swayed and he grabbed onto the sink for support. The White Room's dead noise ringing through his ears caused the walls to close in on him and the floor to shrink further by the second, and when he opened his eyes, he saw white.

The same hell that Tristan had been thrown into time and time again. Simply because he was at the right place at the wrong time? Or because Claude's psycho father had placed a warrant on his head and decided to take away his everything to replace it with nothing? Alter him into an unfeeling, unthinking doll for him to use and abuse to his heart's content only to sell like a meaningless cargo of unwanted flesh?

Because that's how Tristan felt—soulless. A type of unparalleled numbness that could not be compared to the betrayal he felt within his core. Even if Tristan had slipped into a state of learned helplessness, his *alteration* wasn't worth shit if it meant spending another minute with the professor.

But he also knew that he had no other choice.

Panting on the bathroom floor, Tristan began to laugh, a mixture between a strangled sob and suppressed hysteria.

The fucker actually broke me!

❤️ ❤️

Claude returned home to the sound of heinous laughter, and then sobbing. He dropped his suitcase at the front door and raced up the stairs to Tristan's bedroom, nearly breaking the door off the hinges with how violently he kicked it open. He rushed toward the bathroom and forced that door open, too, and saw Tristan on the floor, working himself into a frenzy.

"Tristan!" He collapsed onto the floor and pulled the boy up to his knees, then held onto him tight. "What happened? Talk to me!"

He'd been looking at his security feed a minute ago in the car, and Tristan certainly hadn't been in hysterics. Every day, he watched Tristan on his tablet. The boy barely moved, barely did anything, although thankfully he'd started to eat somewhat. But he'd at least held himself together. So much so that Claude had trusted Oliver to care for him while Claude released the final strings that connected him to his father.

I trusted him!

He knew the boy wouldn't respond to him, so he picked Tristan up and carried him over to the bed. The boy's eyes were wide open, empty, roaming around the walls—

anywhere but at Claude.

He pulled the covers up to Tristan's neck, his hand lingering for only a second, before closing the door behind him.

Downstairs in the kitchen, Munro's washed-out face projected over Claude's laptop screen.

"Galen," he grumbled, and Claude's blood-shot eyes flickered up to meet the doctor's. "What's so urgent that you called me out of surgery?"

"It's... Tristan."

Munro raised his eyebrows. Clearly, Claude calling the boy by his name and not 'subject' startled him. He peeled off his surgical mask and tossed it to the side. "What of him?"

Claude paused, inhaling through his nose. "He's unresponsive. It's like nothing I've seen before," he added, staring firmly into Munro's jaded, brown eyes. "I trust your expertise, and truthfully, I am at a loss of what to do."

The doctor froze for a moment, scratching at his short, white hair. He wasn't old *per se*, older than Claude by two years, but his hair had aged him at least a decade. "How long has it been since he last spoke? And what was the cause?"

"Three weeks. The White Room. I thought he would've pulled through by now, but I fear this punishment may have gone too far."

He almost mentioned the visit from his father, and what encouraged him to blindly tear the boy asunder, but he knew Munro had no desire to hear it. Claude had no desire to confess it. He just wanted Tristan whole again.

He longed for the boy as he was once, not what he had become—because of him.

"I see." Munro's face turned granite. "Seems to me the boy has finally cracked." Now there was something sinister and mocking in the doctor's velvety voice. "Is that not what you wanted?"

"Enough, Munro. My theory is not to break the subjects, but rather remake them. You very well know that."

Munro scoffed. "Remake human beings who do not wish to be altered?"

"Forgive me," Claude spat, equally as scornful, "but if you were so against my father's research, then why did you purchase Joshua? Why did you submit an application requesting him?"

"Purchase, Claude? I like to think of it as *saving*. I saved him from the life you'd later afforded him simply because daddy told you to do so. You make me sick. You're no more than a predator!"

Claude held his features in check. After all, it was the truth, and he deserved it. He'd bent to his father's every command, and it'd taken him decades to refuse him and see him for what he truly was: a monster who'd abused Claude into doing his dirty work for him.

"From your experience, what has been the most effective in curing PTSD?"

"There is no cure, it comes and it goes. I suggest you let him go, Claude, but we both know that won't happen." Munro sighed, throwing a pair of used gloves into the waste bin behind him. "In any case, if I were you, I would reintroduce normalcy into his life again. Let him wander outside. Take him somewhere. A date."

"A date?" Claude's voice came out small. "You mean there's hope?"

A vague, distant relief gripped him as he waited for an answer.

Munro sighed, but he nodded. "What the boy needs now is normalcy. No more punishments. No more White Room. If you're retirement announcement was official, Claude, and that you really are planning on putting aside this lifestyle for good, then focus on healing the poor boy and start treating him as something other than an object. Normalcy, and plenty of rest and wholesome food. Understand?"

"Yes. And Munro, I will let your tone slip by simply because I am in no mood to quarrel with you. But do not forget whose debt you're in and how easily I can take everything you love away from you."

He ended the video call before Munro could argue another word.

❦ ❦

Tristan should've been happy to be outside again. It was just him and Claude, which Claude seemed to enjoy the most. Apparently, if you pretended the White Room never existed, then everything was fine. Tristan wasn't broken, he just needed some coffee to lift his spirits; he was just tired and a little chilly.

Tristan's entire body crawled when Claude put an arm around him and pulled him through the snow. He felt disgusting. He *was* disgusting. Even Fionn didn't come near them, despite being off his leash, not that Tristan blamed him. It felt like years since Tristan had been outside, not a month, and yet he couldn't bring himself to care.

"Are you enjoying the walk?" Claude asked in too sweet a voice. *Talking to me like I'm a fucking toddler!* "If you'd like, we can go on walks more often. You said you wanted that. I have plenty of time for you now that I'm retired."

The thought of being around Claude all the time made Tristan's stomach churn. He kept his head down.

"How would you like to go on a date?" Claude asked, failing with a capital F to ease the tension. "We can go to a restaurant and perhaps see a movie? What kind of movie would you like to see?"

As if Tristan knew what movies were out there. For all he knew, the earth was in ruins, and they were living in some dystopia now.

Still better than where he was.

Because this was torture. A raw, different kind of torture compared to what he'd been through. Every bone in his body begged him to run, and now that he was able to, he simply couldn't. All he could do was let Claude lead him and hope that somewhere along the way he'd find a semblance of his old self.

Everything felt wrenched from him now, no thoughts, no

laughter, and even no hate anymore—the one thing he'd used to fuel his survival.

Besides, he was scared that if he did open his mouth, he'd either vomit or scream and he wasn't sure which one was worse.

Claude squeezed his shoulder and sat him down. He realised vaguely he was sitting on the bench at the lake again. It felt like months since he'd last been here, but it might've only been days.

How *dare* Claude bring Tristan to the lake and try to overwrite the one fond memory Tristan had with them all.

He was unsurprised to find the lake was completely frozen with no swans this time. No animals to make him smile. Not even Fionn, who was burying himself in a mountain of snow, could rouse a hint of emotion from him.

"I'm sorry," Claude said, and his breath came out rushed like thick smoke consuming the night air. "For everything, Tristan."

As if that would fix *anything*.

Tristan wanted to yell and scream and punch... just anything other than nothing! He sat there and numbly watched the lake. He tried not to think of how this would be his life from now on, but it swarmed his head like an aggressive beehive, stinging any semblance of joy and peace that hid deep inside him.

Claude stroked the back of Tristan's head, probably thinking it was soothing, but all it did was aggravate the bees further.

"Oliver's new cat is already a headache," Claude said with a small smile. "He keeps knocking things over, running around the attic during the night. Oliver said he even tripped him up. And apparently Fionn thinks the kitten is his son..."

Claude paused for an answer, but Tristan's mind had turned blank. He tried to picture Oliver with Fionn and the kitten, and Dmitry complaining about their mess, but all he could focus on was the whiteness before him. The constant snow that never seemed to end here, the signs pointing toward the ski resort, and the listless lake and empty trees. Everything was so... *white*, and cold dread washed over him as the memories of the White Room returned.

Finally taking the hint, Claude stopped touching Tristan's hair, and he became silent. He clearly stumbled into one of his own contemplations, for he no longer made pointless conversation and instead fixed his gaze on the lake.

Tristan was numb, but not blind—he could tell how uncomfortable Claude was.

Whatever he was trying to do, he wasn't used to it. Claude was totally out of his depth, and yet, Tristan didn't care, because he couldn't care.

After a long silence, Claude rose from the bench and picked Tristan up. Wrapping his arm gently around his waist, they returned to the cabin together. He thought Claude would take him back to his bedroom, but instead, they wandered into Tristan's old room, and Claude rested him down on the bed.

"I'll get our date organised for tomorrow." Claude leant in and kissed Tristan on the forehead. "Try to rest. I know Dmitry has been wanting to play games with you again. You'd like that, wouldn't you?"

Shortly after Claude left him, Tristan rose out of the bed and stared out the window. Hours must've gone by, but for all Tristan knew—staring into the white sea before him—it could've only been seconds.

He startled when he heard the room door creaking open, but thankfully it was only Oliver. He had the kitten with him, cradled tightly in his ridiculously muscled arms, and tears welled up into Tristan's eyes.

Not because of the blatant adoration he could see radiating from Oliver toward the kitten, or the cute way it meowed and scratched at Oliver's beard, but because Tristan knew at that moment he should be feeling something, yet he didn't. He didn't feel happy or excited when Oliver lay the kitten down onto the duvet. Or even that giddy feeling when its tiny, silver paws galloped clumsily over the bed and toward him.

He walked over to the bed, picked the kitten up, and stared at it. Its light green eyes were sculpted by its immaculately groomed, short grey hair. By all accounts, Tristan knew the kitten was cute, but he couldn't find it in himself to say anything. To *do* anything other than dangle it in the air and stare it down, flinching a little when it sniffed and accidentally head-butted him.

Tristan loved animals, but he no longer felt the joy they

once brought him. Tears stained his pale cheeks, dropping from his chin and onto his chest. He just wanted to feel happy again.

"The little nipper has even grown on the boss," Oliver said, and Tristan could see the hint of anger at referring to Claude. The two must be fighting over something—maybe Claude threw out one of Oliver's Betty Crocker cookbooks. Or maybe, Oliver had finally come to his senses and had seen Claude for what he truly was. A monster. "He's even allowed to be in the house instead of the attic. A first for the boss. He hates cats."

Tristan handed the kitten back to Oliver. Even though they were both stuck in this hell, at least *the kitten's owner* was someone kind like Oliver. Tristan felt a twinge of jealousy over the cat and hated how even the kitten would have a better lifestyle than him. Tristan was so far removed from a human that his competition was a fucking *cat*, who still got better treatment than him.

At least, the cat would be safe. He wouldn't have to endure the constant rapes or White Room torture.

Or Claude Galen and his sick obsession with Tristan.

"The boss is downstairs, and he won't be able to hear us if ya just wanna talk. Even if ya wanna talk about how ugly that tie is he's wearing today, I am all ears."

Tristan sat on the bed and crossed his legs, eyes glued on the kitten crawling all over him. He wanted to speak. He wanted to tell Oliver how frightened he was and that he just wanted to go home. He felt like an empty shell living here, a husk that'd consistently been torn apart for its master's amusement—for his father's amusement. Whichever bastard it was for, it'd ripped Tristan out of his body and placed him someplace out of his reach.

Oliver smiled faintly and picked the kitten up, pinning him to his chest. "Named him Little Nipper. He looks like you, don't ya tink?"

Tristan nodded, and Oliver kissed the kitten on his forehead.

"Watch this," he said, laying the kitten down and turning him onto its back. "Taught him this today. Tried it with Fionn, but he's as thick as shit, that beast."

Oliver tickled the kitten's stomach, who latched onto his stubby fingers, and the second Oliver pulled them away and shouted, "Freeze!" the kitten raised all of his legs up into the air. It had displayed what could only be described as a strangely shocking human expression.

"It's like he's playing dead," Oliver grinned, watching the kitten lay stock-still on its back. "Cute or what? Me tinks Dmitry should learn the same trick. What do ya say?"

There, somewhere deep in Tristan's throat, laughter rose—and it almost escaped him, if not for how tightly he was biting the inside of his cheek. He reached a hand out and stroked Little Nipper's head. The more he stroked, the longer his thoughts swirled around in his head until something fond rushed out, and he found himself inexplicably calm while petting him.

"Ya can keep him here for t'night, if ya want. I'm sure Boss won't mind. He's too busy organising tomorrow's day out anyway."

Just like that, all the crushing force came barrelling down on Tristan. He didn't *want* to be alone with Claude. Why couldn't Claude go, and Tristan stay with Oliver and Dmitry? Why did Claude have to ruin *everything*?

"I'm cooking pizza tonight," Oliver said. "I don't know what ya like, so I'll just make ya one with extra cheese."

Tristan wanted to reply, to say something, but the words kept getting stuck in his throat. He couldn't even make his lips form into a smile. What the hell was wrong with him? Why couldn't his body work like it was supposed to?

Why couldn't he just *feel* again and ask Oliver to help him?

Chapter 21

IT HAD BEEN another month since Tristan was released from the White Room again. The last time Claude had felt this nervous was when his father dragged him from the Dark Room on his sixteenth birthday and said it was time to become a researcher. He hadn't felt this level of anxiousness in twenty-four years. This *vulnerable*. He had delved so deeply into the human mind that he'd stripped it of everything and remade it in ways that hadn't been humanly possible before.

So why he felt nervous about spending time alone with Tristan, in public, was beyond his understanding. So far, Tristan hadn't tried to escape. Claude didn't know if that was a good thing or bad, but the way the boy barely touched his food or looked at anything in the small, but beautifully quaint city, his heart told him it was the latter.

"I have never asked about your tattoo," Claude said, straightening up in his chair. "When did you get it?"

Tristan didn't reply. He simply tore a breadstick in half until there was nothing left but crumbs. Claude hoped the boy would eat something, but unsurprisingly, Tristan left everything else untouched on his plate.

"Is there somewhere else you'd like to go after?" Claude prompted. "Just tell me where you want to go, and I'll take you there." *I'll make things better again, I promise.*

The boy wouldn't even look at Claude. A part of him wanted to threaten the boy, because that was what he was good at—what he'd been trained by his father to do. But what good would that achieve now? Tristan had completely shut down, and Claude couldn't reach him now.

"Just give me a simple 'yes' or 'no' answer, Tristan," he said, voice unaltered. "Do you want to go somewhere else afterwards?"

The boy looked at him this time, but when he gazed into those beautiful, sea-green depths, he saw nothing but pain and misery. Not the kind that he'd witnessed after a mild punishment back at the cabin, but pain that seemed to burn so deeply into Claude's chest that he struggled to breathe.

He'd never felt this kind of helplessness before. Sure, he'd dealt with obstinate subjects in the past, subjects who didn't want to obey or listen to him or follow the theory's script, but this was the first time he'd come across a subject—a human—who had completely surrendered himself. Normally, a subject at this late in the stage would be happy and safe at his new master's heels, but not numb.

Not lifeless.

The fact that I'm still referring to them as subjects... It says it all, really. There's no going back.

And yet he refused to give in. Claude had broken Tristan Kade, but even if it took him the rest of his life, he would make him whole again. He'd have his lively, sweet, and thoughtful boy back, and they could start again.

You're a deluded fool, Claude Galen, and this boy can see right through you.

Claude rubbed a finger across his temple. A headache that snapped like an elastic band around his skull, forever pinging backward and forward, chilled his sinuses. He hadn't slept properly in weeks, but he knew he had to keep trying. He wouldn't give up. Not now. Not even his father's daily threats could persuade him otherwise.

However, dinner didn't go as Claude hoped. Tristan ate little and said nothing the entire time. They had the restaurant to themselves, and Claude had been comforted only by the sound of Tristan's fork hitting against his plate and the pigeons squawking outside the restaurant windows.

He carried the box of food Tristan hadn't even touched, and once Dmitry drove them home, he handed the box to Dmitry.

"Cook Tristan some pancakes."

It was the only thing he seemed to be eating nowadays, except for milkshakes and the occasional bowl of soup.

"Sure thing, Boss." Oliver took the box with a weary frown, watching Tristan walk by them and into his bedroom. He slammed the door shut behind him.

Claude walked into the kitchen and sat down at the table, rubbing his temples. The Irishman set the box down onto the countertop and leant against the edge.

"I've always been faithful to ya, Boss, since ya saved me old da's sorry ass 'til the day he died. For that I'll always obey yer orders, without hesitation."

The Irishman softened his expression, obviously recalling

the day he was brought here ten years ago, at the ripe age of sixteen. He'd been sent to Claude as a way to pay back his father's debts. The Irish gambler had been a sponsor of Claude's research, but when his associates stopped offering the man financial guidance, Claude had offered to dig him out in return for a henchman who would forever serve him diligently.

Claude gazed at him coldly. So far, Oliver had never disappointed him. But since Tristan had arrived... Was the Irishman perhaps still human after all? Claude's father had claimed him a brute of a boy who'd been in and out of jail more times than he could count. His only soft spot appeared to be animals, but with Tristan... One could almost say they were friends.

Claude ground his teeth together. "It is nothing I cannot fix, I simply..." He didn't finish.

Oliver bent underneath the countertop and brought out a bottle of red wine. He grabbed two glasses hanging from the rack above the breakfast table and poured even amounts into each. He handed Claude the first one.

"I *will* reverse this," Claude said, though to Oliver or to himself, who knew. "I will not abandon Tristan, and I'll fix him."

He couldn't bear to think that Tristan's PTSD would last forever. In his PhD studies, he knew of soldiers who had suffered from it the rest of their lives. But that was through prolonged torture and years of combat. That was different than the way he and his father remade subjects. In fact, he knew of no adverse effects, once training was completed. Subjects were prime examples of the perfect slave.

Except for Claude. He'd exposed the ineffectiveness of his father's theory: it was null and void when humanity was concerned, no matter how extensively one combined punishment with pleasure. Humanity, in the end, overrode it.

Claude was not broken like Tristan, though. Had he simply been weaker than Claude anticipated? Or was Claude an even bigger monster than he thought?

He swallowed hard. "The last thing he said was, 'don't let him hurt me again.'"

"And will ya?" Oliver looked like he wanted to say something more, but he held his tongue.

"Of course not. You know as well as I do that hurting Tristan was never my intention. None of this was. He was not intended to be like the rest."

Tristan was not meant to be treated like a slave. Even after Tristan had refused Claude, he'd made sure his men understood that Tristan was different, and they had done so. Claude was the one who went against their plan. *He* was the one who had fucked up, not his subordinates.

Oliver looked taken aback, unused to his employer being so upfront with him. "You had me fooled," he said, and Claude wanted to strike the man right there and then, but that wasn't going to bring Tristan back. In fact, the only one who *could* reach Tristan at all would be Oliver. "Ya know the right thing to do is just let him go, Boss."

"That's not possible," Claude growled, black eyes narrowing into thin slits. "Never suggest that again."

He could not live without Tristan. He knew that, deep down, the moment the brat walked into his office. Tristan was a part of him now—a part of this house even. Claude wasn't giving up his one ounce of happiness just to satisfy everyone else. Besides, Tristan was helpless now—a cat without its claws. Tristan wouldn't be able to survive without Claude, so naturally, the best option was for Claude to stay by Tristan's side and heal him.

Because breaking and healing were what Claude did best.

❦ ❦

Tristan had gotten used to the dates. For days on end, he and Claude would walk around the small, winter-swept village, and Claude would ask him questions that Tristan refused to answer. Whenever he did get asked a question, he'd find himself gazing into space, picturing his would-be life back home in the States, and he'd wonder why in the hell Claude still bothered with him.

On the surface, he'd made little progress in the space of a month; little—as in he forced himself to eat and dress himself. He'd sometimes acknowledge his captors with a brief nod or shake of his head, but inside, a storm brewed within Tristan and waited for the moment it could release itself.

"You'll love the park," Claude said once Tristan had sat down on the living room sofa. "Spring in Aviemore is beautiful." It was springtime already? Winter had felt like it'd just been yesterday. "I've always found it to be so peaceful up here. Everything brought to a stunning, premature stillness. Wouldn't you agree, Tristan?"

Why is he still talking to me?

Peanuts, or Little Nipper as Oliver called him, ran from the couch to the end table next to Tristan. Peanuts had entered his 'knock-everything-over stage, which had given Dmitry a headache since he was the one who had to clean up the mess. Tristan's lip tilted a little. A smile or a frown, he didn't let it grow.

After petting Peanuts goodbye, Tristan followed Claude to the car and sat in the passenger seat quietly—just like he always did in the evenings. He stared out the window as the car pulled out from the driveway and made its way toward the local village.

The snow hadn't vanished from the mountains yet, but for the village down below, the roads were at least visible again. The green of the trees flipped by Tristan as the car sped faster, and at some point, Claude turned on the radio and played rock music. Tristan knew it was Claude's way of trying to 'connect' with him. He'd rather Claude stopped trying to *connect* with him, period, and let him accept his defeat in silence; the fact that he would never truly be the Tristan he once was.

Once they reached the park, Tristan undid his seatbelt and kicked open the door before Claude cut the engine off. He hated being that close to Claude, and he hated how he was stuck in his own head with nowhere to go, with no real escape route in which to choose.

"At least wait until the car is parked, Tristan," Claude said, getting out of the car himself. "You're going to hurt yourself if you keep hopping out like that."

That's rich coming from you!

Tristan walked over to the nearest bench and sat down. He hated these dates, and he hated that Claude kept making him go on them. Last time, it had been the cinema, and they'd watched some awful action movie that'd seemingly broken the box office. This time, Claude had driven him to a park in the middle of the village. The buildings were rustic and quaint with (what Tristan had assumed to be) Gaelic signs hanging in the shop windows. Although the park wasn't far from the lake, the thought of being alone with Claude—albeit in public—made him sick to his stomach.

If only he could use his mind to convince his body to run. With every suffocating date, Tristan felt closer to accomplishing that.

"I'll get us some hot chocolate," Claude said, placing a gentle hand on Tristan's neck. "Extra sugar."

Tristan didn't even look at him or acknowledge his footsteps fading away. His thoughts drifted into mindless contemplation. Nothing like he used to think about—no wondrous contemplations of exotic lizards, or the next video he'd upload to *GamerOn* so he and Jake could gush over it.

Now, his thoughts were hazy as if he were trying to see through contaminated water.

Whenever he did retrieve a thought, it slipped away from him before he could catch it. The only memories that didn't fade were the ones of Claude and the White Room, and how he'd once been happy.

At the rate Tristan was going, it was likely he would convince everyone that he'd never be happy again. That he would never be able to function properly or survive on his own, because Claude Galen had broken him.

"Daddy, look what I found!"

A little girl shot by Tristan, almost snagging his legs as she made her way to the bench next to him. Tristan watched her wave her fist excitedly into her father's face, her pigtails brushing against her purple and pink dungarees.

"What is it, my daft lass?"

Her father clutched the small fist, and Tristan watched the girl uncurl her fingers, only to reveal a blue bouncy ball. It looked just like the ball Tristan had received when he first entered the college. He wasn't sure if he was seeing the right object or not. He peered forward, his body moving as if under the influence of sleep, but the little girl bounced the ball off the side of her father's bench.

"Clever girl! Just be careful now," her dad said softly, watching the ball hit off their bench and then land at Tristan's feet. "Oh, sorry," he added, but Tristan merely smiled at him and raised his hand.

He bent down and picked the ball up. It was completely blue, and he swirled it around, gripping the object between his fingertips. It looked exactly like the one Tristan had been given at the college. The object that had marked Tristan straight out of the gate. His mind raced and his breath constricted as he turned it around, desperate to see if it had Claude's initials on it.

No initials. It was just another plain, stupid-ass bouncy ball. Tristan's eyes widened, his thoughts halting on the train tracks and clicking together. *Just another bouncy ball... Maybe it's just another chance?*

He wanted to laugh hysterically. Comparing his fate to a bouncy ball was the most ridiculous thing he'd ever thought of. But it was accurate, wasn't it? Claude's bouncy ball had changed Tristan's life for the worst. It had pinned him as the victim of a sick motherfucker's twisted obsession before he had a chance to run. Perhaps if he hadn't accepted the ball then he wouldn't be here, trapped in a world forsaken of joy and love and humanity. Perhaps, just maybe, if Tristan accepted the ball, he could change his fate.

He could *choose*: continue to endure the life Claude had forced upon him, or simply seek a new one?

Fight for a *real* one *because this doesn't have to be my life anymore.*

This was the moment Tristan had been waiting for. He'd had enough of pretending, of submitting, of not feeling at all. Claude had stolen half a year of Tristan's life, and he'd be damned if he'd allow him to steal any more of it. If he could just convince his body to move then the six months would be *all* Claude would take from him. All he would ever rip from him and destroy.

"Excuuuse me, but please can I has my ball back?"

Tristan must've looked like a psychopath when he just sat there, staring at the ball, unable to communicate with the girl. His entire body pumped with adrenalin, his heartbeat pounded, his palms turned sweaty, and his legs and arms began to tremble.

They began to move. Clinging onto the object, Tristan realised that there was more to life than just resignation. His freedom was right there in front of him, at his fingertips— literally—and if he made a break for it now, he might actually make it. Claude was preoccupied in the coffee shop, and he wouldn't for a moment suspect him capable of running, not in his state of mind. Not when they'd spent hours together in public already, and Tristan had never made a run for it.

Tristan had convinced him that he wasn't capable of living anymore.

Moreover, they were surrounded by dozens of people, and it was warm, and Tristan could *run*.

He shot up from the bench, dropped the bouncy ball, then he ran—he ran so fiercely that he drove the wind from his aching lungs. He didn't give it a second thought. He just kept on running—in which direction? He had no idea. Where to? Absolutely clueless. He just knew to run for a life that was worth living. He didn't know if he'd find a police station, or a gas station, or just a fast-food joint that would help him, but he was sure that his freedom was there.

As Tristan ran—the park becoming a distant memory the further he sprinted—he thought about what the coming hours, possibly minutes, could bring him. Life. Freedom. Happiness. Love. *Humanity*.

He ran through the village until he spotted the signs leading to a police station.

Was it really going to be this easy? He was almost there. So close… just a little further…

His lungs gagged for air; his heart pounded like a train spiralling off the tracks. But the thought of living in the States again drove him forward; hope and determination sprung his feet through the last of the snow. His options could soon be limitless, but more importantly, he could wrap his arms around Jake and Connie again, and he would never, ever let them go.

Because he was free.

THE END

Epilogue

Two years later

CLAUDE SHIFTED ON the wooden bench and forced himself to hold his posture straighter. *This darn thing is made of toothpicks!* At least the college in Edinburgh had *proper* seating. Oh, well. Sometimes sacrifices had to be made in order to achieve his desires. Something Claude had learned to obtain the hard way.

He pulled out his mobile phone and dialled for Oliver, who still took care of the house at Aviemore while he was away on business. It had taken a while to cool the tides between him and the Irishman, but they were finally back at a steady, if not civilised, relationship.

"Yeh, Boss?" Oliver answered with his usual, grumpy tone. "The flight okay?"

"Yes," Claude replied calmly. "How is everything back home?"

"Quiet…" There was a small pause, followed by a sigh. "I've been here thirteen years and it's never been this quiet, Boss. But I came across something interesting the other day."

"Interesting?" Claude scrunched his eyebrows together. "What was it?"

"A game console," Oliver said. "I know, I couldn't believe me eyes either. I thought Dmitry had binned it once the kid left, but I found it in yer car garage yesterday morning. Actually, Fionn was the one who sniffed it out. Must've been Tristan's scent or somethin'."

Claude's chest pained and his throat suddenly felt drier. He forced his emotions down and kept the same, casual composure. "Interesting indeed. I trust you'll take care and dispose of it wisely."

The house had grown incredibly colder since Tristan left. It had been as if a part of Claude's slowly healing soul had been ripped away from him before it had a chance to mend. Claude had given up everything for that boy, and now he was left with nothing but the scars.

However, the boy had made one fatal mistake—he never went to the police. And Claude knew exactly why that was. Tristan still wanted him. Still *needed* him. *The boy is punishing me as I punished him. He wants me to feel as he did when I placed him inside of the White Room.* Well, Tristan had gotten his way long enough.

"Ya did the right thing, Boss," Oliver said. "Ya letting the laddie go and restart his life in Montana shows yer really a good person deep down, ya know?"

A grin crept onto Claude's face. "Fortunately, I am not a man known for my morals."

"Boss...?"

"I've made it clear from the start that I will gladly take what is rightfully mine." Claude's grip tightened around the phone, his knuckles blanching. "And I will not apologise for whatever I must do to ensure that it happens."

When the dean walked toward Claude, he disconnected the call and put his phone back into his suit pocket. He gave his warmest smile to the older man.

"Ah, Professor Galen," the dean said, taking Claude's hand and shaking it. "Welcome to the University of Montana. I am honoured to have such a prolific scientist interested in our school."

Claude's smile widened. "Believe me, the pleasure is all mine."

WHITE NOISE

The Bound Subject Volume II

Coming to you in 2018 by Katze Snow!

Acknowledgements

And so here we are! The end of what has been my darkest novel yet. I hope you enjoyed it! I honestly have so many people to thank for this novel, but I will first and foremost, thank YOU. The wonderful person who bought and read this novel. I only have one question to ask you… Are you Team Claude or Team Tristan? *wink wink*

Thank you to Jay Aheer who has produced ANOTHER amazing cover for me. I am always in awe of the sheer beauty Jay creates, and I highly recommend her. Check out Simply Defined Art!

Thank you to my lovely editor, Lisa Cullinan, who has encouraged me to keep going when life gets tough. She's a beautiful woman who will soon be teaching me how to bake… because I SUCK at baking and I hear Lisa makes incredible cookies! Hint, hint… Love you, L!

Thank you to Misty McMillen. We have grown incredibly closer since the release of my first MM novel, but it wasn't until we started working on Dark Silence when I realised how much I value, not only your insight, but your friendship! I owe so much to you for helping me get Dark Silence to a stage where I am genuinely happy and proud of it. I am especially proud to call you my friend!

To my amazing betas, Ivy Noha, Toni Wilson, Debbie Bookers, Helen Neale, Patricia Nelson, Dawn Doyle, and

Christine Wright. You guys are my TRIBE, and I love you all! Each of you helped to make Dark Silence a success, and I am so, so, so honoured to know you are a part of my writing pack. Thank you!!

To Raissa Phoenix, Nicholas Bella, Ashley John McLoughlin, Tyler May, and Emily Jean. Raissa, you are my big sister! You always put back together my broken pieces and tell me when I'm being stupid. I love your honesty and your heart. You're an amazing and inspiring woman! NB is my God! I appreciate your help so, so much and don't think I could've done this without you. Ashley, you are my twin. Now hold my poodle!! Thank you for cheering me up when I most needed it. You're an incredibly lovely person. My guru! Tyler, you are like my mother. Whenever I need advice you're there for me, and you never judge. You helped me through a lot this year, and I am so thankful! Emily, my sister from another mister. Thanks for sharing my dream with me, too.

There are so many other people who continuously help me out, and I am extremely thankful, not only for their help, but just their existence. I'm fortunate to be surrounded by so many wonderful, kind-hearted people who just want to make this community a home and the people within it their family. These are the friends and the family you choose, and I will always choose you. Now and always. <3

Until our next journey!

Katze Snow

About Katze

Katze Snow never learned when to shut up. Food and coffee are what encourage Katze to function in a semi-normal, socially acceptable way. Doses of sarcasm and sass are what she lives for, and of course, her furbabies, wolfy Kiba and his best friend, little kitty June Bug. She's been writing since she was a child but finally published her debut novel, *Alpha's Bane*, in Autumn 2016.

While Katze also writes MF, MM is where her heart truly lies. Her writing is dark, gritty, and takes satire to a whole new level. Come and join her! But be warned: Katze likes her men dark, twisted, and all kinds of messed up, and she hopes you do too.

Broken in Silence, Demons and Wolves #1 (MM paranormal)

Tannerian Wulfric is a leader—a strong alpha who bows to no one, especially those who try to undermine his authority. When an opportunity arises, he grabs it with both hands and lets nothing get in his way. Trouble is, his brother has been caught in the crossfire of glorious retribution, and Tanner is in need of assistance.

For many years, Alex Jonas has lived his life in peace. But when fate lands him in the hands of his ex-lover and alpha, he finds himself in the centre of a feud he never knew existed, and must immerse himself in ways he had never imagined. One chance encounter, one night, and everything comes crashing down around him. Alex must fight for his life while Tanner fights for one thing and one thing only—vengeance, which has never tasted sweeter.

Can Tanner avenge his family's death without spilling more blood? Or will his inner demon tear apart everything he has worked for, and lose the man who owns his heart?

Within These Depths, Demons and Wolves #2 (MM paranormal)

Tanner is so close to his revenge that he can almost taste it. With an unusual brand of negotiation skills under his belt, he has everything he needs. Now all that stands between him and destroying Elijah Ravenhill is a dangerous mission into the depths of Hell. Accompanied by his guides, he will enter where loyalties and souls are tested, and few ever return.

Newly mated Alex just wants to keep his loved ones safe. In the sprawling grandeur of Wulfric Manor, he finally has his family under one roof, even if it may only be temporary, and his dreams of having something normal seem to be within reach. Yet what's normal for the wolf is torture for the prey, and chaos descends on Alex with one mysterious phone call.

Can Alex have all he ever dreamed of without sacrificing his life? Will Tanner put an end to Elijah once and for all, or will his revenge go up in smoke within the fires of hell itself?

Alpha's Bane: A MF Werewolf Romance (Twin City Series #1)

Set in the same world as Broken in Silence, Maya Greene has viable reason to despise supernatural beings when one left her for dead six years ago. Now living in Meadowsin City, she doesn't plan to fall in love anytime soon, especially not with a shifter. But Noah Hunter, an elite Halo official, convinces her otherwise. While on the run from Underground weresnatchers, Maya finds herself increasingly drawn toward the older wolf, and Noah's hell bent on saving her life...and her heart.

About Susanna

Susanna Hays has been writing ever since she can remember. She first started out with ghost stories that she would tell to her cousins and best friend. She has always been off in her own little world and spent her time at recess writing stories in her notebook. She is a huge animal lover and adores cats—especially the big fluffy ones! She loves talking to others and enjoys making friends on Goodreads and reading books.

She loves to create characters who have a unique story to tell. She creates protagonists who must overcome their weaknesses and find their true selves.

You can check out Susanna's books on her website!

Made in the USA
Columbia, SC
30 December 2017